IF THIS IS LOVE

JEWEL E. ANN

Copyright © 2023 by Jewel E. Ann

ISBN 978-1-955520-27-0

Paperback Print Edition

Cover Designer: Emily Wittig

Formatting: Jenn Beach

To all the mean girls in school, I forgive you.

PART ONE

A WHITE CASKET AND GRILLED CHEESE

FLETCHER ELLINGTON PURCHASED me for the bargain price of one million dollars. A gift for his wife, Ruthie.

I was four years old.

Ruthie sewed floral sun dresses and ran a boar-bristle brush through my hair every morning. She taught me to read *Magic Tree House* books, paint pictures to express my feelings, and question everything. We spent hours in her gardens, where I learned a tiny seed can turn into a "shit-ton" of zucchini. Fletcher's word, not mine.

Now, she's dead.

"Indie will be so lost," Faye, Ruthie's older sister, whispers to Grandma Hill while Ruthie's casket disappears into the ground. It's a polished white casket, shinier than Greg's casket.

He died last year in an ATV accident. I was sad he died, and his wife and daughter didn't. I know that's bad, but Pauline (Fletcher's sister) and my so-called cousin, Jolene, are terrible people. Everyone on Fletcher's side of the family is terrible. Jolene is seven years older than me, and I hate her. Ruthie told me never to hate anyone, but I can't help it. Jolene never misses an opportunity to remind me that I'm an "impostor." Children purchased like racing horses and livestock are not "blood" family.

Someday, I'm going to get back at her. I'm going to take something that she wants. And I'll stick my tongue out, even though Ruthie always told me nice girls don't have to stick their tongues out. But I'll do it anyway just to see Jolene's freckled face turn red and steam shoot from her big nostrils.

For now, I can't think about stupid Jolene. Instead, I focus on birds chirping while the breeze carries the slight smell of manure up the hill to our gathering around Ruthie's grave. Fletcher falls to his knees next to the grave. I can't imagine feeling worse if he were my real father grieving my real mother. Greg used to say that blood is thicker than water, but Ruthie said he wasn't using the saying correctly. *"The blood of the covenant is thicker than the water of the womb."* Ruthie said it meant the opposite. *"The bonds we make by choice are stronger than the bonds of family (the water of the womb)."* And the only reason Uncle Greg and my mom had this argument was because Greg thought Jolene was more deserving than I was because she was his biological daughter.

I am the purchased livestock.

Ruthie wasn't Fletcher's family by blood. Still, while his body shakes with sobs, hands clenching his white button-down shirt over his heart, I think back to Uncle Greg's death. Fletcher didn't cry. Not once.

In my short ten-year life, I've quickly learned that love is different for everyone. Fletcher must have really loved Ruthie. That's all I can figure out. What must everyone think of him sobbing like this? Like a child. He's a king or maybe even a god. Nobody looks him in the eye, and everyone calls him "sir."

He swears. Smokes cigars. And makes people disappear, according to Pauline. She tells Jolene to be good or "Uncle Fletcher will tie you up and take you for a ride in his truck." Jolene rolls her eyes, but I don't know why. I once saw a man's boot hanging out of the back of Fletcher's pickup truck. And it was attached to a leg despite Ruthie saying it was one of Fletcher's boots.

I know what I saw.

But now? It's as if someone spun the world like one of those globes at school, and everything is backward or upside down. Fletcher Ellington crying?

I wipe the tears. Fletcher's been a good person to me. Good enough. I've always felt like he loved me because Ruthie loved me. Now that Ruthie's gone, I'm not sure Fletcher has a reason to love me. Seeing him on his knees, I'm not sure he'll love anyone ever again. Without Ruthie in the world, I wonder who will cry over my grave if something awful like cancer stops my heart from beating. Will they bury me in the Ellington family cemetery, or will I be composted like some animals that die here on the ranch?

"You'll come with us for a few days." Faye rests her hand on my shoulder. Her silver and turquoise rings clink together. Ruthie wore pretty rings too. But Faye has fake nails where Ruthie painted her own nails to hide the dirt that got stuck under them from so much time in her gardens. "Your dad needs some time alone." Faye gently squeezes me, and my head leans into her touch.

My dad? I never call him Dad. In my head, I call him Fletcher—actually, Fletch because that's what Ruthie called him. To his face, I call him "sir" like everyone else.

"Let's go, Indie." A familiar hand wraps around mine. It's warm, calloused, and huge.

"No," I whisper, slowly shaking my head. "I haven't given her this." I stretch out my other arm with a single pink rose clenched in my fist, sweaty from holding it so tightly all morning.

Milo Odell loosens his grip on me, letting me slide free. I run to the hole in the ground, dirt loose beneath my shoes, and stop on the opposite side of Fletcher. His red eyes find me when my gaze lifts from the shiny white casket. I can't look away. Even now, on his knees, he holds so much power over me and everyone else.

Without taking my eyes off him, the wind whipping my hair into my face, I unfold my fingers one at a time until the wilted rose releases from my palm onto the casket below. His leathery face looks extra sad today. His hair is a little grayer around the bald halo that's constantly peeling.

But his eyes ... they're empty. It's what I imagine someone's eyes look like when they die, when the doctor lifts their eyelids to check for signs of life and there aren't any. Does he know I stole the flower from the garden? Is he upset?

My gaze sticks to his like one of those unfortunate

dragonflies that gets caught in spiderwebs. That warm, calloused hand finds mine again, startling me. And my head whips around to Milo Odell and his pretty face shaded by his cowboy hat. His whiskers are gone. He must have shaved for Ruthie's funeral. She always told him she knew he was a handsome young man behind those whiskers.

I like his whiskers. They make him look mysterious, just like his long, wavy hair that always falls into his eyes.

"Let's go, Indie," he says, giving Fletcher a glance and a tiny nod. Milo is Fletcher's "main guy." Whatever that means. Ruthie said Milo did all the essential stuff so Fletcher could take her dancing and pack picnics for her on Sundays after church.

While everyone else feared Fletcher Ellington, Ruthie loved him. He softened with her.

Smiles.

Laughter.

Hand-holding.

He's not the most handsome man—stained, crooked teeth, scars all over his face, and missing a big round chunk of hair. And he smells like a cigar. Even now, I smell it mixing with the manure. But Ruthie called him the most handsome man she had ever seen. Maybe living on a ranch so far from other people, Ruthie didn't see that many men. And maybe her nose didn't work that well. Either way, she found something beautiful about him that you couldn't see just by looking at him.

He planted wildflowers so he could pick them for her every day.

He woke before the sun rose to do his morning chores.

He showered and made Ruthie breakfast before she opened her eyes for the day.

He carried a dark wood tray to their bedroom each morning: eggs, a muffin, fruit, coffee, and a small bouquet of wildflowers.

I'd peek through my cracked bedroom door to see him wearing the biggest smile or whistling a tune.

I heard them talking and laughing while she ate her breakfast. Then Fletcher would close *and lock* the bedroom door. For the next twenty minutes, I'd listen to sounds ... weird sounds coming from their bedroom. Then the lock clicked open, and Fletcher carried the tray to the kitchen, whistling a different tune, while Ruthie wrapped herself in a silk robe and came into my bedroom.

Even in the morning, she looked pretty with her long black hair tossed over one shoulder, her cheeks rosy from ... hot coffee, I figured.

"Good morning, my lovely girl," she'd say with a warm smile while I played quietly with my dolls. *"I'll have Micah make breakfast while you get dressed for school. How does that sound?"* She'd kiss my head.

I'd nod and pick out my dress for the day. Not every girl in school wore a dress, but I did because Ruthie did. So in my mind, girls wore dresses. Fancy dresses for weddings. Less fancy dresses for Sunday church. And everyday dresses for gardening. Those dresses didn't have to be pressed like the fancier dresses.

While I ate breakfast, Ruthie made my lunch and packed my bag. With a tight hug and a kiss, she sent me out the door to climb into Milo's black truck. It smelled like coffee, cinnamon, and leather. Quite possibly the dreamiest combination ever.

"*Morning, Indie.*" Milo grinned. His shaggy, dirt-colored hair hung in his blue eyes even beneath his cowboy hat.

"*Morning,*" I whispered, tucking my chin and fastening my seat belt. I had a severe crush on Milo Odell. It didn't matter that his brother was in prison for killing their parents.

It didn't matter that Milo lived in the barn.

It didn't matter that he was eight years older than me.

I had a crush—the incurable kind.

Faye clears her throat, bringing my thoughts back to this awful day. "She'll come with me," she says to Milo. "I'm Ruthie's sister. Indie should be with me."

Milo bats away a fly before scratching his jaw. "Sorry, ma'am. Mr. Ellington left specific instructions for me to take Indie."

My gaze rolls between Milo and Faye. *Fletcher made plans for me?*

Faye frowns and so does Grandma Hill. But Grandma Hill always frowns. Fletcher calls it "resting bitch face." I don't know what that means. Ruthie said she only made that face for him.

"She's a young girl," Grandma Hill says just before sniffling and pressing a wad of tissue to her nose. "Indiana needs to be with other women." She steps closer to me while curling my hair behind my ear on one side, like Ruthie would have done. The wind blows it back into my face.

I think she means I need to be with the Hills—Ruthie's family—not the Ellingtons.

"Again, I'm sorry, ma'am. But Mr. Ellington was very clear with his instructions. Let's go, Indie." Milo squeezes my hand.

I feel safe. Safe because Fletcher trusts Milo more than anyone else. Safe because Ruthie always trusted Milo with me. Still, I don't want to be with the Ellingtons. I want to go with Ruthie's family. The Hills are kinder, and they treat me like I belong with them—like I'm their blood even if I'm not.

"I'll check in on you later, sweetie," Faye says while I let Milo lead me to his truck, peeking over my shoulder and giving Faye a nod.

When Milo shifts the truck into gear, he glances at me, but I can't look at him. I don't want him to see me cry, but I sure do miss Ruthie.

"You hungry?"

I shake my head while his truck creeps down the hill and out of the Ellington family cemetery. It's a short drive to the main house, but Milo veers left and parks next to a barn instead of taking me home.

This is new. I've never been inside this barn, the one where Milo sleeps. Am I being moved to the barn now that Ruthie's dead?

"I can make you grilled cheese," Milo says, hanging his hat and tugging at his tie to loosen it before shrugging off his jacket.

It's the first time I've seen Milo in a suit. It's also the first time I've seen him without his cowboy hat, except the time I snuck out of the house and spied on him swimming in the pond behind it. He wore his underwear instead of swimming trunks. When they got wet, I could see the size of his penis and testicles. I never told Ruthie because I didn't want Fletcher to get mad at Milo and not let him swim in the pond.

He glances over his shoulder at me and jerks his head.

With heavy feet, I step past the door and softly close it behind me. "I'm not hungry," I murmur, trying to think about something besides Ruthie dying and the size of Milo's penis and testicles.

"You have to eat. Mr. Ellington insisted I feed you, so ..." He turns toward me and tosses his jacket over the back of a faded brown chair. It looks ancient. The cracked and peeling leather reminds me of the bald spot on Fletcher's head.

I glance around the room. It's plain compared to the main house but nice for a barn. Milo has a real bed, not a bale of hay or a stall of straw like I imagined. That's good.

It's just one room and maybe a bathroom to the right. The door is partially shut, so I can't see for sure. His walls are gray wood. No pictures. No pillows on the sofa. No vases of fresh-cut flowers.

Even though it's very plain, it's clean.

But it does smell a bit like wet leather and hay. Maybe his bed is hay under the sheets. My house smells of lavender. Ruthie loved lavender. She even had Micah add it to her sweet tea, and she put it in her jars of honey from the beehives Fletcher gave her for her birthday.

"Grilled cheese is fine," I mumble, fiddling with the sash of my dress.

"Let me change my clothes, and I'll make it for you." He shrugs off his button-down shirt, but he's not wearing an undershirt like Fletcher. Milo has big muscles and a few tattoos. Bull horns and something else I can't figure out. Before he takes off his pants, he grabs a pair of jeans from a plastic laundry basket and carries them into the bathroom.

Minutes later, he opens the door, and I startle. I'm not doing anything wrong, but everything in here squeaks.

The floor.

The doors.

The windows.

Even the ceiling whines when there's a gust of wind.

I stare at Milo's jeans and white tee while he plucks his tan cowboy hat from a hook and drops it onto his head. Perched on the very edge of the sofa, I smooth my hands over the skirt of my dress.

"I'm going to leave this right here for you. If it's hot, you don't have to wear tights. If it's cooler, then the tights are in the top drawer. Wear your black patent shoes. And Faye will braid your hair." Ruthie prepared me for her death.

Sort of …

She didn't leave instructions for what would happen to me beyond dressing for her funeral. Will Fletcher comb my hair? Will he crawl into bed with me if I have a bad dream? Will he pack my lunch and tell Micah what to make me for breakfast?

"Did he buy you too?" I ask Milo to keep my nervous brain from wondering what happens next. I'm used to being with Milo in his truck when he drives me to school or smiling at him when he comes to the house to talk to Fletcher. This is different.

"What's that?" Milo says with his back to me while he presses the sandwich into the skillet with a metal spatula.

It sizzles and smells a little burnt.

I clear my throat and find a stronger voice. "Did Mr. Ellington buy you too?"

Milo kills the stove's flame and slides my sandwich onto a plate while eyeing me with a funny look. "No. He inherited me of sorts." He sets the plate on the table. "Ketchup?"

"Yes, thank you," I mutter while my shiny black shoes tap along the wood floor toward his small, round kitchen table. The chair squeaks too when I plunk down into it. It wiggles on uneven legs, so I try to hold still. "What does that mean?"

"Inherited?" One of his eyebrows slides up his forehead.

I nod again, tearing the sandwich in half before sucking my fingertips. It's hot, and the cheese is extra gooey. Milo did a good job, even if the bread is a little black.

"It's when something happens to someone, and their property goes to someone else. When my brother and I were separated, Fletcher inherited me."

"I wonder who will inherit me?"

Milo chuckles, grabbing a bottle of beer from the fridge and unfolding his tall body into the chair across from me as he pops the top. "You lost one of your parents, not both. Mr. Ellington is your father. You belong to him."

"He's not my father. He could sell me." I blow on the hot cheese and take a small bite, my nose wrinkling.

Milo pulls the bottle away from his lips; his smile vanishes. "Why would he sell you?" He nods to the sandwich. "Don't like it?"

I shrug. "Because he bought me. For a million dollars." I stare at the black toasted bread. "It's good, just a little different. Kinda ... black."

"Grilled cheese should be charred. It might be an acquired taste. Just dip it in extra ketchup. And who said Mr. Ellington bought you for a million dollars?"

The ketchup bottle farts while I squeeze more onto my plate. It's nearly empty. "A while back, I heard Faye talking to Ruthie. She said Mr. Ellington stole me from my other mom. But Ruthie said a million dollars is hardly stealing. So I asked her what they were talking about, and she said my mom couldn't take care of me like I deserved to be taken care of, so Mr. Ellington gave her a million dollars to let me live here. And I guess my mom thought it was a good idea. I didn't see her much. She worked a lot. I don't miss her anymore, but I miss the other kids there, and I'm going to miss ..." My words catch in my throat, making it impossible to say them.

Milo nods. "We're all gonna miss her."

"I don't think he's going to brush my hair."

"You're ten, Indie. I bet you can brush your own hair. I combed my hair when I was ten." Milo has the best hair. Most boys keep their hair short, like Fletcher. But not Milo. He has brown hair, all in different lengths to his chin. It's kind of messy. Maybe I should tell him he could try a little harder. It's not ugly. Milo's pretty. His skin is tan, and his eyes are the color of the sky around noon when I eat lunch and stare at the fluffy clouds. I used to look for familiar shapes in those clouds, but now I'm going to look for Ruthie.

"Were you mad at your brother for killing your parents?" I ask, trying to be polite and ask questions like Ruthie taught me. It's hard when I'm sad and a little scared. What happens tomorrow? And the next day?

"Jesus Christ ..." Milo's head jerks backward, and he slaps his hand on the table with a hard thud. "Who told you that?"

I shrug. "I heard Ruthie and Grandma Hill talking."

"Indie ..." He removes his hat and tosses it onto the table before running his hands through his hair like he's mad at it. "You need to mind your own business. It's not polite to listen to other people's conversations."

"Were they mean to you? Did they hurt your brother? Is that why he killed them?"

Milo's face remains twisted like someone's pinching him really hard, the way Jolene pinches my arm when she thinks I said something stupid. After a few seconds, the wrinkles disappear, and Milo takes another long drink of his beer and returns his hat to his head. "What do you need from the house? You're gonna stay here for a few nights until your dad is ready for you to stay at the house again."

"He's not my dad."

Milo frowns. "No?"

I shake my head. "He's Mr. Ellington. Sir. I call him sir."

Milo's head dips into a slow nod, and he chuckles. "I'm aware. But he's your father."

"He's not. My father died. That's what my mom said."

Milo blinks several times like he didn't hear me. Then he clears his throat. "Did you think of Ruthie as your mom?"

"No. She was an angel. We all have guardian angels." I push the plate away from me, leaving a few pieces of black crust because I'm out of ketchup.

He narrows his eyes and rests both arms on the table. "Is that what Ruthie said?"

"Yes."

For a few more seconds, Milo doesn't say a word. Then he pops those burnt pieces of crust into his mouth and says, "I see."

"Are you going to be my angel now that Ruthie's gone to be with God?"

Again, he squints. It's funny how his eyebrows look like one instead of two. "Hardly. You can do much better than me, Indie. You have a grandma. Do you think of her as your grandma?"

I shrug. "Her name is Grandma Hill. Everyone calls her that. I don't know her name."

Milo's lips bend like he's trying not to smile. "Fair

enough. Her name is Helen. Let's get back to my earlier question. What do you need from the main house?"

"Everything."

With a chuckle, he scoots back in the chair and takes my plate to the sink. "You don't need everything. I'm thinking some clothes, pajamas, and a toothbrush. Your school bag. You'll go back to school tomorrow."

"Ruthie said I can stay home until I'm not as sad."

Milo rests his backside against the counter and crosses his arms. "Mr. Ellington wants you back in school. Back to your routine. He thinks it's what's best for you."

When did Fletcher start knowing what's best for me? Whenever Ruthie asked him, *"Do you think Indie should wear the red or yellow dress?"* he shook his head and said, *"How should I know?"*

"I should stay with Mr. Ellington. He's sad. I can make him tea. Ruthie used to make him tea when he had a bad day. And she'd ask, 'How would you survive without me?'"

Milo's lips turn upward into a half smile, and he kinda grunts. "What did he say?"

"He said, 'Miserably.'" I shrug. "Whatever that means."

"I'm sure she did take care of him," he says, plucking his beer from the table and emptying the rest down his throat in several long gulps. "But tea won't fix him right now. He needs time to grieve. He needs time alone." The bottle clinks when he tosses it into the bin.

I don't argue with Milo. He's not going to let me stay with Fletcher.

After lunch, Milo turns on the TV for me while he "takes care of things."

Hours later, he returns, sweaty and dirty, with a bag in his hand—a bag of my things.

"Let me know if I forgot anything."

I don't look in the bag. I'm too busy staring at his TV. I've never been allowed to watch this many shows in a row.

Milo showers, makes another black grilled cheese sandwich, and tucks a wrinkled sheet into the sofa before handing me a fluffy blanket and pillow.

"Goodnight, Indie." He shuts off all the lights.

Ruthie read books with me until I fell asleep. She left the light on in the hallway and kept my door cracked. When I had terrible dreams, she was always there to comfort me.

Ruthie is gone. No stories. Just total darkness.

I hold my breath for as long as I can. Tears run down my cheeks, and eventually, a sob breaks free. I quickly press a hand to my mouth. Everything inside my chest burns like I might explode.

"Indie?"

I squeeze my eyes shut and try to hold my breath again.

"Hey, what's wrong?" Milo hunches beside me and presses his hand to the side of my head while I shake with sobs.

I can't speak. I miss Ruthie too much. I'm scared. And I feel unloved. No angel in sight.

"Indie, if you don't tell me what's wrong, I can't help you."

"I-I'm s-scared."

"Of what?"

"E-everything."

Milo picks me up in his arms and carries me to his bed. Then he covers us in blankets while I hug his body like a koala bear in its favorite tree. I feel safe, a little less scared, and a lot less lonely with Milo.

2

DRUNK ON GRIEF

It's been a year since Ruthie died, and Fletcher is not okay. He works, drinks, smokes cigars, and sleeps. And he gets mad about everything.

"I'm hungry," I say just after eight at night while rubbing my rumbling tummy.

Our chef Micah has been on vacation for the past week. Ruthie used to try new recipes when Micah took time off, even though he left her pre-made meals. There are dishes in the fridge, but Fletcher won't let me use the stove or oven. Micah will be back in the morning, but I don't know if my stomach can wait until morning.

"Then eat something," Fletcher mumbles, swirling the golden liquid in his glass while staring at a TV that isn't turned on. A cigar hangs from his other hand. I've been putting them in ashtrays after he falls asleep. Pauline said I should make sure he doesn't burn the place down.

"I haven't had any fruit today. Ruthie always—"

"Well, she's not here, Indiana," Fletcher's voice

booms. After a few seconds, he exhales a long breath mixed with a cough that echoes in the tall ceiling. "There's peanut butter and jelly. Jelly's a fruit. If you can't make yourself a sandwich, you're not hungry. Eat. Brush your teeth. And go to bed." He closes his eyes while puffing the cigar.

There's a chill in the air, so I rub my arms. Since Ruthie died, Fletcher keeps the place really cold. On hot days, I walk into the house and the sweat on my skin turns to icicles. I think it's cold because he's cold. Like the Grinch.

I stand completely still in the doorway, wishing my heart would be quiet, but it only pounds harder in my chest with each breath I take. He never treated me like this when Ruthie was alive.

"I can't open the peanut butter. The lid is too—"

Fletcher's eyes open, and they look black. "If you don't get out of my goddamn sight, so help me, Indiana, I'm going to make sure you can't sit down for the next month. Do you hear me?"

"Yes, sir," I whisper, slowly backing out of the hearth room and sprinting away, but not upstairs. I run out the door, down the lane, and veer to the right, making my way to the barn.

As soon as I throw open the door, I'm met with darkness and silence. "Milo?" I yell, feeling something between a scream and a sob break from my chest.

"What's up, Indie girl?" It sounds like "indigo" when he says Indie girl, which I like because Ruthie used to say she loved my indigo eyes.

I spin around. Milo wipes his sweaty brow while

kicking his boots against an old fence post. He looks tired the way Ruthie looked before she died.

"Are you sick?" I shuffle my feet to him, each step heavy with worry.

He chuckles, squinting at me as the sun, low in the sky, hits his dirt-smudged face. "I'm sick of long days and short nights."

"Are you going to die?"

He peels off his filthy shirt and uses it to wipe his face. I don't know why. It only spreads the dark streaks even more.

"Not today. Why?" He takes heavy steps to the back of the barn, where there's a hose attached to a spigot.

I jump out of the way as dirt splatters in all directions from the hard stream of water.

"If you die, I won't have anyone." I ball my fingers and twist my wrists.

Milo shakes the water from his head like a dog before drinking long gulps from the hose. After he turns it off, he slicks his hair out of his face.

"Who did you have when your parents died?" I ask.

Milo blinks slowly. "I had Fletcher and Ruthie."

I frown. "Ruthie died. And Mr. Ellington is mean to me. I don't have anyone. And I didn't have dinner. No fruit. No vegetables."

"Indie ..." He blows a long breath, one hand on his hip. It reminds me of Fletcher.

I'm annoying Milo too. My chin dips, and I stare at his dirty boots.

"You have me," he says.

He doesn't mean it.

"Indiana?" He leans forward, resting his hands on his knees, water dripping from his hair.

I glance up at him. Even after a long day, all I smell is leather, coffee, and cinnamon. I think it's what my new happiness smells like. It's what I believe a man should smell like.

Milo smiles, his teeth so white. His skin so tan. "Okay?"

"For how long," I whisper.

His dark brows meet in the center of his forehead. "For as long as you need."

"Forever?" I look into his blue eyes; they're a safe place for me.

Standing straight, his long legs carry him toward the front of the barn. "One day at a time, Indie. Let's start with dinner."

"I need fruit. We should go pick figs."

Milo turns toward me, his body slumped. He's tired. "I was thinking grilled cheese."

"Are you going to burn it?"

"Is there any other way?"

I giggle. "But I need fruit for my skin."

"Did Ruthie tell you that?"

I nod.

Looking off in the distance, just over my head, his cheeks fill with air, and he blows it out all at once. "Figs?"

Another nod.

"Lead the way," he says.

With a massive smile on my face, I skip toward the gardens and fruit trees, where Ruthie spent so much of her time with me. Micah takes care of them now but doesn't talk to the plants like Ruthie did.

"Which figs do you want?" Shirtless, Milo rests his hands on his hips, face tipped toward the sky to inspect the hanging fruit.

"The big, dark, droopy ones. And they have to be soft when you give them a gentle squeeze."

"I have a better idea." He squats in front of me. "Get on my shoulders."

"Are you going to drop me?"

"I don't know yet."

I climb onto his shoulders, and he holds my legs while standing straight. "Get your perfect figs, Indie. We'll put them on our grilled cheese."

"Eww ... no." I giggle.

Milo Odell is the most interesting person I have ever met. Sure, he walks around all day with animal poop on the bottom of his boots. He's a terrible cook (but I don't tell him that). And he sucks at helping me comb my hair. Yet I find myself in his barn more than in the house. When Fletcher's away on business, Milo lets me swim with him in the pond behind the house—without a life jacket.

"If you tell your dad, he'll kill both of us," he says just seconds before I jump off the dock into the cool water.

He launches me in the hot summer air and laughs when I land with a big splash.

We race to the other side of the pond and lie in the

tall grass, staring at the cloudless sky. The invisible, fiery flames of the sun lick our skin like a dragon. I close my eyes and pretend it's just Milo and me living on the ranch.

Before bedtime, he takes me on horseback rides. Sometimes, with my arms around his waist and my cheek pressed to his warm back, I fall asleep before we reach the barn.

And ... he makes me a burnt grilled cheese every day —with figs.

Milo isn't Ruthie, but I feel like I did with her when I'm with him. I feel loved. I feel like I fit in this world. I fit with him.

As with all good things in my life ... it comes to an end when I least expect it.

"You're leaving tomorrow. Faye will be here soon to help you pack your bags," Fletcher says without looking up from his phone. He takes a bite of bacon and chews it slowly before licking his greasy fingers.

Micah gives me a sad smile while setting a plate of pancakes on the table. All the same perfect size. Golden brown and dotted with blueberries. The sweet aroma of maple doesn't distract me today.

I don't feel hungry at all. I'm too busy feeling rejected and punished for something I didn't do.

"You're selling me?"

This gets Fletcher's full attention. I've heard the phrase "if looks could kill," but I think I'm seeing it in person for the first time.

"No, Indiana. You're going to school."

"Why do I have to pack my bag? You mean my school bag?"

He shakes his head before taking a sip of coffee. "It's a private school. You'll stay there. You'll get to come home for the holidays and for the summer."

"Are my friends going?"

Fletcher chuckles, shaking his head. "No. You'll make new friends."

"I don't want to go to a new school."

"It's not up to you."

"Why not?"

"Indiana..." he gives me that stern look, the one he gives me when he's had a lot to drink, "...don't press me on this. You need to learn manners and how to respect authority. Start now by saying, 'Yes, sir' and getting any personal belongings together that you think you can't live without."

"I don't want to go." This feeling in the bottom of my stomach feels similar to the pain I felt when Grandma Hill and Faye told me Ruthie died.

Fletcher leans forward, spilling his coffee, but I don't have time to focus on the black liquid absorbing into the white tablecloth. And he seems not to care either.

Smack!

Silence. The room is entirely silent. It's as if life paused. No movement. No sound.

A gasp of breath balloons my lungs. And I hold it while my cheek stings from his hand striking it. My head spins with a dizzy feeling. Tears burn my eyes, and my hand lifts to my face. No one has ever hit me. In a blink, hot tears fall hard and fast.

"Yes, *sir*," he says.

The ringing in my ears makes it hard to hear his words. "Say it, Indiana. Tell me the only two words I want to hear from you."

"Y-yes ... s-sir."

"The trailer's ready, Fletch."

Milo.

I don't want to turn around. He'll see my tears. He'll know that I'm in trouble.

Fletcher straightens his tie, stands, and adjusts his big belt buckle while eyeing me. "Go."

I nod, scrambling to my feet and running past Milo with my chin tucked as far as it will go.

"Indie ..." Milo says my name while grabbing my arm.

I keep my head bowed, trying to hide my face and tears.

"Look at me," he whispers.

My heart beats so hard it hurts my chest.

"Milo, let her go. She has packing to do, and we need to get on the road." Fletcher's boots knock the wood floor, creeping closer to us.

I lift my chin, choking on a shaky breath while keeping my hand pressed to my cheek.

Milo frowns, peeling my hand from my face. In the next breath, something about him changes. He's no longer the kind-smiled Milo who has cared for me since Ruthie died.

"Go to your room," he says, his jaw clenched.

Why does he look so angry? Is he mad at me for upsetting Fletcher?

"Go," he says with a sharp tone.

Shaking, I turn and run toward the stairs, but I stop before going up them.

"If you ever lay a hand on her again ..." Milo says.

"What?" Fletcher laughs. It's evil, like him. "What are you going to do? Listen, boy, don't forget who owns you. Don't forget that every breath you enjoy is a gift from me. I am your god. You don't question God. You obey Him. The one who giveth is the one who taketh away. You best remember that."

Fletcher's boots start knocking against the hard floor again, getting closer. I scurry as fast as I can up the stairs to my bedroom.

Less than an hour later, Faye taps her fake fingernails on my bedroom door.

"Come in."

She peeks her head inside and smiles. Her hair is pulled into a ponytail like Ruthie wore hers when she jogged up and down the long blacktop from the ranch gates to the circle drive. "Micah said you didn't eat your breakfast. I told him you might be hungry now." She sets the plate of pancakes on my desk.

I try to find a polite smile for her while I hug my stuffed bear tighter from the cocoon of my princess bed. I don't know what to say or how to feel. Why did he hit me?

Faye pulls back one of the sheer curtains surrounding my bed and sits on the edge, bringing her floral scent. She clears her throat, face scrunched. "What happened to your face, Indiana?"

I shake my head. "Nothing," I manage without crying.

"Did someone hit you?"

Again, I shake my head. I don't know why I'm lying. Ruthie loved Fletcher. I loved Ruthie. She was a good person. So I know there has to be something good about Fletcher. I don't want Faye to get upset with him. What if she says something to him, and he's mean to her, like he was mean to Milo when he said something about it?

"You know you can tell me anything. Right?" Faye rests her hand on my knee.

"I know," I whisper, pulling at a thread to my quilt.

She sighs, but it doesn't get rid of that look like she doesn't trust me. "Let's get you packed."

"I don't want to go."

Faye squeezes my knee. "I know you're probably scared. You'll make friends. And Thanksgiving will be here before you know it. And you'll be back here with your family."

I still don't want to leave, but I don't have a choice. Faye helps me pack. We say our goodbyes which include a video call to Grandma Hill. She too tries to make it seem as though I will be fine. I will make new friends.

Micah cooks me dinner, and I eat alone. Then I take a bath and brush my teeth. Perched at my window, I wait for Fletcher to come home. A little before midnight, headlights creep into the driveway. I smile, tug on a hoodie, and rocket down the stairs past Micah sleeping on the sofa. So much for him keeping an eye on me until Fletcher gets home.

I wait by the back door. When I hear the front door open, I know it's safe to go outside. There's a dog door for Mud, Fletcher's chocolate lab, that I choose to crawl through because it makes less noise. My anxious feet sprint after the taillights, down the drive, and off to the right. Milo climbs out of his truck, and I throw myself into his body, a shield that protects me from Fletcher.

"Indie girl ..." He stiffens for a brief second like I'm an animal in the night attacking him. "What are you doing? It's nearly midnight."

I don't speak. I can't. The real reason I don't want to go away to school seems to be stuck in my throat.

He hugs me, but my tummy hurts, and I still feel shaky.

"I don't want to go," I manage in a whisper.

His hand rests on my head for a few seconds, fingertips touching my cheek when I peel away from his warm body and glance up at him. The angry expression from this morning returns. "Nobody will hit you at school."

"I don't want to go."

Milo gives me a sad smile similar to the one Ruthie gave me before she told me she was going to die. I hate that smile. Like I hate Jolene. And Fletcher.

I follow him to the barn. "I don't want to leave you."

"It's happening, Indie, and there's nothing I can do to stop it." Milo kicks off his boots, banging them together a few times before he flips on the lights. His keys hit the counter with a heavy clink. After he hangs his hat on the hook, he turns to me.

Milo sweeps a hand through his hair, eyes squinted.

"You said I'll have you forever."

Dropping his head, he exhales a hard sigh. When he raises it again, he curls his hair behind his ears. "I said one day at a time. This isn't forever. I'll see you over the holidays, and you'll be back next summer. You can call me anytime you want."

"I don't have a phone." Fletcher and Ruthie never wanted me to have a phone, a computer, or an iPad.

Books.

They gave me lots of books.

Milo frowns, sliding his hands into his back pockets. "Well, you'll have access to a phone somewhere or computers in school. You can send me an email or write me an actual letter with a pen and a piece of paper. I'll give you money for stamps."

I nod, hugging myself and staring at the floor between us while my fingernails scrape along my arms. His words don't make me feel any better. The only thing that can take away this awful feeling is someone telling me I don't have to go. Fletcher can hit me every day if it means I don't have to leave Milo.

"I'm gonna miss you, too, Indie girl."

I glance up at him and his half grin. "You are?"

He lifts his shoulders. "Of course. Nobody else likes my cooking."

I giggle, and it relaxes my scratching fingers and stiff arms. They fall to my sides with a bit of relief.

"It's late. You leave early in the morning. I'll walk you back to the house."

"Okay," I say, but I don't mean it. Nothing is okay right now. My feet drag along the gravel to the pavement. The night's air is thick with smoke. The workers who live in one of the other barns sit out back for hours around a big fire. I've heard they roast marshmallows, but I've never been allowed to stay up that late. And Ruthie always said I didn't need to listen to their conversations. They weren't for young ears.

Milo reaches back and takes my hand, giving it a tiny squeeze while pulling me to catch up to him. "You're not gonna want to come home after making so many friends. You'll say, 'Milo, who?' I'll be nothing but the hired help with dirt under my fingernails and a bed in the barn."

I like the way my hand feels in Milo's hand.

Safe.

Cared for.

I'm scared of how I will feel when he lets go. Then he does ... he lets go.

"Here." He hands me money from his front pocket.

I don't count it, but I think it's everything he had in it.

"Buy stamps. Buy candy. Just don't forget me." He winks.

I love Milo Odell. Maybe one day I'll marry him. But I'll wait to tell him my thoughts about our future.

Letting the fireflies near the porch distract me from crying, I slip the money into my pocket. "Thank you."

"Are you gonna give me a hug?"

I grin right before throwing myself into his arms, hugging his waist with all my strength. "Bye, Milo."

"Bye, Indie girl."

3

FRISKY BUSINESS IN THE BARN

FLETCHER ELLINGTON DIVES headfirst into full-on alcoholism over the following years. Milo is the only reason I go home for the holidays and summers. Maybe Faye and Grandma Hill too—but mostly Milo.

He makes me his famous burnt grilled cheese, and we add cherries to them during early summer and figs in late summer. He teaches me to saddle a horse and gather eggs from the chicken coops. He even tries to teach me to rope, finding the one thing for which I am not a quick study.

"I don't want to hurt the calf."

"You won't." Milo shakes his head and chuckles.

He's still coffee, cinnamon, and leather—aka happiness. And the epitome of a man. My young heart is so invested in Milo Odell it feels like it stops beating when we're not together.

Fletcher keeps Milo busy nearly every waking hour during the summer, but we still manage to find time to race in the pond and stare at the sky from the tall grass when Fletcher's out of town. I find myself inching a little closer to him, entranced by every word he says. Every look he gives me.

When I can't be with Milo or gaze at him on his horse from a distance, I help Micah tend to the gardens and beehives, and I talk to the plants like Ruthie did. It's my second favorite place to be. Birds sing. Gates squeak in the distance. And I always hope it's Milo. My eyes stay peeled, watching for dust puffing under his boots as they plod toward me. But it's usually not him. It's usually not him when I hear the scratch of knotted rope or the creak of a harness.

Yet my heart always hopes it's him. I yearn for every tiny glimpse, a grin, a wink, the tipping of his hat, or my favorite: when he tries not to smile because Fletcher's watching him. I think I'm his weakness, the tiny crack in even his most stoic expression.

WHILE THE YEARS flip the pages of my life, I learn to raise myself. I make friends. And I honor Ruthie as best I can by not hating Fletcher. It's not easy. Faye says she and Grandma Hill remind him too much of Ruthie, which angers him. So they don't come around very often when I'm home to visit.

I think I too remind him of Ruthie. I'm not sure why he didn't sell me after she died.

There's not a day that passes that I don't thank Jesus and his godly father for Milo, especially today since it's my fourteenth birthday, which Fletcher has forgotten. I bolt out the door, barreling toward the barn on the sweltering July evening, praying Milo remembers and maybe has a cake waiting for me.

"Milo?" I call, throwing open the door to his living quarters, gulping one breath after another.

No one answers.

He isn't in the bathroom either, but his truck is parked out front. Maybe he went for a ride on his horse. I trek around to the backside of the barn that's used for barn things like storing hay, tools, tack, and Milo's horse, Ranger, a beautiful blood bay quarter horse with a white blaze.

Creeping past the stall, I hear something—labored breathing. Milo must be shoveling manure or moving bales of hay around. The sweet scents fill the stagnant air. Fletcher has other guys to do the "shit" work, but Milo doesn't like anyone else in his barn.

However, that's not what he's doing.

That's not *at all* what he's doing. Milo's doing something else. And he isn't doing it alone. The taut muscles of Milo's back form an uneven terrain while his equally firm butt muscles flex and contract.

Holy shit ...

His hands grip two long legs, holding them on either side of his hips while said hips rock against the naked female body he has pressed to the wall.

Sex.

Milo Odell is having sex.

I should turn away, but I can't.

My all-girl school is pretty sheltered and strict. I don't get to see movies with mature content, and my internet searches are monitored. I still don't have a smartphone (because Fletcher is an asshole) or access to the internet outside of school and the library. But I've read books— very descriptive books on sex.

God bless public libraries.

Yet nothing in the public library could have adequately prepared me for this. As old as time itself, the saying "a picture's worth a thousand words" has never been truer than it is now while I watch Milo having sex.

Good sex. Or so I assume. Milo makes little grunting sounds like he's enjoying himself. And the woman's fingernails dig into his back, and she's chanting "oh god" so many times I lose count.

Oh god indeed.

Heat fills my cheeks, and my breathing accelerates. I'm fourteen today, starting my second year as an official teenager. I came to the barn for cake, but it no longer seems like the best time to ask Milo if he'll make me a coffee mug cake. And if I'm being completely honest, the view before me is a better gift.

Do I want to watch Milo having sex? It isn't a question that's ever occurred to me. But as I do, in fact, watch him, the answer quietly comes to me.

Yes.

I want to watch Milo have sex. I like watching Milo have sex. Does that make me a pervert? Is that even the right word?

I prefer curious.

Milo and this woman are teaching me a few things. And I'm diligently taking mental notes. Do I wish it were me having sex with Milo? I mean … kinda. When I'm ready. But I don't think today is that day.

The woman yells his name, and it startles me. My hand flies to my mouth to cover my yelp. He expels a low growl, a sound I've never heard him make. Then he says the F-word three times before he presses his hand to the wall next to her head and eases her to her feet.

Whoa ...

I can't believe I'm witnessing this.

She giggles, then he chuckles, a little out of breath. Milo sounds happy the way Fletcher used to sound happy after taking Ruthie breakfast in bed. Someday, I want this kind of happiness.

I take calculated steps backward before either one notices I'm ... *observing*.

"Would it kill you to let me into your bed?" she asks.

"Can't. Indie pops in all the time."

"Indie. Who names their kid Indie?"

I frown, batting my hand at a fly.

"Her name is Indiana. Indie Ellington. It's a fucking fantastic name."

Again, Milo uses the F-word. I have friends who use it occasionally, but not as casually as Milo uses it. I like how he says it before the word "fantastic" about my name.

"That girl is gonna be messed-up. No mother. A father who ignores her existence. And she goes to boarding school."

"She has me," Milo says. "And she's getting a good education."

"You?" The woman laughs while they make rustling sounds with their clothes. "You're not related to her,

39

which means you need to stay as far away from her as possible."

"Why?"

I hear the zipper of his jeans.

"Because rumors could get started. She's young, but not that young. She's a pretty blonde with long legs; her tits are starting to develop, and her daddy has more money than God. If you cross him, he'll throw your ass in prison with your brother just for looking at Indie."

"You can't be serious. I've been driving her to school since I had a driver's license. Mrs. Ellington trusted me. Fletch trusts me more than his own goddamn family. And I guarantee that's how Indie thinks of me ... like a brother."

"I'm just saying ... watch yourself, Milo."

"Listen, you need to head out. It's her birthday, and I have a feeling Fletch has no fucking clue. I need to do something for her."

This makes my heart swell. *He remembered.*

"How old is she?" the woman asks.

"Fourteen."

"Newsflash, Milo ... I lost my virginity when I was fifteen."

"Your point?"

"Hormones ... She's gonna have a lot of hormones to deal with. Guys will take notice. And while Mr. Ellington is oblivious to her existence, someone needs to ensure she doesn't get into trouble. You know ... young girl with no father figure. Daddy issues. Boom! She's pregnant because she gives it all to the first guy who pretends to care about her."

I cringe when the board beneath me squeaks. Does she think I'm that stupid? Just because she was a whore at fifteen doesn't mean I'm that desperate.

Milo and the woman remain quiet for a few seconds. I don't even breathe. If he caught me, I would be mortified.

"Noted," Milo finally says. "And it's gonna be hard for her to get knocked up at an all-girls school. Now ... move along."

I hear the smack of lips and a tiny hum of pleasure. He's kissing her goodbye. I turn and run toward the house. I'm no longer in the mood for a mug cake.

4

STOLEN DREAMS

"Indiana, where the hell do you think you're going?" Fletcher says when I jog down the stairs, the stench of cigars suffocating me.

"Out." I tuck lip gloss into my purse.

It's the summer before my senior year—less than a year before I get the hell out of here for good.

"Not wearing that, you aren't." He eyes my short denim skirt and crop top.

"You've ignored me for seven years, and now that I'm months from being an adult and a year from going to college, you're suddenly taking an interest in me?" I roll my eyes, tapping my fingernails on the banister.

Milo strolls around the corner, holding a glass of hard liquor in one hand while his other hand slides into his front pocket. He scrapes his teeth over his bottom lip, eyeing me ... differently.

They're drinking together. Fletcher and Milo spend so much time talking shop and drinking expensive whiskey.

In the background, pots and pans clank in the kitchen. The aroma of herbs simmering with something delicious Micah's cooking up saves me from the nasty cigar smoke. Sadly, I won't be here for dinner. That would require me to spend time with Fletcher.

My gaze flits from the vicinity of the kitchen back to Milo.

I'd be lying if I said I didn't still have a hard crush on Milo Odell. I'd be lying if I said he's not whom I think about when I masturbate. And I swear he's looking at me *differently*.

The years have only made him sexier. Thicker beard but still closely trimmed. More scars, like the one by his eye. Broader shoulders covered in dense muscles. He's ... all man.

"Go change or I'm taking away your phone," Fletcher warns.

I fucking hate that he treats me like a child in front of Milo.

"Are you serious? Do you honestly think changing clothes will increase my chances of keeping them on the whole night?"

"Indiana ..." Fletcher growls, eyes narrowed.

I can't help it. I have to poke and prod. I have to goad.

Stupid Milo dares to smirk and quickly rolls his lips together to hide it when I shoot my gaze to him. It's the only way I feel a little independent and not like a piece of property Fletcher purchased for a million dollars.

"Fine, *sir* ..." I say with zero sincerity. "I'll put on a frock so I can milk the cows and gather eggs from the chickens before my date picks me up. Would that make you happy?" I stomp my feet up the stairs. After changing my clothes, settling for jeans and a sleeveless tee, I tiptoe back down the stairs, hoping to sneak out of the house before another lecture on my clothing choice ensues.

"I need you to do something for me," Fletcher says to Milo.

I continue to tiptoe toward the backdoor, but for some reason, Fletcher's tone piques my curiosity.

"What's that?" Milo asks.

"When Jolene graduates from college, I want you to marry her."

What the actual fuck?

I crane my neck in the opposite direction. He did not say that. I had to have heard him wrong. The words spin in my head. It's dizzying. Unreal. Is this what it feels like to hallucinate?

Milo coughs several times. "Excuse me?"

"Listen, Milo. You've done a lot for me, especially since I lost Ruthie. But we know I've done a lot for you too. Some would say I've saved your life many times over. Jolene is a beautiful girl. You'd be lucky to have her."

"Fletch ... do you hear yourself? Do you know what year it is? Do you know what country we live in? You can't arrange your niece's marriage." Milo chuckles again.

Of course, he chuckles. It's ridiculous.

"I promised Greg I would take care of Jolene if anything happened to him."

"Fletch, your sister's alive. She can take care of her daughter. Money is clearly not an issue. And Jolene is a grown woman. I don't think she needs anyone to take care of her, least of all find her a husband."

"It's all going to be hers, Milo. When my sister and I are gone, this will all belong to Jolene. She can't run everything alone. Sometimes the best decisions in life are those that make sense. When we let our fucking hearts rule the world, it goes to hell."

"You married Ruthie because you loved her. Can you honestly say you regret that?"

"Yes," Fletcher says, and my heart deflates into a hollow piece of nothing.

Why would he say that? He loved her. I saw it every single day.

"Look where I am now? I can't sleep. I want to drink myself into the fucking grave. I can't bear to live in this house because she's everywhere. And then there's Indiana."

Me? And then there's me? What about me?

"Yeah, there's Indie," Milo says. "You said when you and your sister are gone, Jolene is it. But that's not true. You have a daughter too."

"No. Ruthie wanted a child, so I got her a child. Indie is not family like Jolene."

"Fletch—"

He cuts off Milo. "Greg made me promise that everything would go to Jolene. And Pauline won't have it any other way either."

"And Pauline is okay with her daughter marrying for business reasons, not love?"

"Pauline is fine with it. Jolene is fine with it."

No. No. No. That can't be true. Jolene hates this

place. She loves the money, but she's not a rancher. She's never been on a horse. She loses her shit if she gets dirt under her fingernails. She's not the woman who will let Milo fuck her in a barn.

My hand rests against the wall next to a black-and-white photo of Fletcher's father on a horse.

"Fletch ..."

"Listen, Milo. You owe this family. I hate having to be such a dick to you about this, but the fact is ... you owe me. And you're going to run the show someday. You need a partner. A wife to have your children. I can't risk Jolene marrying someone who will threaten the ownership ... the legacy my family has built over four generations."

"I'm not blood," Milo says, throwing Fletcher's bull-shit back into his face.

"The day your parents died, you became my blood. My responsibility," Fletcher says.

What does that mean?

"I'm not asking you to marry her tomorrow. I'm not asking you to court her. You can screw whomever you want for now, but don't knock anyone up, and be ready to fall in line when the time comes. Okay?"

Say no, Milo. It's not okay.

I don't hear Milo say anything.

"That's my boy," Fletcher says.

Did Milo nod? Did he agree to this? No. I shake my head and flee on wobbly legs as hard and fast as possible. This isn't real. It's unfathomable, even for Fletcher Ellington.

I sprint to the end of the long driveway, swatting my hands at tiny clouds of swarming bugs, through the seeping trail of smoke from the workers' roaring fire behind their barn. Hopping into the back seat of Camden's red Mustang with Hallie, I swallow down the bile that wants out. The nauseating reality of Fletcher's words and Milo's acquiescence.

Roman glances back at me from the front passenger seat. "You okay?"

I nod, breaths labored. "I will be."

Four hours later, I'm fantastically drunk for the first time and miserably sick. The alcohol doesn't have the same effect coming up as it did going down. Every muscle in my stomach hurts, and my throat feels raw.

"Um ... there's a black truck outside," Hallie says as Camden steps into the half bath and hands me a wash-cloth to wipe the vomit from my cheek.

"My dad?" I hug my stomach and sway slightly on unsure legs toward the window. "I should have turned off my location."

Camden's parents are gone for the night. Nobody needed to know my whereabouts, especially the fucker who stole me.

But it's not Fletcher's black truck; it's Milo's. He strides through the rain with his cowboy hat shielding his face.

Roman scrambles to open the door, no doubt worried that he's in trouble too. Milo brushes past him, straight to me.

"You're such a fucking pussy for marrying Jolene," I

slur my words. I should have drunk until I forgot about Jolene's stupid existence in this world.

Milo stops, eyes narrowed for several seconds. "How much have you had to drink?"

I laugh, stumbling backward a few steps. "Not enough. Not nearly enough."

"What are you talking about?" Hallie asks with a little laugh. "Jolene is getting married?"

Milo scoops me up in his arms. "She's drunk. Don't listen to her." He carries me to his truck and plops my ass in the front seat before belting me into it. Rain drenches both of us.

I start to speak, but he shuts my door. By the time he climbs into the driver's seat, I'm out.

The next thing I remember is waking up with an urgent need to vomit again, but I'm not in my bed. I'm not sure where I'm at when the poison in my stomach causes my muscles to seize, the contents lurching into my throat. "Help ..." I croak, scrambling to my feet in the dark.

"Hold it ... just hold it ..." Milo says, wrapping an arm around my waist and rushing me to the toilet.

I hurl twice before falling back onto my butt. Milo flushes the putrid-smelling liquid down the toilet, closes the seat, and sits on it. My curled body slumps onto the warm, wood floor at his feet.

"What have I told you about eavesdropping?" he asks.

I don't recall him saying anything about eavesdropping. The only thing I remember right now is how my heart shattered when he silently agreed to marry Jolene.

"He's just doing what's best for the family."

I grunt a laugh, hugging my roiling stomach. My mouth tastes like ass. "My friends have parents who do what's best for their families too, but they're not *arranging marriages*. And for that matter, they didn't buy children for a million dollars. Oh my god ..." I groan. "He thinks I'm his property, but not the good kind of property like Jolene." My gaze shoots to Milo's. I can't see much, just a tiny reflection in his eyes from the nightlight next to the sink.

Instant tears.

My lower lip quivers. "H-he thinks I'm h-his p-property ... n-not real f-family." It's not news. I've known this. Alcohol must have a way of bringing up the worst parts of my past and presenting them as new information.

"You're no one's property." Milo takes my hands and pulls me to my feet.

My knees buckle, so he once again carries me, this time to his bed, and tucks me under the sheets. It's been a long time since I've slept in Milo's bed. I don't remember when I stopped going to him for comfort. It just happened.

I inhale a shaky breath. *Leather, coffee, cinnamon ...*

"You're free to marry whoever the fuck you want. You're luckier than Jolene, times *a million*. Now, sleep it off," he says. "Forget about what you heard. He had a bad night with a bad idea. I don't think any of this will come to fruition."

Liar. He knows ... we both know Fletcher gets what Fletcher wants. And he's holding something ginormous over Milo's beautiful head.

"Go to sleep, Indie girl."

Indigo ...

He covers me with an extra blanket and takes another blanket to the sofa, where he collapses for the night. The days of Milo sleeping in this bed with me are over.

I fear many things are over.

5

MY MILO

I'm mad at Fletcher for being such an asshole.

I'm mad at Milo for ... well, I'm not sure, but I'm mad at him.

It's become my new obsession this summer. I spend night after night having nightmares about Milo marrying Jolene. Milo kissing Jolene. Milo having sex with Jolene. I hate closing my eyes at night because I can't make it stop.

This goes on for weeks. Fletcher and Milo go about their business like there isn't a dowery attached to Jolene. And whenever I have the same dream, I awaken feeling out of sorts. Sweaty. Gasping for breath. And ... embarrassed. Not because Fletcher is a horrible human. Nope. I'm embarrassed because *I* want to marry Milo. Jolene probably isn't a virgin. I'm a virgin. Don't dowries go with virgins?

"You're not supposed to swim in the pond alone." Milo catches me ambling into the pond, my fingertips grazing the water's surface after it reaches past my knees.

"I'll be eighteen soon, not eight." I roll my eyes.

"When you were eight, you wore a one-piece with pink ponies."

I glance over my shoulder, eyeing Milo—gauging him. Is he referencing my bikini? The wind picks up, and goose bumps erupt along my exposed skin. Or maybe it's the way Milo's looking at me.

Instead of saying what I want to say, I smirk. *Yes, Milo, I have boobs now. Do you like them? Yes, Milo, more than half of my ass is currently exposed. Does that do anything for you?*

"If you think I'm doing something I'm not supposed to be doing, you'll have to come get me and carry me to my room. I won't fight you." I grin to myself. "Not that much."

"What's with your tone today?"

"Tone?" I ask, diving forward and swimming into the deeper water. When I reach the middle of the pond, I face the bank and Milo sitting on the edge of the dock in his jeans, button-down, cowboy hat, and boots, nearly skimming the water's surface when he swings his legs.

"It's the tone you use with Fletcher," he says.

"I don't hate you *that* much, Milo." I can't help but flirt with him while making slow broad strokes and treading water.

"That much? So you're saying you hate me? What did I do?"

My arms slice through the water, easy breaststrokes in his direction. "You're marrying Jolene next summer. I heard Fletcher talking to Pauline. They're planning your wedding for right after Jolene's college graduation. Did you know that?"

His chin dips into a hesitant nod, eyes tracking my every move. "Yes. I'm aware."

"God ... you're such a slave to him. All these years, I looked at you and thought you were this strong, capable man whom no one dared to mess with. But you're just a pawn. Whatever he has over you must be big." I stop just beneath his dangling legs.

"What if I'm okay with marrying Jolene? What if that makes me financially smart? What if everyone else is the fucking pawn, and I'm the one who's gonna come out on top? And what's wrong with Jolene?"

"She's one of them."

"Maybe I'm one of them."

"You're not. You're like me."

He chuckles, shaking his head and peering out at the pond. A smile plays along his lips. "Nobody's like you, Indiana. You're in your own fucking league."

"What league is that?"

Milo returns his gaze to me. "Self-destructive. You'd burn this whole place down before you'd let anyone tell you what to do, who to marry, or how to think."

A slow grin works its way up my face. He's not wrong, but something tells me it's not meant to be a compliment.

"Jolene is graduating from college. You're getting married. All eyes will be on the two of you. I should thank you. I can graduate and get the hell out of here without anyone noticing that I'm gone." I kick off the dock post and float on my back. "Free. I'll be ... free."

"I'll notice that you're gone."

I lift my head, unsure I heard him with my ears in the water. "What did you say?"

A barely detectable smile tugs at his lips while he averts his gaze and shakes his head. "Nothing."

I swim toward the dock once more and grab his boot. "Tell me."

After a few seconds, he glances down at me, blinking slowly while twisting his lips. "I said I'd notice that you're gone."

There are a million ways I could respond to him. "Well, I'm not gone yet. So get in the pond and race me to the other side."

"I'm in my work clothes."

"Take them off." I grin, tugging on his boot.

"Indie ..." He playfully kicks his foot away from me.

"Last one to the other side cleans out the chicken coops." I circle my arms, swimming toward the opposite side of the pond, kicking up that familiar fishy smell.

"Indiana ..."

"Am I too fast for you, Milo?" I taunt him.

Splash!

I feel him on my tail, and I sneak a glance back. Yep, he's on my tail. His muscular arms cut through the water after me.

With a giggle, I swim as fast as I can. "No!" I scream when he passes me less than five feet from the opposite shore. My motion loses uniformity, and I turn into nothing but flailing arms and legs—a sinking pile of dead momentum.

His hand smacks the grassy edge, and he hurls himself out of the pond two seconds before I reach land.

I try not to stare at his bare chest, tattoos, or shit-eating grin, and I definitely try not to stare at his wet, black briefs clinging to him rather snugly. It's no longer innocent like it was in my formative years. I'm no longer taking note of his size. My mind goes further ... much further. Thoughts as dirty as the water around us.

"There's nothing I love more than watching you clean the chicken coops." He offers his hand and a winning smile.

I place my hand in his, as I've done so many times. But now, even that feels different. Fishing me out of the water, he plunks my ass next to him in the tall grass, bending the blades in wayward directions. On an unavoidable giggle, I fall back and gaze at the clear summer sky and breathe in the earthy scent of grass and honeysuckle. "So you're going to watch me?"

Milo lies next to me. "Absolutely."

"Because you want to make sure I do it or because you like watching me?"

He remains still and silent for a long moment before turning his head. My head lolls to the side to meet his gaze.

I'm so heartbroken. Maybe what I feel for Milo is nothing more than a childish crush. Maybe Milo's love is the only love I've felt since Ruthie died. Maybe my hatred for Jolene has messed with my feelings toward everyone, including Milo. But right now, I'm angry that Jolene is taking *my* Milo.

"Watching you is my favorite job."

"Pfft ... I'm your job? That's ..." I return my attention to the sky. "Well, that just sucks."

He laughs. "Why does that suck?"

"Because it's not authentic. Maybe Jolene is okay with her life being a series of arrangements and transactions, but I want the real deal."

"Indie, I like watching you. And it's real. Does that make you feel better?"

My head flops back to the side, and I smile. "So you really like watching me? Is that what you're saying?"

"Speaking of deals. What's yours today? You're extra ..."

"Extra what?" I ask.

"Just extra."

I roll toward him, and for the briefest few seconds, he inspects my body. It gives me a tiny thrill, a jolt of excitement. I know he's marrying Jolene. I know he's somehow indebted to Fletcher. But for years, he's been mine. My friend. My family. My protector. My angel. My Milo. And before long, he's going to be Jolene's husband. And it's going to crush me.

That's when I'll run. I'll go to college as far away from here as I can get. I'll immerse myself in a life that has nothing to do with Fletcher Ellington.

"I used to have a crush on you," I say, staring at the tattoos on his chest because I can't make this confession *and* look him in the eye. "So it was always weird when you, Ruthie, or Fletcher made the brother and sister reference. I didn't want to think of you as my brother. But now that you're marrying Jolene, I suppose you'll officially be family." I trap my lower lip between my teeth and think about that. "Good thing I no longer have a crush on you."

Biggest. Lie. Ever.

I risk a glance at him.

Milo's eyes gloss over with a distant, sad nothingness.

"For the record," I say, "I hate Jolene. I know I shouldn't hate anyone, but she's worked hard to earn every ounce of my hatred. But I like you, Milo. So as a wedding gift to both of you, I'll try to hate her a little less."

His eyebrows draw together. "Why do you hate her?"

"For the same reason I hate Fletcher. They think I'm an impostor. They think I'm not worthy. The only redeeming quality they have is their keenness for you."

Milo brings his hand to my face, ghosting it over my cheek for a few seconds and whipping my heart into acting like a racehorse.

It engulfs my skin, a wildfire out of control. It's a different feeling than I've ever felt before. Different than it felt when I used to snuggle up to him in his bed after Ruthie died. Different than him ruffling my hair or carrying my drunk ass out of Camden's house. I feel this touch in my chest—a gentle hand squeezing my heart, but not claiming it. More of a reminder that it's always been his.

Drawing a shaking breath, I hold it, trying to conceal what his touch does to me. Can he read my mind? Does he know I can't look at him and not think, *"my Milo?"* Can he feel my pulse racing, my heart bouncing around in my chest from his touch, the endless waves of goosebumps along my bare skin despite the scorching Texas heat?

My composure can't withstand his touch, so I close my eyes and rest my hand over his to steady my emotions.

I turn my head a fraction until my lips brush his palm. It's not a kiss, but it's intimate to me. And it hurts because it's familiar and safe, yet new and exciting. And I'm scared that nothing will ever feel like this again. I'm afraid no other man will ever touch me and make me feel like I do now.

"I have to get back." His words are thick and deep before he clears his throat. "And you have to clean the chicken coop."

I open my eyes when his touch vanishes. He jack-knives to sitting, running his hands through his hair.

Did he feel what I felt? Even a little? Or am I the naive young woman still crushing on Milo Odell as hard as I did as a young girl? I can't sort through my emotions or get a handle on this. It's a lonely vulnerability. I have a long year of school left before I can escape. Really escape.

A long year of yearning for a man who has been promised to another woman. A long year of feeling trapped, owned by a "father" who doesn't love me.

And when I think our little bubble a few seconds ago was all in my head, Milo rests his hand on my leg, just below my knee. He doesn't look at me, just at his hand on my leg.

I wait.

I'd wait forever if he'd keep his hand on me.

Ever so slowly, he slides his hand down my leg to my ankle.

Pause.

My foot.

Pause.

The calloused pads of his fingers tickle my sensitive

skin, but I don't flinch. I'll do *anything* to keep from spoiling this moment and losing his touch.

"Last one to the dock has to clean out Ranger's stall," he says, a breath before diving back into the pond and sprinting to the other side.

I take my sweet time. Ranger's stall is close to Milo's living quarters. I'll happily clean it if it means being closer to Milo.

6

THE END OF INNOCENCE

It's as if that day at the pond never happened.

I clean the coops.

No Milo.

I clean Ranger's stall.

No Milo.

He's intentionally avoiding me.

Until today.

Baking a pecan pie (Fletcher has acres of pecan trees), I use it as an excuse to visit Milo. I take extra time curling my hair. A little makeup. A dab of soft floral perfume. And a cute pink sundress with boots. It's been a while since I've channeled my inner Ruthie with an airy dress and cowboy boots.

I knock twice on Milo's door before opening it.

"Who's that?" a woman says from his sofa as she stuffs her breasts back into her bra, dragging the white straps up her slender, tan arms.

Milo eyes me, but he doesn't say anything at first, quickly averting his gaze while standing in front of the woman. He's only wearing a pair of jeans. Plucking his shirt from the floor, he jerks it over his head while mumbling, "What's up, Indie?"

To keep from losing it, I focus on the pie. Its roasted nuttiness and cinnamon—nope. Not going to focus on cinnamon. Maybe warm notes of sweet vanilla and nutmeg. I bet the buttery crust melts in your mouth.

But I have a feeling Milo already had something else melting in his mouth.

Now, all I taste is acid in my throat, and all I smell is cheap hairspray from her big hair.

While I stare at the pie, the woman adjusts her dress, tugging it up her body while she stands and plasters on a smile like I didn't just see her boobs.

I'm ... speechless. And heartbroken.

It *was* just me. That day at the pond, it was all me. I'm so stupid.

Young.

Naive.

"I made a pecan pie." My voice quivers along with my hands while I quickly set the pie on his counter. "That's all. Sorry to uh ... interrupt."

"Indie ..."

I scamper out the door, slamming it shut behind me. My legs take long, rapid strides from the gravel to the blacktop drive up toward the house.

"Indie?" Milo chases me.

I gulp down my stupid ... young ... presumptuous emotions and turn with my chin up and the fakest, bravest face I can find.

Milo rests a hand on one hip and drops his chin,

staring at his boots. "I'm sorry. I should have locked the door."

He thinks I'm mad because he didn't lock the door? Okay ... not even close. I don't know how to respond without lying or admitting how delusional I've been since that day at the pond. So I don't say a word.

Milo eyes me and exhales through his teeth. "My life is really fucking complicated. I'm sorry."

Sorry? Sorry that his life is complicated? Or is it another apology for not locking the door? Too bad I don't have a voice or a shred of confidence to offer up a single verbal response. So I nod and let him decide what he thinks my nod means.

The weird part? For a few seconds, I feel sorry for Jolene. Awful, mean, vengeful Jolene. The man who has agreed to marry her was enjoying another woman's breasts. Does Jolene care? Who knows? Maybe she's screwing other guys in college. I don't know if she and Milo have officially discussed this marriage. Has there been a formal proposal? Or is this truly an arranged marriage that doesn't involve them until the wedding day when they have to go through the motions of exchanging vows and ... ugh ... it makes me nauseous. They're going to have sex on their wedding night. And other nights. They're going to make babies.

Fuck my life.

Something has to change. Something drastic. Something that helps me escape this hell, this feeling of unrequited love and childish infatuation. This feeling of being owned and imprisoned in this life as the token child of

Fletcher Ellington and kid sister to his right-hand man is torture.

"Say something, Indie."

I shake my head slowly. "Uh ... be careful. There could be a few pieces of shell in the pie. I'm not as good as Ruthie was at making them. So ... be careful." I pivot and putter toward the house, feeling unwelcome and out of place everywhere I go.

"Indie ..."

I ignore Milo, and he doesn't chase me anymore.

I DO the most grown-up thing I can imagine to escape these feelings.

I have sex for the first time, the second time, and many more. The destructive power of loneliness should never be underestimated.

Sex with Camden.

Sex with Aiden.

Sex with Sam.

Sex with a new guy each week, and twice on my birthday, until school starts. Does it make me feel better? Not really. Does it make me feel less pathetic when I occasionally run into Milo? Marginally.

I'll take marginally.

No mother.

No father.

No Ruthie.

No Milo.

And fuck Fletcher. Whoever the hell he is in my life right now.

Sex fills a void. Then the void returns. I need to make it through this year and get out of here. Freedom. I desperately need to feel free.

"I'm going to be gone for a few days. I'll be back by Thanksgiving. Micah left meals in the fridge, and Milo's in charge," Fletcher says as he pokes his head in my bedroom, bringing a nice breeze of stale cigar smoke. "Behave."

I knew I shouldn't have come home for fall break. My nose wrinkles and I slide my bookmark between the pages. "Um ... what about Benton?"

Benton is my new boyfriend. I think. After chatting for weeks, we had sex two days ago when I arrived home for break. So I'm calling it a relationship since I'm open to having sex with him again, and I feel a slight inclination toward monogamy.

"Who's Benton?" Fletcher asks, eyes on his phone instead of me.

"He's my boyfriend. I'm going to see him."

"Not while I'm gone."

"Why not?"

"I'm not in the mood for your questions. Just do as I say." He starts to close my door.

"I'm having him over. Milo can watch all he wants, but I'm having him over." I bite my tongue from reminding him that I'm eighteen now. I don't need him lording my car, phone, or Fletcher-funded bank account over me.

"Indiana, you're asking to lose your car." He adjusts his big-ass belt buckle.

Here we go ...

"And you're being unfair."

"If I find out he's been here while I'm gone, Milo will be in trouble, and you will be without a car for good." Fletcher closes my door as if his word is the final one.

Does that mean Milo won't marry Jolene?

Grabbing a pink decor pillow from my bed, I bury my face and scream. I hate Fletcher. I hate him so much.

LATER THAT NIGHT, Benton arrives just after I clean up my small mess from dinner. Milo's in the barn. And Fletcher is ... who the fuck cares. Miles, maybe even states away from here.

"Fletcher's gone for five fucking fabulous days." I leap into Benton's arms as soon as I open the front door.

"Mmm ..." He buries his face into my neck and grabs my ass with both hands. He's smells like soap and hair gel, not leather, coffee, and cinnamon. I try to convince myself that I prefer soap and hair gel.

"It's weird that you call him Fletcher when he's your dad. But who cares as long as he's gone. Take off your clothes."

I giggle, opting not to explain my complicated relationship with Fletcher to Benton. "We should go to the bedroom."

"Why?" He gathers my skirt with one hand, exposing

my panties, while his other hand slides up my blouse, where he discovers I'm not wearing a bra.

We make it to the stairs in a flurry of kisses and impatient hands before he pulls my top over my head, wetting his lips at my breasts. "Sit down."

My teeth trap my lower lip while I sit on the step with my hands on either side.

Benton kneels on the bottom stair, eyeing me confidently while he peels off my thong, bringing it to his nose and taking a long inhale. Not much embarrasses me, but this kinda does.

The door opens with a sharp creak, and I shoot my gaze to it.

"I'll give you ten seconds to get out before I make a dent in the hood of your fucking car with your head."

My arms wrap around my bare chest while I snap my knees together, feeling the cool evening breeze from the open door. I need another hand to pull my skirt back over my waist. "Get out, Milo," I shriek, heat accumulating in my cheeks.

Milo removes his cowboy hat and scratches the back of his head. He replaces it slowly before balling his hands into fists at his sides. "Ten, nine, eight ..."

"What the fuck, man? Who are you?" Benton scrambles to his feet and stumbles away from me.

"Benton, don't go ..."

"Benton, get the fuck out of here. Seven, six, five ..." Milo stalks him, tracing his steps to the front door and slamming it shut the second Benton gets past the threshold. "Get dressed," he says with his back to me.

"Wow ... is that how you're going to treat Jolene?" Not that I give a shit.

"This is not my house. This is your father's house. And you're not my wife. You're a girl under my care for the next week. Any more questions, Indiana?"

After piecing my clothes back together, I slap my bare feet across the wood floor until I'm at Milo's back, until I smell the leather and resent the feelings that come with a single inhale. "Newsflash. I am not a virgin. Or a girl. I'm a woman. So I don't know what you think you just accomplished by kicking my boyfriend out of my house, but I'm sure Fletcher will give you a bone for being such an obedient little watchdog."

Milo turns, lips curled into a mischievous grin. "Ruff."

It's ... unexpected. And irritating.

Gah!

I don't want to smile. He ran off my boyfriend in the most embarrassing fashion. Instead of a smile, I opt for a subject change or maybe a jab to prove he can't ruin my day without a fight. "Why did your brother kill your parents?"

Milo's grin falls right off his face. "We're not having this conversation."

"Why not?" I plant my hands on my hips.

"Because it's none of your business." He glances around the foyer, avoiding eye contact with me.

"So all of my business is your business, but none of your business is mine?"

"Why don't you finish your homework and go to bed."

"I'm on break. I don't have homework. And I was in the process of going to bed when you showed up."

"You're eighteen."

"I'm aware. What exactly is your fascination with my age?" I cock my head to the side, giving him a challenging scowl.

"You want to be an adult? It's time to grow the fuck up. Stop spreading your legs for anyone with a dick."

Smack!

Fire blazes along my palm, but I don't so much as curl my fingers into a fist. I like the sting. It's what I hope he feels on his cheek. In the next breath, I can only feel how Fletcher's hand felt on my face the day he lost control. The past hitting back with instant guilt.

Like father like daughter?

No. I'm not his daughter. I'm stolen property.

Besides a tiny twitch of his jaw muscle, Milo doesn't budge. His stern glare bores into me without reprieve while his lips pull into a stiff, flat line. I'm probably not the first girl to smack his smug face.

"If you ever do that again, your dad will be the least of your worries. Understood?" His words penetrate my bones.

I don't recognize the Milo saying this. It's not a tone he's ever taken with me.

"Understood," I whisper in a shaky voice. Tears burn my eyes. I am, for the first time, scared of Milo Odell. For the first time, I really ... *really* think about his brother killing their parents and what Fletcher said to him. Could Milo have gone to prison too? Does that mean Milo helped kill them? Have I spent most of my childhood trusting a murderer?

"Go to bed," he snaps.

I nod and bolt up the stairs, oblivious to the tears mixing with mascara and painting black streaks down my cheeks until the bathroom mirror says it all: everything about Milo Odell matters to me. It matters deeply.

His opinion of me.

The way he looks at me.

The tone of voice he uses with me.

And the soul-shattering reality that he will marry Jolene.

After a long bath, drying my hair, and messaging Benton to apologize, I decide to get a snack since I can't sleep. However, my steps falter when I turn the corner into the kitchen. Milo glances over at me from the stove where he's cooking a grilled cheese sandwich, getting it good and black. It's a familiar burnt aroma. His gaze slips a few inches for a brief second ... specifically to my chest.

I cross my arms over my nightie. Ruthie always wore pretty nightgowns. I like to wear them too. I like how they make me feel like a woman—like Ruthie, the most exquisite woman I've ever known. She wore a robe over her nighties. I have a robe upstairs, but I didn't put it on because I thought I was alone in the house. And it's nearly midnight.

And really fucking cold, according to my nipples.

Milo clears his throat and returns his attention to the sandwich. "What do you need?" His voice is thick and tight like my muscles or the ache in my chest.

It's a rare moment to see Milo without his cowboy

hat. Without jeans. Without a shirt. I have never seen Milo in a pair of low-hanging jogging shorts.

"I'm hungry," I manage to say past the frog in my throat. Seeing Milo like this does things to me. I can't stop wetting my lips and gulping down copious amounts of saliva. But seriously, my nipples beneath the thin layer of pink satin ... what's going on down there? A heavy sensation settles between my legs. Why is my body betraying me at the worst possible moment?

I have a boyfriend. He's good for me. I think.

As a young girl, I had a crush on Milo, but I'm no longer that young girl. The way he embarrassed me in front of Benton makes me want to scratch out his eyeballs.

Yet as I stand idle in the kitchen, barely able to catch my next breath, all I can think about is what it would feel like to kiss Milo. To feel his strong, calloused hands touching me intimately. His tongue warm and wet against mine. I imagine what my nipples would feel like trapped between his teeth. His mouth between my legs. Every possible inappropriate thought explodes in my mind. I think of the girl he fucked in the barn, and I imagine it was me. My legs around his waist. My name on his lips.

"You feeling okay?" he asks, glancing over his bare shoulder for a few seconds before sliding the sandwich onto a plate. "Your cheeks are red. Are you running a fever?"

My head eases side to side while I press my hands to my cheeks. They're ablaze. I'm eighteen. Milo's a twenty-six-year-old man. A man who has always treated me like a little sister. Only, I'm not his little sister. And I'm not the little girl he drove to school every day. I'm not the young, scared girl who clung to him at night to ward off bad dreams and keep from drowning in grief.

The young *woman* I've become has raging hormones. They don't care that I'm eighteen and he's twenty-six.

I don't know if it's the time of night, the dark kitchen, my nightgown, his lack of a shirt, knowing Fletcher is out of town, my feeling unloved and lost ... or a toxic combination of everything, but I can't stop my feet from padding their way to him. And while the space between us evaporates, his gaze tracks down my body—*not* like a brother would look at his sister.

"Milo," I whisper.

He takes a bite of his burnt sandwich and mumbles over it, "Indie ..."

I allow my gaze to settle onto his chest, my mind filling with curiosity and questions about his tattoos. The meanings behind them. When he got them. Will he get more?

And then I think about him in the barn with that woman again. That half-naked woman on his sofa. All I can see is the tight flex of muscles along his back and across his perfect ass, shifting and bending with each rhythmic thrust.

I can't help my gulp while I lift my gaze to his eyes. They're unblinking and dark, not the soft blue they are during the day. My hands slowly lift, preparing to rest on his chest, fingers splayed out wide.

"Don't," he snaps while shaking his head.

My hands stop midair.

"Why?" I whisper.

He tears his sandwich apart.

I stare at it. "What do you see when you look at me?" I whisper before risking another glance up at him.

"My grave, Indie." He shoves half the sandwich into my hand and brushes past me. "I see my fucking grave."

7

THE KISS OF DEATH

"DON'T you have stuff to do?" I ask Milo the next night when he settles into the corner of the leather sofa with a drink in one hand and the TV remote in his other hand.

"I'm doing it," he says, staring at the screen and the men with guns spraying bullets everywhere.

"Can't you drink and watch TV in the barn?"

"The barn? You realize there's an entire apartment in *the barn*, right?" He eyes me with one raised eyebrow.

"Sorry, Milo. Did I rub your sensitive side the wrong way? Do you not want anyone thinking you live in a barn?" Not gonna lie ... I'm a little on edge.

Pissed off at Fletcher because he's so fucking deplorable.

Pissed off at Milo because I want him more than anything.

Pissed off that Benton refuses to come over because of Milo.

But what pisses me off the most was the way Milo

made me feel like a fool last night when I wanted to touch him. He made me feel like an errant child.

"Here's the thing, Indie..." he pinches the bridge of his nose for a few seconds "...I have to be here to keep an eye on you because you couldn't wait a full twenty-four hours after your dad left town before doing something stupid. I don't wanna babysit, but I don't have a choice. So to answer your question ... I can't watch TV in *the barn* because I have to stay here and keep an eye on you."

"He's not my dad. And why are you so angry?"

He laughs, shaking his head. "I'm not angry."

"You sound angry."

"Angry? No. Tired? Yes."

"Tired of me?"

He sips his whiskey before eyeing me. "I'm tired of your games."

"Games? What games?"

"This game. You know why I'm here, yet you're pretending you don't. You knew I'd be keeping a close eye on you, yet you invited your boyfriend over to screw you on the stairs. Then for your fantastic twenty-four-hour finale, you wore a little bit of nothing last night while being inappropriate with me."

I roll my eyes. "For the record, I didn't know you were here last night."

"So that's what you wear to bed every night?" He nods toward me like I'm wearing it now, but I'm not.

I tip up my chin and cross my arms. "Yes. Ruthie wore nice lingerie, and I like to wear it too. It makes me feel like a woman." I give him a sly grin.

"You tried to touch me."

With a scoff, I shake my head. "Sorry. You're the first guy who has ever complained about it. Do you only like it when women touch you in the barn next to Ranger's stall or topless on your sofa?"

And just like that ... it's out. He knew about the sofa but not the barn. I said the quiet part aloud, and there's no taking it back.

Slowly taking another drink of whiskey, Milo eyes me for what feels like forever. He licks his lips. "You've seen me in the barn?"

I swallow hard, shifting my weight from one foot to the other.

"You've seen me with a woman?" His eyes narrow a fraction.

After a few seconds of painful silence, I nod.

Milo kills me with his slow reaction. He gives nothing away. Is he mad? Surprised? Embarrassed?

He grunts, shaking his head and returning his attention to the TV. "You're such a fucking creeper."

I open my mouth to protest, but nothing comes out.

"Go." He tosses the remote and flicks his chin toward the stairs. "Shoo. Go to bed. Go read a book. I'd suggest something like ... the Bible."

"I'm an atheist." I lean my shoulder against the threshold.

Milo's brows slide up his forehead. "Are you serious?"

I nod.

"Your grandfather, Fletcher's father, was a Southern Baptist minister. Did you know that?"

"You mean the father of the man who paid my biological mother a million dollars to give me to Ruthie? I wonder what the Bible says about that."

Milo's lips twist, and he narrows his eyes for a few seconds. "Does Fletcher know?"

I laugh. "Does Fletcher know what? That I'm an atheist? That I've lost count of how many guys I've slept with? That I know he paid a million dollars for me? My birthday? The colleges I've applied to? My aversion to arranged marriages? You'll need to be more specific. But chances are the answer to whatever question you asked that started with 'does Fletcher know,' the answer is no. Fletcher is clueless when it comes to me. And why would he be anything less than an asshole? I'm not the chosen one."

"The chosen one?" Milo takes a drink and leans forward, placing it on the sturdy wood coffee table and resting his arms on his knees.

"The one to inherit the family business." I frown. "Not that I want it. I don't. I don't want any of it. I know Fletcher is more corrupt than Satan himself. It's just that Ruthie made me feel like her daughter. I felt loved by her in a way that could not have felt more real had she been my biological mother. She told me Fletcher loved me as much as he could love any child. But she was wrong. I'm not Jolene. This..." I gesture around the room with my gaze "...will be hers. You'll be ..." I bite my lips together and slowly shake my head.

I can't go there.

"I'll be what?"

I shrug. "Her husband."

Milo bites his lips together while he returns a slow nod. "Did you want me to be yours?"

"Pfft ... no."

He doesn't smile. He doesn't laugh. We're joking. Right? Where's his smirk?

"But ... I mean ..." I fiddle with a thread hanging from my shirt. As much as the news of him marrying Jolene sliced my heart into bite-sized pieces, I find the strength to look at him. "I don't think she'll ever know you like I do, so I think you are mine in a way that's hard to explain."

His eyes narrow a fraction, head canted to the side. "What do you know about me?"

"Stuff."

"Stuff? Like what?"

"I know you drum your fingers on your lower lip to keep from grinning when you don't want to let anyone see when you find something funny. I know your hat always hangs on the hook with the front facing down. I know you sprinkle cinnamon into your coffee, but I'm not sure why. You have conversations with Ranger about your to-do list before you feed the chickens. And I love that because it reminds me of Ruthie and her talking to the plants in her garden. And I suspect you've had a bad day on the nights you're extra quiet because Fletcher's probably asked you to do something awful like put down an animal or fire some poor guy for being two minutes late to work. Maybe worse because I think he asks you to do some morally questionable things. I ..." I shrug. "I notice things."

Milo holds the silence for a moment or two after my

long spiel, keeping time with nothing more than a few little nods. "And that knowledge makes me yours?"

"Yeah, a little bit."

"You don't want me, Indie. I have a feeling you're gonna get into enough trouble all on your own."

"What's that supposed to mean?" I ask, crossing my arms.

He leans back again and laces his fingers behind his head. "What's your endgame? Are you gonna graduate and leave Texas? Are you getting a job and cutting all ties with Fletcher? Are you feigning independence while using his money to pay for college? Or are you gonna get pregnant and shit all over your future before you get the chance to have a future?"

"I think the guy marrying someone for their money has no right to question my motives. I'm willing to leave it all. Fletcher. The family name. The money. All of it. Unlike you."

"You think I have a choice?" He raises his brows.

I shrug. "I don't know, Milo. Again, all of my business seems to be yours, but nothing about you is my business."

"Indie, you don't wanna know my business. It's not pretty. It can't be changed. I'm in debt beyond any amount of money. I chose my future years ago, and now I'm accepting it. Not all duty comes with honor. Sometimes you have to accept fate."

"And Jolene is your fate?"

"So it would seem." He scratches his jaw, stifling a yawn.

"Do you love her?"

Milo laughs. "I don't know her. I've had a handful of

interactions with her over the years. She's ... fine. She was nice enough to me. She's graduating from law school. She's mentally stable. Really, what's there to complain about?"

My face sours. I can't help it. "That's so sad, Milo. You're going to marry someone you don't love. You're going to have children with someone you don't love. What's the point?"

"You're assuming love is the reason for living."

"Isn't it?"

He gives me a blank expression and a one-shoulder shrug. "I just do my thing. I love fresh air and sunshine. I love not being in prison like my brother. I love the freedom I've been granted. That's my love."

Milo leaves me speechless and sad for him. Turning, I head toward the stairs, but before I round the corner, I have to speak my truth. "I love your touch. I've always loved your touch, Milo. For different reasons. You've touched me in ways I'm sure you can't imagine, maybe in ways you never intended. Your arms absorbed the grief I felt after Ruthie died. Your fingers have wiped so many tears from my face. Each swipe is like a salve to my soul, healing it with something as simple as a *touch*. And when your hand pressed against my cheek and down my leg in the grass by the pond..." I glance over my shoulder, resting my chin on it without fully lifting my gaze to him "...it made me feel beautiful. For that fleeting moment, I thought maybe you felt something for me. Something more than duty. Something more than loyalty. More than sympathy. Then you were gone. But your touch is still on my skin. I wonder if a day will come when I don't feel your touch?" I laugh a little, and it's a pain in the pit of my stomach. "I hope so because it hurts."

When his silence cuts my last thread of bravery, I disappear to my room. But the pain won't dissipate anytime soon. At least I said all the words that have been knotted in my throat for months ... maybe years.

After a shower, I slide a white silk nightie over my body and lift my leg onto my vanity stool. While applying lotion, I glance at the mirror. Milo's reflection stares at me from my bedroom doorway.

My heart pauses, choking my next breath. Turning toward him, I rub the lotion into my hands. I'm out of words. I've said all of them. So I wait. Milo's in my doorway for a reason.

He takes a step toward me for a reason.

Another step.

Milo takes *all* the steps. He looks so sad and weary. "A million dollars, huh?"

A shuddering breath spreads like an earthquake across my chest. I want to nod, but I can't. I'm shackled with grief. I'm stolen, yet I belong to no one. And when I leave for college and Milo marries Jolene, I will *have* no one.

His hand finds the side of my neck, and his thumb brushes along my pulse point. "What a bargain for someone so priceless," he whispers.

Tears fill my eyes. He has no idea how long it's been since someone has touched me, really touched me like this. How can a touch so light reach so deep? "M-Milo ..." I stutter his name.

He gives me a sad smile while his head cants to the

side. "Indie girl ... I'm gonna kiss you. And it's not gonna change anything, but it's gonna mean everything. Okay?"

I blink, setting the tears free while nodding several times. His mouth brushes my wet, salty lips before he kisses me. It's not my first kiss or my second kiss. I don't know how many times I've been kissed, but I know this ... with this one kiss, Milo resurrects the parts of my heart that died when Ruthie left this world. He may never say the words, but I feel loved. I feel like no matter how far apart we are, part of Milo will always be with me. I will *feel* him forever.

My hands press to his chest, and this time he doesn't stop me. His tongue teases my lips, and I open my mouth. Milo makes everything feel like nothing and no one before him was real.

His other hand finds my neck, his touch so gentle and intimate. I keep my eyes closed when his lips leave mine, ghosting along my cheek. I'm so scared this is a dream. What will happen if I open my eyes?

"Indie girl ..." he whispers in my ear before kissing my neck next to his thumb. "You're my fresh air ..." He drags his mouth to the other side of my neck.

My head tips back, mouth falling open, letting tiny breaths escape while his words lull my mind into a safe place. With him, I'm not scared. I'm not lost. I'm not abandoned.

"You're the sun ... so fucking bright, blindingly beautiful." Milo kisses up my neck to my jaw, my cheek, and back to my mouth.

It's a perfect kiss, our tongues making slow but deliberate strokes. He grins against my mouth when I hum. I can't help it.

My fingertips sneak beneath the hem of his shirt and tease his abs.

Milo slowly pulls away and rests his forehead on mine. "It can't go any further. I'm sorry." His hands take mine, guiding them away from his stomach, interlacing our fingers behind my back.

I swallow the thick lump of reality. And my hatred for Jolene grows exponentially.

My Milo.

MY. MILO!

I squeeze his hands, and he squeezes mine back. They fit perfectly. *We* fit perfectly.

"Sweet dreams, Indie girl." Milo dots several kisses along my cheek to the corner of my mouth, where he pauses and inhales slowly. His words feel like the wind's breath, warm and soothing.

And then ... he's gone.

I open my eyes only for them to blur behind a new round of tears. Milo gave me a glimpse of a life I will never have. He's going to marry Jolene, and it will feel like a death, like the day Ruthie died. If I go to their wedding, I will wear black. I will mourn the loss of *my Milo*.

8

FAVORITE PLACE IN THE WORLD

THE NEXT NIGHT, Milo checks in on me after dinner and once again a little before midnight. I hear my door creak, and a sliver of light peeks inside, but I don't move or say a word.

He kissed me. And maybe he said it wouldn't change anything, but it changed *me*. That one kiss made me feel wanted and special. And scared to death. I'm afraid that when I see him again, all I'll see are deep lines of regret on his face.

He keeps his distance for the next two days, only proving my point—he regrets it.

But now my car won't start, and I have errands to run.

"Milo? My car won't—" I freeze, covering my mouth with my hand after barging into his place. His barn. "Sorry," I mumble behind my hand.

He smiles, taking a step back from the woman sitting on his counter, holding a cup of coffee. She's new.

"Your car won't what?" He seems unfazed.

Lucky him.

I clear my throat, sending a nervous smile in the woman's direction. "Start."

It's official. I hate my life—more like my lot in life.

"Rae, this is Indie. Indie, this is Rae. Let me grab a shirt, and I'll look at your car."

"I can run errands later or call a friend. Don't uh ... let me interrupt." I back my way out of this situation and his apartment. There's never a black hole to fall into when you need one.

Milo's gaze cuts to the pretty redhead on his counter. She gives him a grin and a shrug while gently swinging her legs.

"Let's go. I'll look at it now." He pulls on a tee and snags his truck keys from the end of the counter.

"Nice meeting you, Indie," Rae says before taking a sip of her coffee.

"You too," I croak, skittering toward the main house without waiting for Milo.

My measured strides keep me a foot or so ahead of him where I don't have to look at him. The balance between losing my shit (it's what I want to do) and ignoring him proves to be wobbly. It could go either way.

Pretend the kiss never happened. Pretend the best night of my life never happened.

"Indie ..." Milo says, chasing me toward the blacktop.

"Rae seems nice."

"Indie ..."

"Does she know that you're marrying Jolene? Did you try to tell her things couldn't go any further? Did you sleep with her?" I lose my emotional balance, falling hard off the cliff into a sea of jealousy.

"Not recently."

I spin around, blocking him from taking another step. "So you have had sex with her?"

"Why are we having this conversation?" He frowns.

"Because you kissed me, and you're marrying Jolene. I think it's time you set some moral boundaries."

My last morsel of control catches in the breeze and scatters miles away.

"What do you suggest?"

I open my mouth, but nothing comes out.

"I didn't sleep with Rae last night. She stopped by to chat this morning. I'm marrying Jolene, but I'm not rehashing the reasons why. So it would appear the only moral boundary I need to set is with you. I won't kiss you again."

"Stop. Just ..." I blow out a long breath before it suffocates me. "Stop making this about me. It's about you, Milo. It's all the things about you I'm not allowed to know. It's about your indebtedness to Fletcher. It's about your complete and utter lack of self-worth that you're willing to have sex with literally anyone. Except for me, of course. And you're willing to marry someone you don't love."

"Are you really giving me a lecture on self-worth, Indie?"

I turn and stomp the rest of the way to my car. "Yes. I am. Thanks to you, I have less self-worth than anyone right now, so I'm a bit of an expert on it."

Milo pops the hood and inspects things. "I'm not in prison, Indie. I'm. Not. In. Prison." He pokes his head around the hood and eyes me. "I don't care where I live.

I'm not in prison." His gaze drops, and tension lines his forehead. This simple change in demeanor sits heavily on my heart.

"I don't care what job I have. I'm not in prison. I don't care who owns my debt. I'm not in prison. I don't care who I have to marry. I'm not in prison. My brother's on death row. I'm. Not. In. Prison."

Stone still, breath held, every selfish emotion vanishes. Milo is alive. That's what he's saying without actually saying it. Fletcher did something big for Milo. I don't think I will ever know what, but the unspoken truth is a wall between us. An unscalable wall.

It changes nothing, but it will mean everything.

"I don't want to be your moral boundary," I say just above a whisper. One. I have one person in this world, and his name is Milo Odell.

He grunts, returning his attention to my car. "The sooner you realize you'll never get what you want inside the boundaries of Fletcher's world, the easier your life will be."

Emotions knock around in my chest while I stare at my boots and lean against the side of my car. "You. You mean you. I'll never have you."

After a few minutes, he shuts the hood. "Start it."

I inspect him, hoping for a tiny sign of acknowledgment. Pretending the kiss never happened isn't what I want. The car starts right up. Just as quickly, I kill the engine and brush past him toward the house.

Two feet inside the front door, his hand encircles my wrist.

"Let me go," I whisper.

"I will."

When I turn back toward him, he releases my wrist, and my heart sinks in my chest. Loneliness has never felt so instant.

My hand catches his a second later. "Just ..." I gaze up at him. "Not yet."

This is it. Right here. Everything shifts and I know I can't stop it. I know it's going to hurt. And I know I'm going to do it anyway.

That's pretty much the miserable definition of love.

Milo stares at our hands.

"I'm sorry your brother is going to die."

He nods slowly. Milo has never looked this tortured. "We're all gonna die, Indie."

I release his hand and slide my arms around his neck, pressing my face into it, not caring if he hugs me back. "The world doesn't care about us. It doesn't wait for us. Why should we care about it? Why should we wait for it? We're not like everyone else."

"Indie ..." His strained voice cuts into me. "Fletcher will kill me. And I mean that in the most literal sense." He lets his hands rest on my hips.

"Fletcher doesn't have to know." I kiss his neck. "And if the world doesn't end before summer, I'll leave. You'll marry Jolene. We'll both be miserable." I kiss my way to his jaw, lifting onto my toes. "But we'll have the best memories." I pull him down, softly pressing my lips to his cheek. "Make memories with me, Milo. Be mine ... until you're hers. I promise ..." I kiss the corner of his mouth and whisper, "I'll let you go." I kiss him again, but he doesn't kiss me back.

Deflating, I fall flat on my feet and take a step back, blowing a long breath out my nose.

The concentration on Milo's face elicits hundreds of questions. I'm sure none of which he'll answer if I ask him. But I try anyway. "Is Rae your girlfriend?"

"She's Ty's sister."

"Who's Ty?"

Milo chuckles. "Wow. You know nothing about Fletcher's business dealings."

"I know you're his right-hand man. I know he owns ranches and some solar company, yet he still drills for oil. He owns movie theaters and a chain of restaurants that sell chicken. I hate eating chicken, coincidentally. Does Ty have something to do with chickens? There must be more than just what's in the coop behind your barn."

Milo laughs some more. "Ty is the two-hundred-and-fifty-pound guy who's always one step ahead of Fletcher. He's his bodyguard."

"Ken? Fletcher's bodyguard's name is Ken."

"Ken Tyson. Everyone calls him Ty," Milo says.

"Well, that's weird."

"It's *known*, not weird. Well-known." Milo tucks his fingers into his front pockets.

"Not to me," I mumble.

I wasn't jealous when I saw him having sex with the woman in the barn, but Rae was different. She wasn't naked. He hadn't reduced her to a quick fuck next to a horse stall. In some ways, I feel like walking in on them having coffee, her sitting on his counter, was more intimate than fucking around next to Ranger.

"Rae has mad sewing skills like Ruthie had. I don't

know if you've noticed, but I no longer have missing buttons on my shirts."

"Sorry, I hadn't noticed missing buttons, so it's highly unlikely I'd notice mended ones. Was she your girlfriend two nights ago when you kissed me? How old is she?"

"Girl and friend. Not girlfriend. And she's twenty-three. Are you done asking questions?"

"Is it serious?" I ask since I can't let it go. Milo is eight years older than me. Sure, a brother of sorts, but I don't like that comparison. I should be happy for him. He deserves something for himself. Fletcher takes advantage of him at every turn. How have I forgotten that he was eighteen when Ruthie died? Do *I* have what it takes to care for a ten-year-old like Milo looked out for me? The way he fed me. Drove me to school. And let me hug him like a security blanket at night. Milo has always been exactly what I needed him to be. That deserves something, I suppose.

"Does she know about Jolene?" I take several steps backward and sit on the stairs.

"No."

"Why not?"

"Why do you care?"

"I don't, Milo. I don't care about Jolene or Rae or … the random women you screw. I care about you."

His Adam's apple bobs before he drops his gaze. "I don't know what you want me to say."

"Say you care about me too."

He flinches. "You know I do."

"Did you want to do more than kiss me the other night?"

"Indie ..."

"It's just a question. Like ... if you could go anywhere in the world, where would it be? Doesn't mean you'll go there." I hug my knees, praying for an honest answer from him.

Milo blinks several times, expression unreadable. "Well, there you have it. You just answered both questions yourself."

I squint at him. What's that supposed to mean?

He turns and opens the front door.

"Hey. You have to tell me what you mean." I stand.

With his back to me, he slowly shakes his head. "If I could go anywhere in the world, Indie ... it would be inside of you."

Click.

The door shuts behind him.

My lips part. My heart thrashes out of control. And my feet want to chase him.

However, I can't move because his confession weighs more than my car. I'll never breathe again.

9

THE UNCROSSABLE LINE

MILO

Indiana is my death row.

I don't know when it happened. She was a young girl. I felt protective of her. Fletcher and Ruthie always trusted me with her. And that meant a lot. Then I blinked. I can't recall whether it was a slow or long blink. All I know was that she wasn't a young girl when my eyes opened.

Indie is a woman.

As hard as I try to envision the young girl, I can't. I didn't steal her from her mama. I didn't buy her for a million dollars. I'm not her father. I'm not her brother. There are so many things I am not.

But her?

Every one cell in my body, every thought in my head,

every fiber of my being tells me she's mine. Fletcher has unknowingly stolen her from me, or maybe he stole her *for* me.

I spend the day traveling long hours to check in on Fletcher's businesses. He has his fucking hand in everything, and it's my job to make sure no one tries to cut off said greedy hand.

It's after eight by the time I pull onto the Ellington ranch. The second I open the front door and reach for my hat to remove it, I realize the floor lamp is on. And Indie's asleep on the sofa with an open book hugged to her chest. Lips slightly parted.

I ease the door shut, not wanting to wake her.

Is Indie right? Does the world not care about a harden-souled man like me or the stolen child of a mother who was in over her head with the father? Do we have to play by rules that don't mean a damn thing in our lives?

Indie's wearing a T-shirt of mine, and hell if I know what's on her bottom half. With my fucking luck, she's not wearing anything but my T-shirt, which looks like it's swallowed her whole.

Why is she here? Fletcher comes home tomorrow.

I take a quick shower and emerge to the aroma of garlic and Indie pulling a plate out of the microwave.

"Milo, you need to go grocery shopping."

I dry my hair with a towel while she lets her gaze slide across my bare chest, hypnotized, nostrils flaring while she inhales slowly.

This isn't good. I'm fucked.

She clears her throat and offers a nervous smile while

her eyes flit upward to my face. "I uh ... brought you some of the pasta Micah left in the fridge."

"Micah makes something besides steak?" I narrow an eye at her.

She grins. "Yes. For me, he makes pasta."

I sit at the table when she sets the plate on it. "What happened to your clothes? I think that's my shirt?" I twirl the pasta around the fork.

Indie stands a foot away from me, her toes pointed inward, her bare legs on full display, and her hands folded quite innocently behind her back. "I wanted to wear your shirt."

"Because?" I take a slow bite, attempting to act unaffected by her half-naked state. I'm anything but unaffected.

"It smells like you."

I chuckle. "Sweat?"

"Leather, coffee, and cinnamon." She grabs the neck of the shirt and pulls it to her nose. My gaze drops to the extra two inches of legs she's showing me.

Dead.

That will be my physical state if I touch her again. Fletcher will make sure I don't live to see another day.

Clearing my throat, I return my gaze to her face, her pink cheeks and cherry lips. "You think I smell like leather, coffee, and cinnamon?"

"Mmm ..." She nods, wetting her lips. "I do."

Stop. She has to stop right now.

"I let Benton know I'm no longer interested in seeing him."

"Whatever you want, Indie." I focus on the pasta. It's thinner than spaghetti.

"*Whatever* I want?" She takes a step closer until her legs touch the side of my chair.

"It's a figure of speech." I lick the sauce from the corner of my mouth.

She curls her blond hair behind her ear on one side before wedging between me and the table, sitting on one of my legs with her back to me. Lavender overtakes the aroma of garlic. It's the way the main house smelled when Ruthie was alive.

I set my fork down and hold my hands away, *far* away, so I don't touch her. "What are you doing?"

"I'm hungry again." She pinches a piece of pasta between her fingers and slurps it into her mouth while her toes brush the top of my bare foot. Turning her head, she grins at me, upending my carefully constructed wall of control.

I zero in on her lips, and her smile fades before she rubs them together. I wanna kiss them so fucking badly.

Her hand reaches for mine, guiding it to her knee. We stare at each other, sharing an occasional slow blink.

Not a word.

Barely a breath falls between us.

She swallows when my hand slides an inch or two up her silky inner thigh. I might as well load the gun and hand it to Fletcher. Do I have a death wish?

Maybe.

All I can hear is the blood in my ears, pulsing, rushing, and racing to keep up with my heart.

"Keep going," Indie whispers before holding her breath when my hand remains idle on her thigh.

There's a dagger of guilt twisting into my conscience, but even that doesn't stop my hand. The tips of my fingers skate along the crotch of her underwear.

Her breathing becomes a little ragged.

My fingers bend, dragging my fingertips over the thin cotton, feeling the outline of her flesh beneath it, the thin material quickly becoming wet to the touch.

She closes her eyes while her hand grips my other leg. I curl my fingers to cup her, and her fingernails dig into my leg while her pelvis makes a tiny jerk.

Fuck ... I'm torturing myself.

I rub her with the heel of my hand several times, pulling more breaths from her open mouth, each one harsher than the previous one. Her toes reach for the floor, lifting herself toward my touch; her other hand grips the table's edge.

I'm so fucking mesmerized by her.

Her slow blinking eyes.

Her lower body moving in tiny waves with my touch.

Her teeth trapping her lower lip just before she turns and drops her chin to watch my hand between her spread legs.

Every sane, self-preserving idea I've ever had gets ransacked. If I ever had a true conscience, it's now unrecognizable.

My free hand covers hers on my knee, my fingers sliding between hers while my right hand dips into her underwear. And she is so. Fucking. Wet.

"M-Milo ..." Her weight collapses onto my leg again, and she swallows hard when my middle finger strokes the warm, wet path between her legs, circling her clit with slow strokes. She grips my leg harder, and her nails dig into the wood table, making a soft scratching sound.

My middle finger slips inside her, and I rub her clit again with the heel of my hand. She drops her head back against my shoulder.

Chest heaving.

Back arched.

It's taking unimaginable strength to keep from unzipping my jeans and burying my cock inside her. I deserve a medal.

Indie moans. It's long and soft. And I feel it everywhere. Then she melts; her muscles relax, molding her body to mine. Her flesh is pulsing ... gripping my finger inside her.

"Tell me you know I'm marrying Jolene," I whisper in her ear. I'm not trying to be an asshole; I think I am one by circumstance.

Instantaneously, she stiffens—every inch of her.

"Tell me, Indie. Tell me you know." This need I have to protect her feels admirable until I realize the person I need to protect her from the most is ... me.

She says nothing, but her head moves in a barely detectable nod before lifting it from my shoulder.

It's like someone presses rewind. My hand disappears from her underwear. Her feet grip the floor. She lifts her body from my lap. In silence, she peels off my tee. I don't look at her. I focus on the pasta, knowing my stomach is too knotted to take another bite tonight. Only when the door clicks open do I glance up at Indie.

"But you will be mine," she says.

I'm not sure I'm hearing her correctly, but then she glances back at me. "You will marry Jolene, but you will never be hers."

10

KEEP YOUR ENEMIES CLOSE

INDIE

I've made an informed decision. I'll take Milo for however long I can have him. And then ... I'll walk away. Let's hope this makeshift wall around my heart holds up.

"Mathias is going to ask you to go out Friday," Hallie says as soon as I slide into her car the day before Thanksgiving.

"I'm busy," I say, shooting her a nervous smile.

"What are you talking about? Did you hear what I said? *Mathias Crowley,* hot running back, looks like he's a senior in college, is interested in you. Are you sick?"

I can't think about Mathias Crowley when I still feel Milo Odell's hand between my legs. "I met someone." I shouldn't tell Hallie or anyone about Milo, but I have to give her a reason to stop harassing me about Mathias Crowley. Sure, before Milo kissed me, I would have been interested in Mathias the way I was interested in Benton and Camden and every other guy I filtered through to not think about Milo and *not* make Fletcher proud of me.

"Oh, tell me more." Hallie gobbles up every morsel I offer her.

"He works for Fletcher."

"That's not good. The last thing you need is your dad grilling some employee over what he did or didn't do to his daughter. What if his henchman finds out?"

I open my water bottle and take a sip. "Henchman?"

"That hot piece of ass in the cowboy hat who dragged your drunk ass home from Camden's house. He's one of your dad's henchmen. You can tell."

I pause my gulping and slowly lower my water bottle. "Milo?"

"Yeah. He seems to know your whereabouts all the time. You know he'll be the first to know if you're messing around with one of your dad's employees."

"I've told you ... Fletcher isn't my dad. And Milo won't say anything."

"How can you be sure he won't say anything if he finds out?"

I bite my lips to hide my grin. "I just am." My gaze shifts to the window and the endless acres of flat, emerald-green land passing by us.

"How old is he?"

"Who?"

"Duh ... the guy who works for your dad ... er ... Fletcher?"

"Twenty-six."

"Twenty-six? Are you fucking kidding me?" She

shoots me a sideways glance, eyes popping out of her tiny head.

I smirk.

"Have you had sex with him?"

"Does it matter?"

"You're still in high school, and he's twenty-six. Yeah, it matters."

"I'm eighteen. Seventeen is the age of consent anyway."

"So that's a yes? You've had sex with him?"

"It's a 'none of your business.' Why do you care?"

"Jesus ... what's up with you? I thought we talked about this stuff. You've told me about every other guy you've hooked up with."

"He's kinda taken. So I'd rather not overshare. Not that I think you'd say anything. I know how easily information can get leaked."

"Taken? Married? He's married?" Her voice escalates.

I shake my head. "No. Maybe like ... engaged." My nose crinkles.

"Indiana! You can't be serious. You're involved with someone who is engaged? You're not that person. I'm sorry, but he's an asshole. A grade A asshole for cheating on his fiancée. Why would you do that?"

Because he's mine.

"Speaking of marriage ... want to know who's getting married?" I don't know why I've decided to walk this thin line, but it's out.

"Who?" Hallie takes the bait.

"Jolene."

"Oh god ... that's right. That's what you said that night at Camden's. She's marrying Milo?" Hallie expresses the same level of detest I have for Jolene "Well, I feel sorry for that poor bastard."

"Yeah ..." My smile fades while I mumble, "So do I."

AFTER HALLIE and I finish shopping, I change into jeans and boots and make a quick sandwich. Then I run to the barn to clean Ranger's stall and the chicken coops. Finally, I take the eggs to Milo's apartment so he can disperse them to some of the workers. When I open the door, my momentum crashes.

"Howdy," Rae smiles at me while pulling a tray of cookies from Milo's oven. "Get your car fixed?" She turns off the buzzing timer and tosses the hot pads aside before crossing her arms and leaning her backside against the counter.

"Yeah," I say, slowly setting the box of eggs on the counter. My gaze slides to the table and the chair where Milo touched me. I shouldn't feel like the intruder. Yet I do.

"Sorry for the brief introduction the other day; I'm Ty's daughter. I've heard a lot about you from my dad and Milo. I feel like I know you."

My eyes narrow for a few seconds while I chew on the inside of my cheek.

"Ty is in charge of your dad's security," she says with a little laugh.

"Yeah." I return a slow nod. "I know. I didn't know everyone called him Ty."

"Well, I call him *Dad*. I'm sure you call Mr. Ellington 'Dad' instead of Fletcher."

"No." I fold my hands behind my back. "I call him sir to his face, Mr. Ellington to other people, and asshole to my friends."

Her eyes go wide, and she releases a nervous laugh. "That's ..."

"Life." I return a toothy grin. "He's not my real father. If he were, I'd consider calling him 'Dad' or something endearing like 'Papa,' but if he were still an asshole, I'd probably reference him as such in front of my friends."

"So, are we friends since you're confessing this to me?" Rae asks.

"Well, any friend of Milo's is a friend of mine."

"I think it's cool that you two are close. I bet you love having a big brother of sorts in your life if your relationship with Mr. Ellington is rocky, and you lost your mom when you were so young." Rae turns and lifts the cookies onto a cooling rack.

"Milo's not my brother."

"I know. I just mean he looks out for you like a brother."

"What about you?" I drum my fingers on the counter. "Is Milo like a brother to you too?"

"Uh ... no." She chuckles. "That would be a bad comparison."

"Oh? Why is that?"

Rae glances over her shoulder, biting her lower lip.

"Well, we're sometimes ... more than friends. If you know what I mean."

My teeth clench, and I find a smile to go with my lack of enthusiasm for Rae. "I think I do."

"He's..." she shakes her head and returns her attention to the cookies "...not like my boyfriend or anything. Just more of a ... companion."

"Like a dog?"

Again, she shakes her head and laughs. "No. Maybe you don't understand what I'm saying. And that's fine. I probably shouldn't be saying—"

"You and Milo have sex."

Turning toward me, Rae wipes her hands on a towel. Her lips roll between her teeth while she nods several times.

Are we friends? Do friends tell each other when they last had sex? Has she had sex with Milo since he kissed me in my bedroom? Will he have sex with her tonight because she's in his kitchen making him cookies? After all, the way to a man's heart is through his stomach. Is that how one gets to his cock as well?

"I bet your family puts on quite the spread for Thanksgiving."

I nod. "Micah will spend the morning preparing everything before going home to have dinner with his family. We'll commit a solid act of gluttony in the early evening. The men will retreat to the hearth room for expensive whiskey and cigars, and the women will sip wine in the formal living room while gossiping about everything and everyone. I'll go to my room and read a book. So basically, if your family opens a can of Spam with day-old dinner rolls but spends an hour or two actively conversing with you over a box of cheap wine, then you'll have a better Thanksgiving."

Am I purposely trying to make Rae uncomfortable? I don't know yet. I really haven't decided if she's a friend or foe. I can't hold it against her for sleeping with Milo. I'd jump at the chance.

"My grandparents live in San Antonio, so we'll spend the day there. And we'll have turkey, not Spam." She chuckles. "I hope. But that sucks that your family isn't engaged with you since you're gone so much."

"Well, I have Milo."

He's mine. Mine. Mine. MINE!

She eyes me with an unreadable expression.

"So ..." I clear my throat. "What do you do, Rae?"

"I'm a pharmaceutical rep. I work for Ellington Pharmaceuticals." She gives me a sheepish grin before turning to wash the baking sheets.

I didn't know Fletcher owned a pharmaceutical company. I haven't kept up with all of his businesses. But I'm not real family, so why should I?

"Does everyone in your family work for Fletcher?"

"Not yet." Rae laughs, squirting dish soap onto the cookie sheet. "But since Fletcher seems to own everything, I'm sure it's only a matter of time." She sounds impressed. "Are you going straight into the family business, or are you going to college first?"

"College. I'm not interested in the family business."

Rae's penciled eyebrows slide up her forehead when she glances at me over her shoulder. "You might change your mind. I understand what it's like to be your age and not feel like you want to make life commitments yet."

"Mmm ..." I nod slowly.

Rae dries her hands and grabs her phone, staring at the screen. "Milo's having dinner with your dad. Looks like I'll have to fend for myself and wait to surprise him with these cookies later."

"Well, good luck with your surprise. I was just dropping off the eggs." I make a calculated retreat to the door. "See you around."

Only ... I hope not.

"Absolutely," Rae says. "Have a happy Thanksgiving."

"You too." I slam the door shut and pound my brown cowboy boots into the dirt as I make my way to the blacktop and up to the main house where Milo's truck is parked by the fountain in the circle drive.

"Is that you, Indie?" Fletcher calls when I close the door.

I take a deep breath and contemplate answering him or just running to my bedroom.

"Come here, darlin'."

Darlin'? I hate when he calls me that. It was endearing when Ruthie was alive, but nothing is endearing about him anymore.

Tugging off my dirty boots, I grumble my displeasure before brushing off my jeans and shuffling my socked feet to the dining room.

"Have a seat. Milo and I were just discussing holiday plans. Jolene will be here tomorrow. You two can catch up. Maybe she can help you pick out some colleges to apply to."

Go fuck yourself, Fletcher.

I smile at him but keep plenty of disingenuousness to share with Milo sitting just to Fletcher's left. The table seats twenty. I like tables that seat four or fewer. Anything more is excess, and I'm over all the excess.

But mainly, I wonder if Milo's thinking about colleges for me *or* what it felt like to have his middle finger inside me last night.

"I'm good. Jolene and I don't have the same taste in much."

"Well, have a seat. Micah will fix you a plate," Fletcher says.

I shake my head. "I already ate. I also cleaned out the chicken coops. You're welcome, Milo. Oh ... and Rae is at your place. Spoiler alert." I wrinkle my nose. "She's making you cookies. But don't tell her I said so. Just act surprised."

Milo stiffens, pausing his fork an inch from his mouth.

Fletcher shoots him a look. "You two still seeing each other?"

Milo lifts a shoulder, averting his gaze for a second before taking that bite of medium-rare steak. "Sometimes."

"Enjoy it while you can," Fletcher gives him the go-ahead. "I don't fault you a bit. Make sure she knows you have nothing serious to offer her. Ty won't appreciate anything less than honesty."

Milo sneaks a glance at me. I don't blink. I silently

dare him to say one word. He swallows and clears his throat before wiping his mouth with the white napkin while offering Fletcher the tiniest nod.

"Christ ... what now?" Fletcher looks at his phone. "Excuse me." He stands, bringing it to his ear and heading toward his office.

"Indie ..." Milo says, setting his fork down and scooting his chair backward.

I stop him with a firm headshake. "Enjoy it while you can." I turn on my heel and head out the back door. I can't even be in the same house as those two.

Mud, Fletcher's chocolate lab, follows me to the trail that borders the secluded pond and connects to the pasture where the horses graze. "Your master is an asshole," I say to Mud, "but I like you." I stop just long enough to scratch him behind the ears.

Then grabbing strands of tall grass, I pull off the rows of seeds as the sun descends in the distance. It seems so close, but it's the same sun everyone in the world sees. More proof that nothing is what it seems. Happiness is as much an illusion as the intimacy of the sun setting.

My stroll takes me to the far end of the pasture, where I sit against the white fence post. Mud lies down beside me. I think he loves me more than Fletcher. He's getting gray, and I have no doubt I'll be more broken-hearted when he dies than when Fletcher dies. Ruthie got Mud for Fletcher. Maybe that's why I'm partial to the old lab.

When only a pink hue is left in the sky, I stand and brush off my backside. Mud barks, drawing my attention to Milo and Ranger approaching us, slowing down as they get closer.

"It's not a good idea for you to be out here this late," Milo says, bringing Ranger to a halt and jumping off him. He removes his cowboy hat and rests it on the saddle's horn.

Milo is many things, but sexy cowboy tops the list. He can rope. Brand. Herd and drive cattle. Repair fences. Hit any target with a shotgun. And scare the living bejeebers out of the ranch hands if they fall out of line. I've heard rumors that he's killed people too. I used to not believe that, but now I think it might be true.

"I've never been a fan of good ideas," I say.

"I know." He steps closer to me.

I back up until the fence post stops me. Milo slides one boot between mine. He looks ethereal in the sunset's faint residue.

"Rae went home. We ate cookies. I told her the only thing I could offer her was friendship without benefits. She's Ty's daughter, so I must navigate things gingerly with her." He feathers his knuckles along my cheek. "She said you two chatted for a while."

"Yes," I whisper. His touch is still so new but familiar. It's perfect, yet Fletcher has manipulated Milo's world, tainting what we have and giving it an expiration date.

"Rae said you seemed sad. She thinks your relationship with Fletcher is strained."

I lean into his touch, resting a hand on his chest. "What do you think?"

"I think you were sad because Rae was in my kitchen.

I think you thought I'm an asshole who doesn't care about you."

I lift my gaze to his. "Are you?"

He slides both hands to the back of my neck and bends down, stopping just before his lips touch mine. "I'm certainly an asshole, but I care about you so much that the passing of time feels like torture."

I rest my forehead on his chest. "Do you regret what we did last night?"

Milo's hands disappear from my neck and skim down my arms. His fingers slide into my back pockets. "Indie, I have many regrets, but you will never be one of them. The world is a fucking dumpster fire. There's so much hate. There's so much judgment. I refuse to bend to anyone's opinion. They don't know us."

I love you, Milo.

It hurts to swallow my emotions, but I do it because Milo is not a choice. My heart never chose him. It tangled with his years ago, and I'll only get pieces of it back when this ends.

I glance up at him. "Have you ever killed anyone?"

His forehead wrinkles. "Indie ..."

That's my answer. Right there, in his eyes.

"I don't care," I whisper, lifting onto my toes and pressing my lips to his.

He kisses me. *Really* kisses me back. It's an all-consuming kind of kiss. The way I imagine you kiss someone when you're coming completely undone.

Hungry.

Sensual.

Mind-blowing.

Milo doesn't take it a step further, but my need is a tangible pain. A clawing desire, unlike anything I've felt in my life.

He ends the kiss, our labored breaths swirling between our lips, making me dizzy; I'm wound so tightly I think I might explode.

I reach for his fly, but he stops me. This level of rejection is wearing on me.

Milo takes a step back and adjusts himself before sliding on his hat again. When he meets my gaze, he grins. It's vulnerable. It's innocent. And I pretend he only shares it with me. He only lets me see this side of him even if he won't let me have all of him.

"Up you go, Indie girl." He gives me a slight boost onto Ranger.

I don't need it, but I won't complain about his hands on my ass.

Milo climbs on behind me and guides us back to the barn with a slow gait. His lips occasionally find my neck. I love the tickle of his short whiskers on my skin. The warmth of his breath. The illusion that we are real.

I giggle when he teases me with his teeth. My shoulders lift, and a shiver works its way along my skin.

"Tomorrow, you should tell Fletcher you want to tour Rice University." He slides off Ranger just outside of the barn and helps me down.

I follow him to the stall, resting my chin and hands on the smooth rail. "I'm not going to Rice. Nowhere in Texas."

He removes the saddle. "Indie, I don't give a shit where you want to go to college. I have some business to take care of in Houston on Monday. And if you tell Fletcher you want to tour Rice, he'll make me take you with me." He turns.

My lips roll together. I'm trying to play it cool, but it's hard. Milo wants to spend the day with me.

When the gate latches, I step into his space, wrapping my arms around him.

"Get to bed, Indie girl."

I grumble into his chest, and he chuckles.

"Fuck if I know," a deep voice sounds from somewhere close.

Milo pulls me around the corner to an empty stall filled with hay bales on one side and horse blankets draped on the other side. It's not well-lit, cloaking us in the shadows while several workers use the spigot just outside the barn.

I peek between two of the blankets hanging over the stall's rails. The men take their time rinsing buckets, shrugging off their dirty shirts, and drinking from the hose.

Milo's arm snakes around my waist, his warm chest pressed to my back and his face tucked into the crook of my neck. He sucks the sensitive skin below my ear.

I release a tiny hum.

"Shh ..." he whispers.

Biting my lips, I angle my head, giving him better access.

His kisses grow demanding as they did in the pasture. My fingers grip the railing over the blankets.

One of Milo's hands splays along my stomach, pulling

me closer to him. That's when I feel him—his erection, through his jeans, pressed to my backside. My breaths quicken, making it hard to keep quiet. Milo's other hand skates up my body, over my breast to my neck. He cups my jaw, angles my head back to him, and kisses me hard.

Hard like his body flush with mine.

Hard like his erection.

Hard like his pelvis rocking against me.

This is so fucking unfair. *Now* he does this? When we're feet away from workers? When we're fully clothed? When we can't make a sound?

I'm angry and frustrated, but it doesn't mean I don't want it just the same. My tongue flicks against his while I arch my back. Milo releases my jaw, his head dropping back to my neck, sucking and biting his way to my shoulder while both hands grip my hips.

I lift onto my toes, and his fingers dig into my hips as he grinds his erection along my ass, his hips jerking hard and slow.

The men cackle with laughter while lighting cigarettes, seemingly in no hurry to leave their circle around the spigot.

Milo hugs me tightly, one hand sliding up my shirt and beneath my bra while his other hand keeps my hips from moving away from his.

I suck in a harsh breath when his calloused thumb strokes my nipple before his hand squeezes my breast.

"Shh ..." he whispers in my ear again.

His adept fingers flick open the button and pull down the zipper of my jeans. Then he steals my right hand from the railing and guides it down the front of my underwear.

"Touch yourself," he breathes heavily against my cheek, gripping both of my hips and increasing his pace, each thrust a little faster ... a little harder, just like his labored breaths at my neck.

My fingers slide through the warm wet space between my legs, over my sensitive clit. And I close my eyes, imagining his erection sliding between my legs, dipping lower, pressing inside me. I lose it; my knees weaken with my orgasm. My head drops to my arm anchored to the bar with a death grip.

Milo bites my shoulder, muffling his low groan while he holds me painfully tight and circles his hips before stilling, body rigid for several seconds. Then he slowly releases a long breath while his muscles relax along with his grip on my hips.

I turn in his arms, but it's too dark to see his eyes. His hands frame my face, and he takes me under again in a passionate kiss. It's easy to dismiss the sexual release as something animalistic, the human need to fuck, to feel that release. But this ... this kiss is not physical. It's emotional. It's everything I know he can't say with words. It's a promise he can't keep. A life we can't have.

My fingers clench his shirt, my weight on the balls of my feet. The men's voices outside of the barn fade in the distance. And Milo slowly pulls away. His thumb caresses my lips, and he softly kisses them again. I swallow the words I want to say, the case I want to make for the unfairness of life. He said I could have him.

You have me.

For how long?

For as long as you need.

Forever?

"Sweet dreams, Indie girl."

I bury my nose in his shirt, inhaling deeply one more time before whispering, "Good night."

11

THERE GOES MY HEART

"Since Jolene is home, we're having dinner tomorrow night. Our first ..." Milo keeps a close eye on his men herding the cattle into the tractor trailers. Even on Thanksgiving, Fletcher's men work in the morning.

I rest my arms on the fence next to him so our elbows touch. "Your first date?"

Without taking his eyes off the cattle, he nods.

"This is unreal," I say. "You've been in the same room with her a handful of times. You've never gone on an actual date. You've never held her hand or kissed her. You didn't propose. Yet ... just like that ... you're getting married in seven months. Make me understand what Fletcher did to deserve this level of loyalty and gratitude from you. Did he give you a kidney? Part of his liver? This can't be loyalty because he took care of you after your brother went to prison. It ... it doesn't make sense." My words spill out, each one sounding a little more desperate.

Just the mention of Jolene's name makes my stomach

twist. I don't want to see her. And imagining her and Milo going on a date crushes everything inside me.

"Indiana, this is not a surprise. This has always been part of the deal. You know your freedom has a price. Well, so does mine."

I turn, crossing my arms and resting my backside against the fence so I'm facing the opposite direction as Milo.

The cattle protest, their hooves clapping the ramps while the men whistle to get each other's attention.

The breeze carries the pungent scent of the cow piles.

"Don't kiss her, Milo. Don't let her into your bed. Don't smile at her. Don't ... just ... don't." Emotions burn behind my eyes, but I keep my composure. I keep my head above water, but just barely.

"She's home for a week. Then she'll go back to school. She'll come home again for Christmas, but then she won't return until after graduation."

I grunt. "Did you know our graduations are on the same weekend? Whose graduation will you be attending?"

Milo doesn't answer.

I turn my head, but he's a statue with a cowboy hat shading his solemn face. He can't make this go away by ignoring it. And I can't stop it by resisting the events that will take place whether I accept them or not.

I hate it all.

"Milo?" one of the workers calls him from the trailer.

He pushes off the fence, and I take off toward the house.

"Indie?"

Nope. I can't look at him. I can't speak. And I'm done listening to the painful truth. If he can't help me understand, then I don't want to listen to him.

"INDIANA ..." Jolene squeals when she and Pauline spill into the foyer with their designer luggage and overbearing perfume.

My posture jerks to attention like a good girl, like I don't have a choice. Fletcher's made it clear that I don't have a choice. He owns my car, my phone, and my whole fucking life.

For now ...

I stiffen when Jolene pulls me in for an awkward embrace. Why is she hugging me? Why is she smiling like she's happy to see me?

"Listen, honey ..." she pulls back, keeping me at arm's length.

Honey? Why does her term of endearment sound so condescending?

"I don't have room for you to be a bridesmaid, but I'm making you my personal attendant. How does that sound?"

It sounds like I should take a bus to anywhere but here before the wedding.

Fletcher clears his throat, shooting me a stern look while he helps them with their bags.

I smile on cue. He knows Jolene and I have never been friends. He knew it when Ruthie was alive. Ruthie and Fletcher didn't argue often, but her protecting me against Jolene's vileness brought out the fighter in her.

If Jolene took a breath to really look at me, she'd see the confusion on my face. *How can you marry a man you don't love?*

"What time are your dinner reservations tomorrow?" Pauline asks Jolene.

"I made them for six," Fletcher says as everyone funnels toward the dining room for Thanksgiving dinner. Two of Fletcher and Pauline's cousins have joined us, along with their wives.

"Come on," Jolene says, retreating a few steps and grabbing my wrist. "I feel like we left things on a bad note. I don't even remember what all the fuss was about." She pulls me toward the table. "Silly childish stuff, I suppose. After dinner, I want to show you the fabric swatches for my dress." Her words barely register. They're an echo, like a weird dream.

No. This is a nightmare.

She's not being nice. She's torturing me under the guise of a truce. Jolene is rubbing this in my face. The wedding. The inevitable inheritance. The attention. And she's claimed me as her personal attendant—that's code for I've been deemed worthy of waiting on her hand and foot. Like Cinderella, but I don't think there's a glass slipper in my future.

"You're being rude, Indie." Fletcher eyes me while sipping his whiskey after I take a seat.

From the high-back chair next to him, Pauline glances at me. Her red lips pull into the same smile Jolene gives me. I hate that she knows I was the million-dollar purchase for Ruthie, whom she never liked. Pauline always hated how Ruthie had Fletcher wrapped around her finger. At least, that's what Faye said.

"How am I being rude?" I ask, giving everyone else at the table a quick scan.

"You're staring at your phone instead of conversing politely with our guests."

I begin to formulate a snide remark to his comment, but Milo appears around the corner.

"There he is," Fletcher says with fatherly pride. It's what I imagine a father's pride looks and sounds like. I don't have much experience with it.

Milo gives me a quick glance before smiling at Fletcher and everyone else. The glance is so fast I don't have a chance to blink, let alone give him a silent plea to make all of this stop.

"Pauline." Milo gives her a polite nod.

He's not cowboy Milo. He's funeral Milo. It's not the same suit he wore to Ruthie's funeral, but it's still a suit. And Milo Odell doesn't wear suits. He's a cowboy. Jeans. Chaps. Boots. Hat. Everything about him right now screams impostor.

"Milo ..." Pauline smooths her hands along her red, off-the-shoulder dress. Her brown-dyed hair cascading in soft waves around her shoulders.

She's made-up pretty much like Jolene. Makeup and money go a long way.

Ruthie had all the money in the world, but she didn't need it or any makeup to be beautiful. Her beauty came from within and shined brighter than the Texas sun. You can't fake that kind of beauty, but Pauline and Jolene try.

"Hi, Jolene. Did you have a nice flight home?" Milo asks.

I roll my eyes. It was a private jet; how bad could it have been?

The clinking of dishes between the cousins nearly drowns out Jolene's response. *Nearly* ...

Jolene sighs. "We were delayed a bit in the hangar because the pilot got stuck in traffic. I wish I had known. I get a little claustrophobic."

It's a jet that seats twelve, and it was only her, the pilot, and an attendant serving her food and champagne. Poor thing.

Milo nods and smiles. That smile falters a bit when he catches my scowl aimed right at him.

The older adults continue to steal the conversation. I barely eat anything on my plate while watching Jolene inspect Milo, who stuffs his face to keep from looking or talking to anyone.

I'm done. I can't sit here any longer, so I excuse myself before Fletcher can object, and I hightail it to my room.

THE NEXT DAY, I don't leave my room. I don't eat. I don't do anything but stare out the window until Milo arrives to take Jolene on their first date.

A black town car pulls up next to the fountain. The driver holds open the door for the happy couple.

Milo glances up at my window at the last second. I don't hide. I let him see me. When he eats bloody meat and drinks expensive wine with her tonight, I want him to see me.

The town car pulls away from the fountain and down the driveway.

There goes my heart.

12

THE WRONG WOMAN

MILO

THIS IS MY LIFE. It's true. A fact.

But it doesn't make it any less tragic.

Tragedy defines my life. It defined the look on Indie's face when I left the house with Jolene. I've never felt like less of a man. If I love her, I should protect her. Her feelings. Her heart. Her honor.

I'm damned if I do, damned if I don't. Either way, it won't get me Indie.

"So ..." Jolene gives me a shy smile when we're seated at the restaurant, everyone dressed to the nines, champagne flowing, and more utensils on the napkin than one person could possibly need for a meal. "Did you ever imagine this happening?"

"Dinner?" I force a smile to accompany my equally forced humor. The waiter passes us with an assortment of fresh bread. I find them more appealing than my date. Add some soft butter, and there's no competition.

Jolene laughs a little. "I was meaning this uh ... arrangement."

I lay my napkin on my leg and look over the menu. "Nothing surprises me anymore. My life has been far from expected. But you're getting ready to graduate from law school. I'm a little surprised you agreed to this *arrangement*."

She's not ready to say marriage, and neither am I.

Jolene nods several times, a little distracted by the waiter serving the table next to us some dessert that's on fire.

"I can see why you'd be surprised," she begins. "I'm an independent woman. I can't wait to graduate and take the bar. However, I'm fiercely loyal to my family. And I know you are too. That's what's most important to me. The law degree. My independence. Those things will only enhance my ability to take over the family business." She smirks. "All of the family businesses." After nodding to the waiter to pour her white wine, she shifts her gaze back to me. "You know everything Fletcher knows. I think we will be great partners, one day, running this empire. But for now..." she holds up her glass for a toast "...we'll make our partnership official. You'll be family."

I hesitantly lift my glass and tap it to hers. "And love? You don't need a grand proposal? A long engagement? The fairy tale?"

Jolene sips her wine and nearly chokes on it with a laugh. "Fairy tale? No. Those don't exist. I don't need a knight—a Prince Charming. Love is overrated. I'd rather marry a man I respect and who respects me. Love is fool-ish, and it's most certainly blind, but not in an endearing way. My parents weren't head-over-heels in love, but they had mutual respect. And over time, I think that grew into love. A good love. A smart love."

Taking a sip of the bitter wine, I let her words sink in. I was hoping she'd be on the fence. I don't have a choice in this *arrangement*, but I think Jolene does. If she decides this isn't the life she wants, Fletcher and Pauline will be disappointed, but I don't think they'll disown her. Unfortunately, I don't see her budging. She's all in.

"What about you? How do you feel about what we're doing?"

I feel like I've chosen the prison that doesn't involve an actual cell and orange jumpsuit.

I loosen my tie. It suddenly feels like a noose, tightening an inch at a time. "I feel indebted to your uncle. I like my job. I like the people working with me. The ranch. Indiana. I can't imagine not having that life."

Pausing her next sip, Jolene cants her head. "Indie? Huh." She sets her glass on the table next to the flickering candle. "I guess you did take care of her a lot after Ruthie died. The sister you never had?"

My days of using Indie's name and *sister* in the same breath are over. I shrug. "She's a ... friend—all grown up. I do feel close to her. I think Fletcher let her fall between the cracks after Ruthie died."

"She's seventeen." Jolene's gaze cuts to the couple who ordered the flaming dessert. He gets down on one knee. Great timing.

I shake my head. "She had a birthday."

Jolene snorts, bringing her attention back to me. The proposal does nothing for her. Figures. "Sorry." She shakes her head. "*Barely* eighteen. And Fletcher took her out of poverty and probably an abusive home. Who knows? Her mom happily traded her for a million dollars. Ruthie coddled Indie. She thought she was a miracle instead of a business transaction. Indie's had a charmed life. But she's graduating in the spring and needs to figure out her place in this world. She's not a real Ellington."

"Neither am I."

Jolene nudges my leg with hers. "Not yet." She flicks her wrist. "I don't want to talk about Indie. Let's talk about the wedding. And where we're going to live. Fletcher has offered to move out of the main house, but I'd like to build something new on one of the other properties. Something closer to Dallas. And when Fletcher and Mama pass, we can decide where we want to live to run things efficiently."

She talks about them dying like it's all part of the plan. They could both live for another thirty-plus years.

"I'm not planning on carrying babies, so we'll need to discuss finding a surrogate."

Fuck my life ...

"You have fertility issues?" I ask.

"Pfft ... no. I'm not taking time off from work to be pregnant and dealing with all the physical limitations I'll have for nine months ... not to mention what pregnancy does to a woman's body. I have a friend who used a surrogate. I'm going to check with her. Nanny. Private schools. Our kids will have the best life." Jolene's enthusiasm settles into a sad smile. "A much better life than you had."

I'm curious what she knows about my life. What did

Fletcher tell her? Or what did he tell Pauline? I'm at a disadvantage right now.

"Doesn't take much to have a better life than I had." I shrug.

"I'll let you plan the honeymoon." She's clearly done talking about my life. I'm sure it's a nuisance.

"But I'm fair skinned," she continues. "So don't assume I want to spend a week on a yacht. Be a little more creative than that."

"If you're not accustomed to being disappointed, then I suggest you plan the honeymoon."

She laughs like I'm joking. "You're adorable."

I signal to the waiter so we can order and get out of here. It's hard to breathe with Jolene demanding so much oxygen. Entitlement is suffocating. I'm going to die a miserable man. Maybe prison would be better.

THE TOWN CAR drops us off at the main house where Jolene and Pauline are staying through Thanksgiving break. I hold open the door until she steps onto the cobblestones and adjusts her dress.

"Dinner was lovely. Thank you, Milo." She touches her fingertips to her lips for a second. "Is Milo short for something?"

I loosen my tie even more before it strangles me. "No. Just Milo."

"What's your middle name? I'm trying to decide if our son would take my father's name, Uncle Fletcher's name, or if you have a strong middle name."

"Omar."

"Oh dear, sweet Jesus ..." Jolene covers her mouth like my middle name offends her. "Well ..." She giggles. "That answers that. We'll stick with one of my family's names. Milo Omar Odell. What was your mom thinking?"

I grit my teeth behind the smile that will be pinned to my face from now until eternity or Hell. Whichever comes first.

"Are you coming in for a drink?"

I shake my head. "I have to be up early."

She holds her small handbag with both hands in front of her and shifts her weight from one foot to the other. "If you want to kiss me goodnight, I wouldn't be opposed to it."

Will every single detail of my life be this orchestrated?

I glance up and can't say for sure, but I see a silhouette in the window. It has to be Indie. Before I return my gaze to Jolene, she presses her lips to mine. I stiffen.

Jolene takes a step back and grins. "Night, Milo Omar Odell." She waltzes to the front door, giving me a flirty glance over her shoulder.

My focus returns to the window, but the silhouette is gone.

I close my eyes for a few seconds. "I'm sorry, Indie," I whisper.

13

MINE!

INDIE

"Good morning, Indie. Are you having breakfast with us?" Pauline emerges from her bedroom just as I pass it on my way to the stairs. Bacon and coffee overwhelm my senses.

"Afraid not. I'm cleaning the chicken coops."

"Oh ..." She follows me down the stairs. *Clickety-clack.* Why do she and Jolene wear heels all the damn time? I hope they have mangled toes and bunions the size of mushrooms.

"That's a lot of coops," Pauline finishes. "Don't we have someone else who does that?"

"It's a small brood of chickens for the family and some of the ranch workers. They're not the chickens that get slaughtered for restaurant chains. Milo takes care of them most of the time since they're close to the barn. But now that he's marrying Jolene, I'm taking over the job.

You know … since I'm not a real Ellington." I pull on my boots and give her a toothy grin.

Pauline clutches her invisible pearls. Have I made her uncomfortable by saying the quiet part aloud? Too bad. I'm fresh out of fucks to give.

My boots scrape along the blacktop and then scuff through the gravel.

"Too late. I already cleaned them."

I look back at Milo as he steps out from the shadow of the barn, tugging off his work gloves and then removing his hat to wipe the sweat from his brow. Milo in those fitted jeans … that shirt molded to his chest … and brown chaps. I could get pregnant just from looking at him.

"Um …" I swallow a mouthful of drool. "Breakfast is being served at the house. I'm sure you're invited."

"So why aren't you eating instead of looking for shit to do?"

"Why are you asking a question you already know the answer to?" I flip out my hip and rest my fist on it.

He jerks his head toward the barn. "I'm heading inside to burn some toast and slap a crap ton of butter on it. Then I'm going to make coffee thicker than motor oil. Care to join me?"

I don't answer. I don't move. Stubbornness paralyzes me. Well … that and the sexy cowboy in front of me. All I can do is squint against the cresting sun, which works well because it feels like an appropriate scowl.

Milo shrugs. "Suit yourself."

My options aren't great this morning, but I choose Milo over my family, even if I'm mad as hell at him for no good reason. He doesn't acknowledge me when I open his creaky door and close it behind me.

"Sugar in your coffee?" he asks with his back to me.

I lift my foot and pull off one boot, giving it a toss. When it clanks against his wood floor, Milo twists his head.

With another quick tug, I send my other boot flying next to the first one.

"Make yourself at home," he says with a chuckle.

"I'd like to, but you're marrying Jolene."

"Not today." He drops two pieces of bread into the toaster.

I snag his empty coffee mug and set it on the counter. Using his metal scoop, I dump sugar into it until it fills at least a fourth of the cup. Then I pour the coffee.

"You like coffee with your sugar?"

Stirring slowly, I glance over at him with a grin. "I do."

"I like mine black with cinnamon."

I know, Milo. I know you.

"Are you trying to make us incompatible?"

He shakes his head before sprinkling cinnamon into his coffee and taking a slow sip.

While we have a stare down, I smell smoke and turn around. "Your toast is on fire!" I wave my hand over the smoke.

Milo presses the cancel button, and the black pieces of toast pop into the air. "It's not on fire. It's just done."

"What's the deal with you and burnt bread?"

"I thought you liked my signature grilled cheese.

You've eaten them for years. And you've made me think I need fruit on it." He douses the burnt toast in butter.

"I like you, Milo. The burnt grilled cheese has been an acquired taste."

"You ate it because you liked me?" He hands me a piece of toast.

Butter drips down his arm. I can't help but grin. I take a bite, and butter runs down my chin. Milo licks his wrist and forearm.

"Why burnt bread? You have to tell me." I giggle, chasing butter with my tongue.

"You didn't answer my question." He manages to stuff half the slice of toast into his mouth.

"Yes. I ate burnt grilled cheese because I liked you."

He hums, chewing slowly. After he wipes his lips with the back of his hand, he smirks. "Do you still like me?"

I use my thumb to wipe butter from the side of his mouth, and by wipe, I mean I smear it along his cheek.

"Don't do that. You don't want to play this game with me." He narrows his eyes.

I grin, taking a step backward. "What game?"

Milo stalks toward me like a predator. And I don't see what's in his hand until it's too late.

Until he's rubbing the stick of softened butter all over my face.

"Milo ..." I bat away his hand.

He comes at me again. I run around the sofa.

He jumps over it.

"Stop," I squeal with nowhere to go. I run to the bed, jump on it, and bolt toward the front door.

He hooks my waist with his arm. My knees give out, and we fall to the floor. I claw a chunk of the butter from his hand and smash it into his face.

"You're gonna pay ..." he says, wearing a huge grin before burying his buttery face into my neck.

I wriggle beneath him, smearing the butter on his shirt, jeans, and hair while freeing myself. I crawl to my feet, but he grabs my ankle, a move straight out of a horror movie.

"Milo!" I kick my leg, and my side hurts from laughing.

"*What* is going on?"

Milo and I jerk our attention in the direction of the door.

Jolene parks her hands on her hips, brown eyes unblinking, matte red lips molded into a big O.

Fletcher steps inside the door just behind her. He looks more upset than surprised, his scowl more intense than usual.

"We were having toast, and I accidentally got butter on Milo's face." I scramble to my feet; butter smeared all over me. Clumps of it in my hair. "He thought I did it on purpose, and things got..." I give Milo a glance "...out of hand."

Milo slicks back his greasy hair, lumbering to his feet. "It was childish. Sorry."

Jolene nods ever so slightly, but it doesn't soften her expression. "I ..." She shakes her head as if doing so will change what she sees before her. "I was inviting you to breakfast, Milo."

"Milo, get showered and meet me in my office in

twenty minutes," Fletcher says while keeping his evil glare aimed at me. "Indiana, go hose yourself off behind the barn before you go into the house. Put on something appropriate and behave while we have breakfast. Understood?"

How is this my fault? And why does Milo get to go straight to his shower, but I have to hose off like the dog?

"Let's go, Jolene." Fletcher makes his authoritarian exit.

Jolene shoots a full round of daggers in my direction before spinning on her heels and closing the door behind her.

"Hose off behind the barn?" I whisper, staring at the closed door.

Milo doesn't move. "Hose won't work. Butter removal requires hot water and soap."

"He was trying to humiliate me because he thinks I just humiliated him."

"Yes," Milo says, making his way to the door and locking it.

Shirt off.

Chaps off.

Jeans off.

Milo retreats toward me in nothing but his black briefs. "Take your clothes off, Indiana." He grabs my face and kisses me before I can sputter a word.

My hands hold onto his arms for support, my head spinning from this kiss. He releases me just as quickly as he grabs me, making me even dizzier. On a sudden pivot, he struts into the bathroom, pushing his briefs down his butt just as he disappears.

It's the sexiest move I have ever witnessed.

The shower turns on.

I gulp, rooted in place.

"Don't make me late to Fletcher's office," he calls from the shower, steam wafting out the partially open door.

My feet inch in that direction, and I peek around the corner. Butterflies flutter in a frenzy deep in my belly. I've seen his naked backside before … in the barn, nailing a woman to the wall. This is different.

Every thought I had sorted out in my young mind gets tangled. Are we just showering together? Will we have sex? Am I ready to let this happen? Is he?

Milo pokes his head out from the curtain, the rings tinging along the metal rod. Water rivulets bead on his butter-covered skin. "Clothes off."

I unbutton my jeans.

He watches me, and it feeds those butterflies.

I discard every scrap of clothing sans my bra and underwear.

Milo's gaze shows no signs of hesitation before surveying my body. "All. Of. Your. Clothes."

I scrape my teeth along my lower lip several times.

"You know," he says, "someone once told me, 'The world doesn't care about us. It doesn't wait for us. Why should we care about it? Why should we wait for it?' So what are you waiting for, Indie?"

I grin. He recited me. *Me!* Every single word. We repeat things that resonate with us. This means I resonate with him.

Quickly discarding my bra and underwear, I step into

the tight quarters of the steamy shower. And I have a moment ... an I'm-naked-in-the-shower-with-Milo moment.

Breathe ...

My chin drops when I realize just how invested my heart is in Milo Odell.

"Indie, look at me."

I shake my head. "You're marrying *her*," I murmur.

"Not today." He squirts shampoo onto my head.

Over the next few minutes, he meticulously washes every inch of my body while I find it impossible to peel my gaze away from his erection. It's just ... there. Begging for attention. He turns me when I reach for it so my back is to him. After rinsing the soap and shampoo from my body, he proceeds to wash his hair and body.

And I gawk.

Milo shuts off the water and hands me a towel.

I hug it because I can't comprehend what's happening. We're showering? *Just* showering?

The brush of the towel across my sensitive nipples nearly makes me whimper.

Not Milo.

He's drying off like I'm not here. Except for his erection ... it hasn't forgotten my presence.

Naked Milo saunters out of the bathroom and returns seconds later with a shirt and a pair of jogging pants. "You'll swim in these, but they'll get you to the house."

I nod.

"Indie?"

And finally, I manage to look at his face instead of his erection.

"Have you not seen a dick before?"

Several slow blinks later, I grin. "Not yours."

For the first time since we removed our clothes, Milo looks a little ... affected.

"You quoted me to get me into the shower. *Just* to shower?"

"I've got like ... ten minutes, Indie." He squats before me and holds the sweatpants open for me to step into them.

For the second time today, I feel humiliated and treated like a child. Like ... I'm not good enough. Though, it hurts far worse coming from Milo. I step one foot into them and then my other foot, but Milo grabs my ankle first. He pauses, then rocks forward to his knees, and everything happens at once.

He hooks my leg over his shoulder and plants his mouth between my legs.

My stomach lurches into my throat then bottoms out like flying down a big hill on a roller coaster. Everything inside me explodes into unexpected euphoria. One hand reaches for the vanity behind me while my other one tangles in his hair. "M-Milo ..."

He closes his eyes while his tongue explores me. The attack on my senses makes my head heavy, my eyes unfocused.

"Fuck, Indie ..." he growls, his breath just as stimulating as his mouth and fingers. "This is my new favorite thing."

I groan, barely recognizing the sound as my own. If someone pushed me out of a plane with ten seconds to pull the parachute cord or strapped me to a bucking bull at the rodeo, I wouldn't feel more alive than I do now. Nothing will ever compare to this moment. He doesn't disappoint. I imagined the cowboy who fucks in the barn to be perfectly unsophisticated while seducing a woman.

Spontaneous.

Raw.

A little rough.

Expectations exceeded.

With both hands, I grip his hair, pulling him away and unhooking my leg from his shoulder. And I grab his face and kiss him like he did to me.

"Indie ... I have to go."

I shove his shoulders while kissing him harder. Milo sits back on his heels, gripping my hips, pulling me to straddle his legs.

"Milo," I whisper, leaning back just enough to look into his beautiful blue eyes. "Remember where you said you'd go if you could go anywhere in the world?"

He studies me with a serious expression for a breath before nodding.

"Go there," I move closer, bringing his mouth toward my breasts.

Milo's hands hold them while he teases them with wet kisses and tiny flicks of his tongue, tugging my nipples with his teeth.

Lowering my body, I feel the wet, smooth head of his erection pressed between my legs.

"Indie ..." He grabs my hips, fingers digging into them to stop me when he's already nearly an inch inside of me and I'm *dying!*

It's so warm. So erotic. So mind-blowing.

I need all of him. Anything less would be cruel. We're not stopping. I just ... can't.

"I won't wanna leave," he says.

It takes me a second. Not leave the barn? Not leave the property? Texas? I grin. He won't want to leave his favorite place in the world.

Me.

"Then don't." I draw a harsh breath when I lower all the way when he's completely inside me. "D-don't ... move." I close my eyes and rest my forehead on his shoulder.

"Am I hurting you?"

"No. It's perfect. I ... I don't want you to rush perfection."

"Indie girl ... I'm kinda dying here. I *need* to move."

Biting my lips to hide my grin when I lift my head, I nod.

We kiss. My legs wrap around his waist while he lays me on the floor. And then he moves inside of me. Slow and deep at first, then faster. I love when he breaks our kiss to tip his chin and watch us. Watch himself moving in and out of me.

I love how distracted he gets with every inch of my body. Grabbing my ass and squeezing it, moving us together at his pace. My breasts and nipples tempting both his hands and his mouth. His tongue along my skin and exploring my mouth.

Milo releases a sexy groan when I trap his lip between my teeth.

"Indie girl ..." he says on a labored breath, lifting onto his knees, hands holding my legs while he pumps into me harder and faster.

My back arches.

He spits on his fingers and smears it on my clit in slow, deliberate circles, gaze locked to mine the whole time. I come just from that sight alone. Milo curses, pounding into me several more times before he stills, head back, stretching the thick, corded muscles in his neck. His abs are tight, and every inch of him is so ... fucking ... perfect.

Peeling open his eyes, he lowers to his elbows on either side of me, slowly dragging his tongue up my body, eyes hooded. I feel claimed in every way humanly possible.

I stroke his hair, closing my eyes and committing this moment to memory.

The residual smell of burnt toast mixed with soap.

The warm, uneven wood floor pressed to my back.

The silky strands of his hair teasing my fingers.

The pulsing of his chest pressed to mine.

The tickle of his lips skating from my neck to my jaw.

The hum of appreciation as he continues to devour my skin with his tongue. Kinda animalistic, but incredibly sexy.

"You were made for me, Indie girl." His teeth trap my nipple while his fingers lace with mine above my head.

In the next moment, tears burn my eyes, saddened by the cruelty of this world. Living life with a shitty hand of cards yet feeling guilty for having so much more than so many other people.

I would take less.

So much less.

Just give me Milo, and I'll leave everything else—my car, my clothes, my bank account, food, shelter ... everything. Just give me Milo.

I make the mistake of blinking. In that blink, I feel a void where he was seconds earlier.

While he dresses, Milo gives me a glance. "Stay out of sight for a while. I need to get up to his office before he sends a sniper to take me out," he says while stepping into his boots and donning his hat.

Dragging his sweatpants up my legs, I nod.

Milo steps in front of me and takes the drawstring, cinching it tight and tying it. A simple act that feels intimate. Then he lifts my chin with one finger.

"Did you like kissing Jolene?" The second the words are out, I regret them. My heart has a way of speaking without permission from my brain.

Milo sighs. "Indie ..."

"It's okay. You probably should like kissing her."

"I like kissing you."

"Did you discuss the wedding?"

"I don't want to talk about her when I'm with you."

I frown. "We should talk about something ...your brother? Your parents? What Fletcher's holding over you?"

He drops said head, shaking it. "Indie, if this is too much for you, too unbearable, too cruel ... then we stop. I'm not sure something is always better than nothing. Sometimes, nothing hurts less."

Taking a step back, I hug myself and lean against the

wood beam where he hangs his hat. "It's too late. It's already something, and it already hurts."

THE BOSS'S DAUGHTER

MILO

"HAVE A SEAT." Fletcher tosses his reading glasses onto his desk and leans back in his chair while I take a seat on the opposite side. "Is there anything I need to know about you and Indiana?"

I have a million answers to his question. They all involve me being an asshole to the one person I don't have the liberty to be an asshole to. "We've secretly acted immature for our ages for longer than I want to admit to you. After Ruthie died, I spent a lot of time with Indie. And we've always had a special bond."

Fletcher scratches his jaw. "Like a sister?"

I shrug, not missing his subtle jab. "I don't know. I haven't thought about it in such detail."

He seems to think about my explanation for a few seconds.

"We should have been more respectful of Jolene and Pauline being here," I continue. "Had I known I was gonna be invited to a formal breakfast, I would not have engaged in ... the butter incident."

Kissing Fletcher's ass robs little bits of my soul. The alternative is rather soul-crushing as well.

"When was the last time you visited Archer?" Fletcher punches me in the gut with his swift subject change. They've been friends since they were ten, twelve years before I was born. I'm one of those "oops" kids whose brother is old enough to be my father.

I slowly shake my head.

"Jesus, Milo ... he's your brother. He's in prison because of you, and you've never fucking visited him?"

"Because of me?" I shake my head, unable to bring my gaze back to Fletcher's. "He committed murder."

"And why is that?"

I force myself to make eye contact with him. My jaw clenches for a second. "How many times are we going to have this same conversation?"

The lines in his leathered forehead deepen. "Go see him. Make things right before he dies."

"Make things right? Christ, Fletcher ... nothing is *right* about what happened. Nothing is right about his life being cut short like this. Nothing is right about ..." I bite my tongue. God, it hurts, but I do it.

Nothing is right about you putting yourself in the position to own my whole fucking life. The puppeteer.

"Jolene said you had a nice dinner last night." Again, Fletcher whips the conversation in another direction and picks a subject I don't care to discuss.

"I did. I got the prime rib. It was the best I've ever had."

He glowers at me, as usual, not getting my humor.

I sigh, tapping my fingers on the arm of the chair. "We discussed this arrangement. I wondered if she felt as enthusiastic about it as you and Pauline. But she's..." I twist my lips "...dedicated to this family."

"And you?" He cants his head, crossing his arms.

"Is that a real question?"

Fletcher concedes with a single nod and stands. "Breakfast is waiting. Please don't encourage misbehavior from Indiana. She's been unusually challenging and unbearable lately."

I disagree. I've thoroughly enjoyed her behavior lately.

We make our way to the dining room, where the ladies are already seated.

"Mimosa?" Jolene nods to the champagne glass next to hers.

I take a seat, glancing up at Indie, her wet hair braided in pigtails and a mischievous smirk plastered to her beautiful face.

"Mmm ... sounds good." I take a sip.

"Mine is just orange juice." Indie sips her juice before offering everyone a toothy grin. "Can't wait until I'm old enough to have and do adult things."

I clear my throat, so I don't choke on my drink. Visions of her drunken gaze, eyes drifting shut while my head was between her spread legs, rush to the front of my brain. It was "adulting" at its best.

Indie wets her lips, trying to hide her knowing grin. Of course, she knows where my mind's at right now.

"Mom, Milo hinted that he might need some help planning the honeymoon."

Pauline's spine straightens. "I'd love to help you plan your honeymoon. Although I'm not sure location matters if you're not likely to leave the bedroom."

Jolene blushes.

Fletcher rolls his eyes.

I remain neutral.

And Indie shoves half a croissant into her mouth, keeping her chin tipped toward her plate.

"Have you decided where you're living?" Fletcher asks.

"You should stay in Milo's barn," Indie mumbles with her mouth full, which earns her disapproving scowls from everyone but me. "I used to stay there after Ruthie died. The bed is so comfy."

I hope Fletcher realizes that I did not start this conversation and therefore didn't present the perfect opportunity for Indie to "misbehave."

"You stayed with Milo?" Jolene's perfectly symmetrical brows stretch up her forehead while she rearranges all three berries on her plate with her fork.

"Yes. God ... I've slept with Milo so many times, I've lost count."

Fuck, Indie girl ... you're killing me.

Fletcher clears his throat. "Indiana ..."

I have to swallow my amusement. Indie deserves to be free of this life. Her personality is too big for the stuffiness of this kind of sick wealth and entitlement.

"That sounds bad, Indie," Pauline scorns before sipping her mimosa. "You need to clarify that he let you sleep in his bed while he slept on the sofa, right?" She shifts her gaze to me with desperate hope in her eyes.

I pick up a piece of bacon and pause it at my lips. "Of course." I smile before tucking the whole piece into my mouth.

"That's a cute idea, Indie, but I don't think I'm cut out to live in a barn." Jolene scoffs.

Indie shrugs, stuffing more croissant past her lips, not waiting to swallow or even chew before responding. "When you love someone, they are your home. As long as you're with them, you can live anywhere." She chews slowly while Jolene avoids eye contact with everyone. "Unless ... you don't love Milo. God ... you're marrying him. I hope you love him."

"What do you know about love, Indiana?" Jolene brushes aside Indie's comment. "Have you ever been in love?"

I wait for her to look at me. I expect her to look at me. Does she love me? I don't know. But I hope she trusts me with whatever she's feeling. When she doesn't look at me, I feel like shit for not being who she needs me to be. That's who I've been for her. I've always been her safe place. Her protector.

"That's none of your business," Indie mumbles.

"That's a no." Jolene laughs along with Pauline.

Indie slides her gaze to Fletcher. "I've seen love ... with you and Ruthie."

In the next breath, the room falls silent, all eyes on Fletcher.

He wipes his mouth with the white napkin. "Yes. I loved Ruthie very much."

"What about Switzerland?" Pauline pulls her shoulders back and smiles. "Jolene has never been to Switzerland. It would be a lovely destination for your honeymoon."

Switzerland.

Honeymoon.

Married to Jolene.

Prison ... I'm not in prison.

"Have you been to Switzerland?" Jolene asks.

We know nothing about each other.

"Milo's never been anywhere but Texas and Oklahoma," Indie says matter-of-factly while pushing back in her chair. "If I were getting married, I'd know shit like that about my fiancé." She gives Jolene a stiff smile and ignores the rest of us. "Now, if you'll excuse me, I need to go dry my hair."

I don't allow myself more than a few seconds to stare at her while she heads toward the stairs. Fletcher's watching me, distrust heavy in his gaze.

"Is that true?" Jolene asks.

"Truth." I shrug.

"That's ..." She blinks at me. "Crazy."

"It's not crazy. Milo's young. He's my right-hand man, and he's loyal. Where exactly do you expect him to go?" Fletcher doesn't help me sound any more worldly.

World traveler doesn't seem to be on the list of prerequisites to marry her, so I couldn't give less of a shit if she's in shock right now.

"So you don't even have a passport?" Jolene blinks several times.

I shake my head, eating the frittata.

"Looks like we have a lot to do before the wedding," Pauline sing-songs. "Nothing to worry about. I'll make sure you have a passport. I'll make sure you two have a fabulous destination for your honeymoon. I'll take care of everything."

I'm not sure if I should feel grateful or emasculated. None of it seems to faze Fletcher. He's been protective of me over the years, but he's not jumping to my defense right now. He's not telling Pauline I can get my passport by myself and plan a honeymoon without her help. Did his mom help him when he was my age? When he married Ruthie, did she handle this kind of detail?

15

THE TRUTH HURTS

INDIE

I CAN'T SNEEZE without Fletcher a mile up my ass.

What am I doing?

Where am I going?

Who am I texting?

What I would have given for him to have shown a fraction of this level of interest after Ruthie died.

And when he's not hawking me, he has Milo at his side drinking whiskey or enjoying cocktails and fancy appetizers before dinner with Jolene and Pauline. I have two days before I have to be back at school. Milo's waiting for me to suggest a visit to Rice University, but I've decided now is the best time to get the hell out of here. After the butter incident, I don't think Fletcher will suggest I go anywhere with Milo.

"Where do you think you're going, darlin'?" Fletcher asks while I lug my bag to the front door.

"School."

"So soon?"

"I have some work to do, and it's easier to concentrate when I'm there instead of here."

No surprise, Milo steps around the corner, holding a mug of coffee. "Need help?"

I shake my head, offering him a stiff smile.

"I'll carry your bag to the car while you tell your dad goodbye."

My dad? He needs to stop saying that. "No need."

"I'm already on it." Milo gives me no choice. He steals the bag out of my hand and carries it to my car.

Fletcher eyes Milo and waits for him to disappear out the front door. "That boy's taken." His gaze slides to me.

"If you have a point, I'd appreciate you getting to it so I can get on the road."

"Have you picked a college?"

"I haven't picked a major. Makes it kinda hard to pick a college."

Fletcher twists one side of his mustache. "Then you'd best be focusing on what's important and stop wasting time distracting those of us who have actual jobs and responsibilities. Do you understand what I'm saying?"

Yeah. I understand what he's saying. What I don't understand is what Ruthie saw in him? Has he always been this awful?

"Is it too late to return me?" I take a step closer.

He glowers. "What are you talking about?"

"Do you think my mom invested that million dollars? Do you think she'd refund your money and take me back?"

A dark mask slides along his face, hardening his

expression. "You don't have a goddamn clue what you're talking about."

"No?" My head tips to the side. "So you didn't give my mother a million dollars in exchange for … me?"

"Ruthie was your mother, and I never want to hear you suggest otherwise. Understood?"

"Understood?" I laugh. "No. That's just it. I don't understand. I don't understand why you took me from my mom, only to bring me here and treat me like you wish I didn't exist. I don't understand how you loved Ruthie, but you can't stand to look at me. I don't understand why you treat everyone around you like property. I don't understand why Milo obeys you like—"

Whack!

The familiar sting of his hand across my face.

Before I can gasp or suck in the tiniest of breaths, Milo charges through the front door, past me, and collars Fletcher's neck with his bare hands, pinning him to the wall. "If you ever lay a goddamn hand on her again, I will end you," Milo says, his fingers white from gripping Fletcher's neck with such force.

Fletcher's face turns red like his head might pop right off his body. He claws at Milo's hands, but Milo doesn't budge; every muscle in his body is rock-hard and steady.

After a few seconds, Milo releases him. Fletcher coughs and rubs his neck, eyes narrowed at Milo. "You can't end me. Your whole fucking world depends on me. You better *never* forget that again, or I'll be forced to remind you how quickly the hand that giveth can also taketh." Without another word or so much as a glance in my direction, Fletcher ascends the stairs.

Hands fisted at his sides, Milo watches Fletcher slowly disappear, and he turns toward me, lips in a frown. "Come on."

"I'm fine," I whisper despite my shaky hand covering my cheek, despite the tears burning my eyes.

It's not that my cheek hurts, although it does. It's the gravity of everything around me. Fletcher's deplorability. Missing Ruthie. Milo marrying Jolene. I'm lost. No direction. No home. No family. When grief's not clawing at my chest, I feel hollow inside.

"Indie, follow me."

I hold my ground, shaking my head.

Milo takes my hand and pulls me to the kitchen. Micah glances up from the island and a chopping board full of diced onions. Milo gives him a slight gesture with his chin. Without hesitation, Micah sets the knife aside and exits the kitchen.

Retrieving an ice pack from the freezer, Milo wraps it in a towel and presses it to my face while his other hand cradles my good cheek.

"Come with me," I whisper, my words breaking as they fall from my lips. There's such a heaviness in my chest as desperation grows out of control.

"I can't, Indie girl." Milo leans in and kisses my forehead. "I just can't ..."

"He doesn't own you."

Drawing his brows together, he nods slowly. "He does."

I try to shake my head, but he's holding it with his hands. "Milo, I don't understand."

"That's good. I don't want you to understand. I want

you to take what's left of your innocence, your memories of Ruthie, your determination, and your kind heart and go. Finish school. Go to college. Go absolutely anywhere but here."

"You're here. I can't leave forever. I love ..." I swallow the last word, choke on it, and let it poison everything inside me.

I love you.

My gaze lifts to his. Did he hear me slip? Does he feel the same? Would it matter?

"What's he going to do to you?" I ask.

Milo sets the ice pack on the counter and feathers his fingertips over my cheek for a few seconds. "Nothing I can't handle." He nods toward the entry. "Let's get you on the road."

I hesitate for a second before tucking my chin and making my way to the car with Milo behind me. He opens my door, and I turn to him, giving a glance in the direction of the house and the windows.

"We're being watched," Milo says.

I return a slight nod. "I want to kiss you."

With his back to the house, he twists his lips, giving me a kiss from too far away. I'm heartbroken and don't feel like smiling, but his tiny grin brings one out of me as well.

"Can I hug you?"

He doesn't answer with words. Instead, he pulls me to him, wrapping me in his arms. The warmth. The faint scent of leather. His hand on the back of my head.

My good cheek rests against his heart. "Milo ..." The rest of my words die, vanish before they reach my lips.

I'm not sure what I want to say. Or maybe I do know; I just don't know how to say it.

"Indiana Ellington ... I love you too."

With a single blink, a tsunami of tears surges down my face. If this is love, then love is overrated.

No. It's flat-out cruel.

16

IMPRISONED

MILO

"Did you fuck my daughter?"

I tighten the saddle on Ranger two days after Indie returns to school. It's taken Fletcher this long to broach the topic. Ranger rears his head a bit, and Fletcher strokes the bridge of his nose with one hand while holding the bridle in his other hand.

"Daughter. That's a bold word. Is Indiana your daughter now?" A cooler fall breeze slithers past my neck, or maybe it's just Fletcher's proximity.

"Milo, your bravery is admirable ... but stupid. Whatever you feel toward Indiana is inconsequential. You will marry Jolene. Indie will pursue her own life."

I laugh. "Well, that we agree on. Indie should pursue her dreams as far away from here as possible."

Fletcher strokes his gray beard, eyes squinted in the shadow of his cowboy hat. "Gotta say, I wasn't expecting you to be so agreeable."

I remove my hat and wipe the dirt along my brow. "I can be agreeable. It's obedience I struggle with."

Nodding, Fletcher gazes off in the distance at the guys unloading fence posts from the back of a tractor trailer. "Have you submitted a request to visit Archer?"

"Christ, Fletcher ..." I mount Ranger. "Why do you care?"

"Because I think we're legally out of options. This train will leave the station, and I can't stop it."

I squint against the sun. "You know I never asked for any of this."

"Doesn't mean you shouldn't be grateful." Fletcher turns, heading back toward his truck.

Grateful.

I don't know what that means anymore. Existing seems to be the best I can do. Gratitude feels like a luxury just out of my reach.

WITH INDIE GONE and my impending nuptials creeping closer, my life feels void of emotion and filled with meaningless tasks.

It takes three weeks to get my application approved to visit Archer. Indie hasn't sent me a single text. Not one call. Until today. Her timing couldn't be more impeccable. From my truck in the prison parking lot, I lift the phone to my ear.

"Hey."

"Hi," she says in a soft voice.

I want to drown in it. I want to crawl through the

phone and bring every inch of her body as close to mine as possible. And if I die at that moment ... so be it.

"Tell me something good. I *really* need to hear something good right now." My head tips back to the headrest while I close my eyes.

"I'm not coming home for Christmas."

I deflate even more. "Indiana, you suck at this game."

"I'm going to stay with a friend in Colorado. Snowboarding. Shopping. Maybe smoke a joint or two and pretend her family is my family."

It's not an execution, but I feel like Indie's news is the equivalent of my stay of execution being denied.

No Indie.

Merry fucking Christmas.

"Milo?"

I clear my throat and open my eyes. "Yeah. I'm here. That's, uh ... great. That's great, Indie. I'm happy for you. Guess I'd better get your present in the mail if that's the case."

"You bought me something?" Her tone escalates, and I gobble up every ounce of joy that leaks from it.

"Maybe."

She giggles. It's a better high than anything she'll smoke in Colorado.

"Well, I got you something too."

"Liar." I can't help my grin. It feels out of place on my face, given why I'm parked where I am.

"Guess you'll just have to wait and see," she sing-songs.

"Guess so."

A pause—a long one—wedges its way into our conversation. I stare at the dash because what's beyond is too tragic, too unimaginable. And I picture Indie and her wavy blond hair tousled from the wind. Her short sundress whipping in waves. And her boots scuffing along the dirt, kicking dust on their way to me as I finish a long day, covered in dirt and sweat.

"So ... where are you? On Ranger?"

I force myself to lift my gaze to the top of the guard tower over the endless horizon of razor wire. I force myself back to reality. "How'd you guess?"

"I miss Ranger. I'm sure he misses me too."

"Yeah." I pinch the bridge of my nose. I miss my Indie girl something fierce. It tugs at my chest, leaving permanent marks. "He misses you," I mumble.

"Just him?"

"The chickens miss you too. You were much gentler with their eggs than I am."

Again, she giggles, and again, I tuck every little note of it into my memory because I know someday she won't be laughing like this in my ear.

"I'm sure you're busy, so I won't keep you. I just wanted to tell you about my plans."

"Have a great time." I clear the agony from my throat. "Send me pictures of the Rockies."

"You ... you haven't seen the Rockies. I forget. Now I feel like an asshole for calling you about it. I feel like Jolene."

"Don't. I'm happy for you. And you are not Jolene."

Again, a pause settles between us. I don't have anything magical to say to make her feel better. But I don't want to end the call, and I don't think she does either.

"Milo, I want to be happy for you too, but ..."

I stare at the windowless walls of my brother's home. "No buts. You can be happy for me. My life could be much worse."

"Yeah," she whispers. Indie knows I compare every situation in my life to my brother's current situation, even if she doesn't know the details. I hope she never knows those details. Nobody should have to share headspace with the unfortunate incidents of my past.

"Have a great time. You'll be missed this Christmas," I say.

"Pfft ..."

"I'll miss you."

"Milo ..."

I clear my throat. "I gotta go."

Another long pause.

"Do you still love me, Milo?"

I grunt a laugh. "Yes, Indiana. That won't ever change."

"I love you too," she says like our love is a lost cause ... because it is.

Before I can say anything else, the call ends. Should I feel guilty for loving her? For letting her know I love her? For taking things this far with her when we have nowhere to go?

I don't know. I don't know anything anymore, except this ...

I love her.

It takes eons to get through the crawling line of security. When I do, I stand idle for a moment, afraid to sit in the chair on the opposite side of the glass as Archer. It's been years. Until now, I never realized how much guilt I've harbored—guilt for *so* many things.

His blue eyes look gray, like the bark of a dead tree. The chair screeches along the floor as I pull it out to take a seat. The acrid odor of chlorine and human misery seeps into my skin until I can taste it. Until I fucking choke on it.

Archer's old enough to be my father, and he looks it today. His shaved head, white whiskers, and deep wrinkles by his eyes and mouth. We stare at each other for several seconds before I reach for the phone, as does he.

"What are you doing here, Milo?" His voice is rough from layers of tar in his lungs.

"Thought I should come say ..."

"Goodbye?" He laughs, which sends him into a coughing fit while he fists his hand at his mouth. "Years. It's been years, and you decide to show up to say a final goodbye? Listen, little brother, I told you to forget about me. I told you to pretend I'm dead."

"Well, that will be easy to do before long." I frown. "I heard."

Archer's smile fades, dry lips covering his nicotine-stained teeth. "Fletcher told you? And that's why you came?"

I shake my head. "Your attorney told me a date's been set."

"So it *is* why you're here."

"I talked to your attorney *after* I decided to come."

"After Fletcher told you to come?"

"Does it fucking matter?"

He sweeps his hand along his head like he's slicking back his nonexistent hair. "Is he taking good care of you?"

It's hard to keep from choking on his words. Is he serious? "Sure."

"Sure? That's not an answer."

"I'm alive. I have a job. Oh ... and I'm getting married to the woman he chose for me. So yeah ... it's all good."

"No shit? You're getting hitched? Is she hot as fuck? If she's not, just lie to me. One of us should get to fuck an actual woman."

I try to hide my flinch. "It's Pauline's daughter."

Archer's eyebrows make a slow ascent up his forehead. "Well, done, Milo. Marrying into the Ellington family. Well fucking done."

I don't react. The last thing I'm going to do is give my dying brother some whiney bitch speech about marrying someone I don't love or really know for that matter. Suppose I was the one in this god-forsaken place with an execution date. In that case, the last thing I'd want to hear is some asshole playing his fucking violin because he has to marry into a wealthy family, eat medium-rare steak every night, and screw some long-legged brunette when it's time to have a family.

"How's Fletch doing? I hope he's moved on since Ruthie died. Life's too short to spend it grieving the dead or visiting the near-dead," he rasps before coughing.

"Moving on? I'm not sure what you mean by that. He works. Drinks. Smokes. Eats. Sleeps."

"But is he getting some pussy?"

"Christ ..." I sigh, rubbing the back of my neck. "I dunno. We don't discuss pussy."

"Why the hell not? Oh ... I forgot ... he has a daughter, doesn't he? Didn't he adopt some girl for Ruthie?"

For a moment, I study Archer. Does he really not know Indiana's story?

"Adopt is a generous word," I say. "But yes, he purchased a girl. She's eighteen. Her name is Indiana. And she hates Fletcher because he lost what was left of his humanity after Ruthie died."

"How do you know she hates him? Are you two close?"

"Someone had to take care of her after Ruthie died."

He smirks. "That's ... sweet. You make sure you take care of her like I took care of you."

I slowly shake my head.

"Hey!" He slams his palm against the glass, and the guard gives him a warning, but he ignores the guard, eyeing me without blinking. "I. Took. Care. Of. You. Don't you ever forget that. Fletcher took care of you. Make our sacrifices count. Do you fucking hear me?"

I grit my teeth to hold my shit together as Archer's eyes turn red and gloss over with unshed emotion.

Swallowing hard, I return a slow nod.

"Time's up, Odell," the guard says.

Time's up ...

It's been years since I've seen him, but there's comfort in knowing that someone exists in your life, even if you don't see them. I find comfort in knowing that Indiana will go on to live a great life. There's no comfort in knowing you can't see someone even if you want to see them. Unless I choose to watch Archer die, this is our forever goodbye.

Slowly, I lift my hand and press it to the glass against his. Life isn't fair. I have more days than Archer has to think about anything. To make good and bad decisions. To ride a horse. Swim in a pond. And fuck a woman. Any woman. I need to remember this.

"I'd do it all again because I love you, Milo." Archer hangs up the phone while using the heel of his other hand to erase his tears before the guards see him.

I fucking choke on the words. They jam in my throat, a train wreck of regret and unchangeable circumstances. As they open the door to take him away, my hand balls into a fist against the glass, and I bang on it several times.

"Hands off the glass," the guard behind me warns just as Archer glances over his shoulder.

Hands in cuffs.

Ankles shackled.

I swallow repeatedly until I find enough composure to mouth the words. "Thank you." I think he needs those two words more than a million "I love you's."

A tiny smile touches his lips while he returns a single nod.

17

NEVER A BRIDESMAID

INDIE

> Indie: Why do you never answer your phone?

> Milo: I'm rarely alone

> Indie: Even at night? In bed?

> Milo: No. Hearing your voice at night would be torture

I GRIN, staring at the calendar on my computer. My spring break plans got canceled, so I'll be going home in one month, but Milo thinks I'll be in Palm Beach.

> Indie: Still marrying Jolene? Lie to me

> Milo: Jolene who?

I giggle.

> Indie: I'm thinking of spending the summer in Canada working at a resort with a friend of mine.

> Milo: Canada is good. It's still in North America but a solid distance from Fletcher.

My grin dies. I know what he means, but I hate that he's so desperate for me to be far away from Fletcher because that means I'm far away from him too.

I fiddle with the ring he sent me for Christmas. It's a white gold stacking band with encased crushed turquoise. It was his mother's. I wear it on my left ring finger because ... fuck Jolene.

It made the silly belt buckle I sent him seem impersonal.

> Indie: I have to study. Call me.

> Milo: Good night, Indie girl

Indigo ...

OVER THE NEXT MONTH, Milo and I text. Just text. He asks me about my spring break trip. I lie to him.

When I pull into the drive on the Friday before spring break week, I see him out in the pasture on Ranger along with Fletcher on his horse Zeus in a cloud of dust around the herd of cattle.

My sexy cowboy ...

I step out of the car and inhale the unsterilized air, a welcome break from the halls and desks doused in disinfectant. Neither man glances in my direction, so I head into the house with my bag.

"Oh, hi. Mr. Ellington said you'd be in California for spring break," Micah says when I poke my head into the kitchen after depositing my bag by the stairs.

Ugh ... I could die. I don't have to see it to know that he has pies in the oven. The kitchen's filled with the sweet and sour blend of strawberries and rhubarb. I can already taste the zingy tartness.

"Yeah. I was supposed to go with some friends, but one had to cancel, then another, then ..." I shrug. "Well, eventually, it was just one other girl and me, so I suggested we cancel the trip. I didn't tell Mr. Ellington because I wanted to surprise ..."

Milo.

"Uh ... him." I fake a grin.

"Can I make you something to eat?"

"I'd kill for some of that—"

"No. She has to fit into her dress."

I turn toward Pauline's voice behind me. Again, I fake a grin.

She smirks. "Fletch said you wouldn't be home, but I'm glad you are. We need to get you fitted for your dress."

"My dress?" I squint. "I'm a personal attendant, not a bridesmaid."

Pauline fiddles with my long bangs. "Yes, dear. But Jolene doesn't want you picking out your dress."

I take a step back to stop her fiddling. "Because?"

She scoffs. "Don't take it personally, Indiana. You and Jolene have different tastes in fashion, that's all. And we don't want you picking out something in lavender that will clash with her orchid bridesmaid dresses, or even worse ..." Her nose wrinkles. "White. You never wear white to a wedding."

I hadn't planned on wearing white. Black. I want to wear black to mourn the marriage of Milo and Jolene.

"Why don't you shower and do something with your hair? We can make it into town and have you measured before dinner."

I sniff my armpit and run my hands through my slightly damp hair. "I showered a few hours ago. All I've done is drive here."

Micah chuckles, earning a scowl from Pauline.

"Fine. But at least change into something that doesn't have holes in it and run a brush through your hair. Maybe put some color on your cheeks and a little lipstick too."

I glance down at my ripped jeans, but Pauline's gone before I can defend my fashion choice.

"If I didn't think I'd get fired, I'd offer you a stiff drink," Micah mumbles.

Eyeing him for several seconds, I smirk. "I've missed you. And save me a piece of pie."

PAULINE DOESN'T SAY a word to me while her driver takes us to town. I get fitted for a hideous green dress that looks like something an older woman might have worn fifty years ago. It's itchy, and the waist hits a weird spot on my torso. Then we pick out shoes, also elderly looking, yet surprisingly toe-crushing. I bite my tongue until I taste blood because I just want to get home to Milo. It's been four months since I've seen him.

Since he's kissed me.

Since he's been inside me.

"Dinner's in an hour. Don't be late," Pauline instructs when I hop out of the car and start to run toward the barn.

"Indiana?"

My strides die so quickly it feels like I've run into an invisible wall. Sighing my annoyance, I turn toward Fletcher on Zeus.

"What are you doing here, and where do you think you're going?"

Wow. No, *Indiana, so good to see you. What a great surprise. Let me give you a big hug, my darlin' girl.*

Nope.

He's already angry, and I just got here.

"My trip got canceled, so I'm going to see Milo." I glance down the drive at one of the workers carrying a dead chicken by its neck.

"Milo's busy." Fletcher jerks his head toward the main house. "You'll see him at dinner. Go get changed."

How many times do I have to change my clothes today?

"I won't disturb him. I just want to say hi."

"Indiana." Fletcher gives me that look and that tone. He's done negotiating. Will he hit me again if I say more? Will Milo come to my rescue? Will he *end* him? God ... someone needs to.

Deflating, I mope back to the house and up to my bedroom, where I stay until Fletcher and Pauline beckon me to dinner.

When I reach the top of the stairs, Milo comes in the front door, freshly showered and looking hotter than ever in his light blue button-down, sleeves rolled to his elbows, dark jeans, and boots. As he removes his hat and sets it on the entry table, I bite my lips together and watch him. Admire him.

In the next breath, his gaze lifts to mine. And he grins. I feel it *everywhere*.

Barreling down the stairs, I try to suppress my squeal.

"Indie, please help Micah set the table. We're about ready to eat." Pauline's request shoots out of nowhere like an animal triggering a trap in the woods. More like a sword being plunged into my stomach. If I don't feel Milo's embrace soon, I will die.

He swallows, tamping down his smile.

Leather. Coffee. Cinnamon.

I can almost taste him like the pies baking in the oven earlier. My skin tingles, anxious for his touch. Balling my hands into fists, I inhale slowly and turn toward Pauline. "Of course." Never before have I helped Micah set the table. Not that I wouldn't. It's just never been asked of me until now.

When we sit for dinner, I can't look at anyone, not even Milo. Why did I think that coming home was a good idea? Is this what I have to look forward to for the next week? Pauline and Fletcher keeping constant watch over Milo and me?

Reeling with a mixture of anticipation, frustration,

and the desire to do physical harm to Fletcher and Pauline, I ease into my chair.

"I don't have the final count yet, but I think we're going to be around four hundred," Pauline says.

"Four hundred what?" Fletcher asks.

Dishes and utensils clink and ting as everyone digs into the rare meat, roasted potatoes, and garlicky asparagus.

My anxious hands rub along my soft denim jeans, building warm friction.

Milo's boot nudges my foot under the table. Reluctantly, I lift my gaze from my plate to him.

"People attending the wedding," Pauline says.

If Ranger sat on me, I'm not sure it would feel this painful on my chest.

The wedding ...

Milo smiles with his eyes, sliding his foot against mine again while he slowly chews. It's as if he's not listening to a word Pauline's saying. How can he be so immune to the death of us?

It's not his hands or his lips. But I'll take whatever touch I can get from him.

"I thought it was going to be a small wedding."

"Fletcher, we started with close to eight hundred. Four is small."

"When is the wedding?" I manage to ask, giving Pauline a fleeting glance.

She frowns. "How can you not know this?"

I shrug. "Nobody tells me anything. Just when to change my clothes and when to get fitted for my dress.

I've been gone. Remember? You sent me away to an all-girls school so, I'd be out of your hair."

"Indiana, that's enough," Fletcher warns, glancing up from his plate while cutting his crimson slab of meat.

Pauline blots her mouth. "It's June first."

Ten weeks. In ten weeks, Milo will be Jolene's husband.

"Will you be bringing a date?" she asks.

Milo stiffens a second before sliding his foot away from mine. I give him a measured glance, but he keeps his gaze on his plate.

"You should bring a date, Indiana."

I raise my eyebrows at Fletcher. Did he really suggest that? Then it hits me … of course. If I have a date, nobody worries about me trying to steal the groom from his bride.

"Do I have to decide right now?"

"No. But you need to let me know before you return to school," Pauline says.

I nod several times, waiting for Milo to look at me. He doesn't give me another glance for the rest of the meal.

"Thanks for dinner. I have a few things to check on, so I'm going to excuse myself if that's okay?" Milo says.

"Of course." Fletcher smiles and nods.

"Good night, Milo," Pauline says.

He gives her a quick nod and mumbles, "Night."

"Good night," I say with the most confidence I've had in my voice all night. Can he please look at me?

Then he does.

Milo's gaze finds me again, but all I get is a curt nod and a barely detectable smile.

Minutes later, I get excused from the table and lock myself in my bedroom.

> Indie: WTF?

Milo doesn't reply.

> Indie: You're MARRYING HER! And my getting asked if I'm bringing a date to YOUR wedding earns me the cold shoulder?

I wait nearly thirty minutes for an answer.

Nothing.

I call him.

Of course, he doesn't answer.

When I decide to sneak out just after ten, I hear Pauline and Fletcher in the formal living room.

"I'm sending him to Oklahoma City for the next week. I wasn't going to go, but given Indie's unexpected trip home, I think it's best he is not here," Fletcher says. He's puffing on a cigar.

I can smell the sweet, spicy wood aroma. I swear I'll smell it long after he's gone. And that can't happen soon enough.

"Oh, I'm so relieved," Pauline chirps. "It's exhausting keeping her away from him."

"Agreed." Fletcher chuckles.

I'm glad he finds my love life so amusing.

Sneaking out the dog door, I make my way to Milo's barn and open the door; all the lights are off.

"Milo?"

No answer.

Blowing out a frustrated breath, I check the back of the barn. He's sitting next to a small fire, a beer in hand and several empty bottles on the ground beside him.

"Why are you ignoring me?" The smoke wafts in my direction, and I blink hard several times.

He inches his gaze to mine before taking a swig of his beer. He seems in no hurry to answer me.

"Are you drunk?"

"Getting there." He drains the rest of the bottle and tosses it next to the others.

"You can't be mad if I bring a date to your wedding."

Milo nods. "I'm aware." He folds his hands over his stomach and stares at the orange and yellow flames.

I cross my arms. "I don't want to talk about your stupid wedding."

"Neither do I."

"Fletcher is sending you to Oklahoma City until I return to school."

He nods slowly. "I'm aware."

"Do you leave early in the morning?"

Again, he nods.

"Milo, I ..." My voice begins to crack from the emotions eating away at my heart. "I came home for you."

He blinks at me a few times, the flicker of flames reflecting in his eyes.

"I'm dying here, Milo. I want to touch you so badly, but you're sitting there like it hasn't been *months* since you touched me. Is it Jolene? Are you screwing her now? Some other random woman? Rae?"

He narrows his eyes a fraction before slowly inching

his head side to side as if he does not fully understand me.

"Fuck it. Fuck you. Fuck everyone. I'm done here." I pound my boots toward the blacktop, my heart crumbling into unfixable pieces.

"Touch me ..." Milo's voice is barely audible, laced with anguish.

I turn.

He stands a good ten feet from me, hands limp at his sides. Shoulders slumped. "If you want to touch me ... then touch me."

Oh, Milo ...

He breaks my heart, more pieces crumbling to the pit of my stomach—over six feet of thick bones, solid muscle, and tortured soul.

I force my feet to make their way back to him.

His drunken gaze slides along my body while his lips part, tongue darting to wet them. When Milo looks at me, really looks at me, it feels like he's silently screaming, "Help me!"

But I don't know how to help him. I can't change his past any more than I can change my own. In ten weeks, he's going to marry Jolene. And as much as I want to hate him for allowing it to happen, I can't.

It's in his eyes.

I don't know if he could stop it, short of taking a gun and killing himself.

"Milo ..." I whisper, unbuttoning his shirt. The fire behind us crackles. "Do you love me?"

"Yes," he rasps, drunk eyes hiding behind heavy blinks.

I unbuckle his belt while pressing my lips to his bare chest. "When you say 'I do' to her, will you still love me?"

"Yes."

My hands shake while removing his belt and unbuttoning his jeans. I'm scared of how bad life will hurt when he's wearing the wedding band she slips on his finger. When she decides it's time they start a family.

The gravel digs into the knees of my jeans while I lower before him, taking him into my mouth.

I close my eyes and claim every part of him before Jolene. And one day ... I will tell her I had him first. One day, I will plant my foot in her face and make her feel like an inadequate wife, like a failure as a woman, like a second choice. She might feel entitled to a marriage certificate with his name, but he will *always* be my Milo.

"Fuck, Indie ..."

I open my eyes while Milo's head tips back, and a low groan escapes from his open mouth. He's warm against my lips, controlled while moving ever so slightly, yet I feel it fleeting. The ache inside. The undeniable need.

His fingers sliding into my hair.

His abs tightening when my nails dig into them.

"Come here, baby," he rasps, grabbing himself, and teasing my lips.

I flick my tongue along the head; his hips jerk once, a sharp hiss sliding through his clenched teeth. "I-Indie ... I can't control it any longer."

My lips forge a trail up to his chest, neck, and lips. "I don't want you to control it," I whisper.

Milo grabs my face with a firm grip, kissing me hard. We stumble our way back to the barn. I reach for the door handle, but my hand slips when he grabs my thighs, lifting me, and pinning me to the cold metal.

He jerks the skirt of my dress out of his way along with the crotch of my panties.

All control is lost while he moves inside me.

Never ... not *ever,* have I felt this wanted. This needed. He's not just inside me; he's flowing through my veins and filling my lungs.

"Inside," Milo says between labored breaths, sliding out of me while easing me back to my feet.

He opens the door, backing me inside.

Hands on my face again, kissing me—branding me.

I push his unbuttoned shirt over his shoulders, and he releases me long enough to send it to the floor. Eager hands tear off my clothes, hungry lips devour my skin, as desperate and tortured as the look in his eyes.

A voice in my head whispers, "*If this is love ...*"

It's. So. Unfair.

Milo Odell was made for me. And I was made for him.

Then the devil inside Fletcher came to life after Ruthie died, and he won't be satisfied until the world submits to his form of hell.

My back hits the mattress, and he spreads my legs, consuming me with hungry strokes of his tongue. Then he flips me onto my stomach and kisses the back of my legs and ass. My fingers curl into the sheets when he nudges my legs apart and plunges into me with a hard grunt. "Mine," he says, gripping my hips.

"Yours ..." I echo, out of breath, while my hands

stretch above my head to grip the top edge of the mattress.

If this is love, why is it wrong?

If this is love, why can't we be together?

If this is love, why does it hurt my heart so much?

If this is love ... I don't want to live without it. Without him.

"Milo ..." I cry his name so loudly someone might hear me.

I want them to hear me. I want the whole world to hear how Milo makes me feel.

He sits back on his heels and hugs my back to his chest. Kissing my shoulder, one hand slides to my breast while his other hand snakes between my legs, where he was just seconds ago. "Mine ..." he rasps like he's angry.

Closing my eyes, my head lulls back onto his shoulder. "Yours," I whisper while several tears work their way down my face.

Time doesn't care that Milo's leaving tomorrow. It ticks on relentlessly all night. Milo does his best to spend most of the night in his favorite place, but he may have had too many beers.

All too soon, it's over. The way we will be over forever. Too. Soon.

"Indie girl." He kisses my back while I sleep on my stomach. "I have to go."

"No ..." I protest with my face buried in the pillow. It's not even light out yet.

He chuckles. "Sorry. Sleep as long as you want. Just be smart about sneaking back into the house."

I roll over. He's dressed. My arms wrap around his neck.

"Stay."

Again, he laughs. "I can't."

Standing on my knees, I press my naked body to him, my hand grabbing his crotch.

His abs tighten while he tries to pull away a fraction. "Indiana ..."

"I'll let you lick butter off me." I bring his hand between my legs, my fingers guiding his inside of me.

"Is that so?" He stares right into my eyes, slowly moving his fingers.

I bite my lower lip, blinking heavily while nodding.

"I have never..." his voice gets husky while his lips turn into a grin "...seen anything or anyone as sexy as you are right now."

"Don't..." I rest my chin on his shoulder "...stop. P-please." My teeth dig into his shirt and the thick muscles beneath it while my hips rock into his touch.

Milo chuckles. It's deep, vibrating his whole chest. "I have to go, Indie girl."

"Milo ..." I grab the back of his neck to steady myself. "J-just ..."

His other hand grabs a fistful of my hair, gently tipping my head back so his mouth can cover mine. His tongue dives deep into it while his fingers move inside me.

Groaning into his mouth, I claw at the back of his neck when I orgasm.

Out of breath and heart pounding. Grateful. And ... sad. I collapse onto the bed.

Milo rubs his middle finger and ring finger along his lower lip a few times before sucking them into his mouth and humming.

If you ever stick those fingers inside her, I will cut them off.

It's an awful thing I wish didn't float into my jealous consciousness. Everything behind my ribcage constricts to the point that it's hard to breathe. I can't look at him. I'm ashamed of even thinking those thoughts after such an intimate moment.

And I'm hurt because I know he can't promise me anything, and that's a chronically unbearable pain I will have to live with for the rest of my life.

"What is it, baby?" He plucks one of his shirts from his basket of clean clothes and pulls it over my head.

I love it when he dresses me.

I find a smile just for him. It's a bandage with fun characters so no one sees the unsightly wound beneath it. No one sees the pain.

"Nothing." I shake my head. "I *hate* these cards. Every day I wake up hoping I've been dealt a new hand where you're marrying me, not her. And when we're together like this, I can't stop counting down the days. I fucking *hate* it." And I hate the images of him with her that are not even real—yet—but still an unstoppable poison spreading through my head.

Milo rests a finger under my chin and tips my head to look at him.

He's extra cinnamon today.

"I will never stop looking for a way out." Wrinkles crease his forehead. "But that could take a lifetime ... and you deserve a life that doesn't involve false hope, slim chances, and unimaginable images in your head."

Tears burn my eyes, and with one blink, they release. Milo bends down to kiss away every single one of them.

"Have a good spring break. I'll text you when I get to Oklahoma City."

"When will I see you again?" I sniffle.

With a sad smile, he shakes his head. "Dunno."

"Graduation?"

He continues to shake his head.

No. He won't be at my graduation because Jolene graduates on the same day. Aunt Faye and Grandma Hill will be there. That's it. No Fletcher. No Milo.

"Bye, Milo."

His knuckles skate across my cheek. "Bye, Indie girl."

18

MILO'S WOMEN

MILO

"Hey," Rae says, stepping out of her car as I brush the dried mud off my boots. She flips her red hair over her shoulders and slides her hands into her pockets. Her familiar vanilla scent wafts toward me. "It's been a while since I've seen you. I was at my dad's place yesterday, and you'll never guess what I saw on his refrigerator."

I scrub the mud from my boots, glancing up at her again. "What's that?"

"An invitation to your wedding. Milo ..." She coughs a laugh, shaking her head. "You're getting married ... to Jolene Ellington? Is this some joke?"

"Sadly, no." I refocus on my boots.

"Sadly, no? What does that mean?"

"It's a business arrangement more than a marriage."

"An arranged marriage?"

God, I hate how that sounds. "A marriage of convenience."

"Wow. I never saw you as that guy." She digs the toe of her boot into the dirt.

"That guy?" I toss the brush aside and carry my boots to my place.

"The guy who marries for money," Rae says, following me.

"Try again." I set my boots inside the door and wash my hands in the bathroom. The soap stings the cuts along my arm from my run-in with a wire fence.

"What do you mean try again?" Rae asks the second I return to the kitchen. She tosses her handbag on my sofa.

It's been a month since I've seen Indie. We text, but the elephant in the room keeps getting bigger. When I'm desperate to hear her voice, I call her just to say good night. I'm a little on edge about this wedding, and the last thing I need is Rae questioning what kind of guy I am or am not.

"I'm marrying Jolene because I'm loyal to her family, and they've done a lot for me. I'll never be able to repay them unless—"

"Unless you marry Jolene?"

"Something like that." I open my fridge and survey the mostly empty shelves. Something needs to go. I wrinkle my nose. I think it's raw milk that's weeks past its freshness.

"Do you love her?"

I glance over my shoulder. "Yes. We've had a handful of interactions around the holidays. We've been on one date. I don't even have her cell phone number. But yeah ... I love her."

"Jesus ..." Rae winces. "We've had sex, and I wouldn't marry you this quickly."

I grunt, opting for the usual—burnt grilled cheese. "Thanks. The feeling is mutual."

Rae laughs, crossing her arms while resting her backside against my counter. "You know what I mean."

"I do. And if your dad has told you much of anything about the Ellington family, then you know this marriage is nothing more than an extension of the business. An insurance policy, I suppose." I nod toward the loaf of bread while I fetch my slices. They're so dry they practically crumble in my hand. "Do you want a sandwich?"

"I've seen your sandwiches. They're black. No, thank you. Let me say ... if you find a woman who eats black sandwiches, *she's* the one you should be marrying. But I highly doubt you'll find her. So yeah ... marry Jolene Ellington and die a rich man."

"Indie eats my burnt grilled cheese." I give Rae a quick sideways glance.

"Senior-in-high-school Indie? Fletcher's daughter Indie?"

I nod, buttering my bread.

"Well, there you go. Ask Fletcher to let you marry Indie instead of Jolene. I'm sure he won't have an issue with you marrying his *eighteen-year-old* daughter." She laughs more.

Ignoring her, I press my sandwich against the pan with a firm hold on the spatula. Maybe in another life, Indie's age would matter to me. She's a woman with a woman's body. She wants me. I fit inside her. And she orgasms from my touch. If she wasn't supposed to be sexual, God fucked up and let her hormones rage a little too early. I have no time, patience, or desire to conform to societal standards.

"You're a good man, Milo. You're marrying someone you don't love and barely know, yet you're being faithful to her even before your vows."

"Why do you say that?"

"I assume she's why we're now friends *without* benefits?"

Despite my urge to set the record straight, I keep my chin down and my mouth shut.

"*Right?*" she asks again.

I chuckle and shake my head. "Sorry. Was that a question I needed to answer?"

After helping herself to one of the last beers in my fridge, she sits on my sofa. "I mean ... who would know? Really? You're not breaking any vows to God yet. And it's not love. I bet she's getting some."

I shut off the gas and slide my sandwich onto a plate. "Jolene can do whatever she wants." Plopping my tired ass onto the end of my bed, I inspect the black sandwich before taking a bite that sears the roof of my mouth.

Rae laughs when I open my mouth to release the steam. "What do *you* want to do?" She gives me that flirty smile that's worked so well for her before now. Before Indie.

"Need me to mend any of your clothes? We could barter."

I smirk over my bite of the sandwich before mumbling, "Sex for sewing on a button? I can't be the only guy who's willing to fuck you."

"Screw you, Odell." She rolls her eyes.

I chuckle.

"You're easy, Milo. Uncomplicated. And can I say *good in bed* without it going to your head?"

"Too late." I take another bite and chew it several times. "It's already gone to my head."

My phone vibrates on the counter. Before I can stand and grab it, Rae jumps up. "Is it your boss? Or your fiancée calling you for the first time?" She snags my phone.

"I'm sure it's something to do with my car's extended warranty," I mutter.

Rae giggles. "Oh ... it's Indie. Why is she calling you? I've got this."

"No—" I reach for the phone just as she turns away.

"Hey, Indie. How the heck are you? It's Rae."

"Rae ..." I set my plate on the counter and hold out my hand. "Give me the phone."

"Oh, he's right here. How's school? What are your plans after graduation?"

"Jesus Christ, Rae ... give me the fucking phone." I rip it from her hand.

Her head jerks backward while she shoots me a grimace of disbelief. "What the hell? I was just kidding."

I hold the phone at my side for a second, releasing a long breath. "Sorry. I'm not in the mood to kid around." I nod toward the door. "It's late."

She blinks a few times before nodding. "O-kay ... Wow." Snagging her bag from the sofa, she walks back toward the door, shaking her head and wearing a look of complete confusion. "Bye."

I pinch the bridge of my nose.

When the door clicks shut behind her, I bring the phone to my ear. "Hey. Sorry about that."

"It's ... um ... why is Rae at your place?"

"She's not. She just left."

Indie tries to laugh, but it sounds tight and forced. "Okay. Sorry. Why *was* Rae at your place?"

I collapse onto the sofa and run a hand through my hair. "She stopped by to visit, I guess." If I say she stopped by to ask me about Jolene, it will make Indie even more uneasy.

"Visit?"

"Yeah."

"The woman you were screwing still stops by to visit?"

"She's a friend."

"Like I'm your friend?"

"No. Fuck ... just ..." Another heavy sigh makes its way past my lips. "Indie ... can we not talk about Rae or Jolene or the past or anything beyond right now? Can you just tell me about your day or what you're wearing or studying or watching on Netflix? Literally, anything that's not my fucked-up life?"

She says nothing for what feels like forever, magnifying how much I depend on her to anchor me to something resembling sanity in my life.

"Dahmer. I'm watching the Jeffrey Dahmer story on Netflix. I'm studying AP Bio. My day was shitty until I heard your voice. And I'm wearing a black Twilight tee and ripped jeans."

Lying on my side, I keep the phone pressed to my ear

and close my eyes. "Mmm ... keep going."

There's another long pause. I know she's working through everything in that beautiful head of hers. I've seen her do it so many times. Ruthie used to take her time before answering people's questions, always offering a calculated response. I don't think Indie knows how many learned behaviors she has because of Ruthie.

"My roommate's boyfriend broke up with her, so she's in the corner of the room with soundproof headphones and a pint of cookie dough ice cream hugged to her chest. And I found a date for the wedding."

Fuck my life ...

I open my eyes.

"A friend's brother. He'll be home from college. We've texted a few times. He's pre-law. I almost didn't ask him because I officially hate lawyers since that's the profession of your future wife."

She just pissed all over my night. Do I deserve it? Probably.

"I'm worried about you. Why Dahmer? There are a million other shows to watch that won't give you nightmares."

"His name is Judah ... like son of Jacob. He has one more year before he graduates. He wants to be a judge. And he's willing to wear a tie that matches my ugly-as-fuck green dress. Isn't that wonderful of him?"

Sitting up straight, I scrub a hand over my face. "AP Bio, huh? I never took any smart classes like that. Maybe that's why I didn't graduate."

"Just because the dress is ugly-as-fuck green doesn't mean I can't wear something sexy under it. It's the least I can do for a guy willing to buy a matching tie that he will never wear again."

"Christ, Indie ... what are you doing?"

"I'm having dinner with my fuck buddy. I'm marrying a woman I don't love. I'm an obedient little dog to a real son of a bitch. Oh wait ... that's you, not me. What am *I* doing? I'm hitting back. I'm trying to give you a tiny fraction of the pain you've given me."

"Indie ..."

"I must go before my roommate drowns in her bucket of ice cream."

"Indiana—"

She ends the call.

My thumb hovers over the *send* icon, but I don't touch it. As hard as that is to do, I toss my phone aside and give her space, then I shower and brush my teeth. I keep moving forward. Routine has always been my greatest comfort. It's about to become my best friend as well.

Snagging my phone from the sofa on the way to my bed, I find a message on my screen.

> Indie: Sorry. It might be that time of the month for me. I'm an asshole. An asshole who loves you. <3

I grin.

> Milo: That's my title, not yours. "Asshole who loves you." Good night, my beautiful Indie girl <3

19

FREEDOM NEVER FELT SO MISERABLE

INDIE

"Where's your family sitting?" Lexie Ebert asks while we're ushered into the frigid auditorium for graduation. It's a symphony of echoing chatter just before the band plays. "Mine's over there." She points.

"I'm not sure. I haven't spotted them yet." I squint my eyes like I'm doing just that. It's embarrassing. I haven't spotted them because it's just Grandma Hill and Aunt Faye. Everyone else is at Jolene's graduation today. Once we're seated, my head swivels in every direction until I find Grandma and Faye.

They give me a wave, and I force a smile. Ruthie would have been here. I hope she is here in spirit. She would have insisted Fletcher be here too. And he would have been nice because he was an actual human being with Ruthie.

The ceremony lasts to infinity times infinity. Nobody's supposed to have their cell phones, but everyone does, heads bowed to them. It's a middle finger to the teachers and administrators who will no longer dictate our lives.

My phone vibrates in my right hand as my row lines up to walk across the stage and receive our diplomas. I lift the sleeve of my gown, which reeks of perfume from so many hugs, to sneak a peek at the screen.

> Milo: You look stunning today. And I thought valedictorians were supposed to give speeches. Why didn't you speak?

I raise my head, spinning in one direction and then the other. There's no way he's here. It couldn't happen. Fletcher wouldn't allow it. Still, my heart holds enough hope to send it into a frenzy at the slightest possibility. Grandma and Faye give me another smile and wave when I look in their direction, but Milo's not seated near them.

Because he's not here, stupid.

"Indiana Ivy Ellington," my name is called, and I wobble on shaky legs across the stage to accept my diploma with a sweaty hand. I smile until I nearly cry because ... I'm FREE.

I'm eighteen.

I have a diploma.

And I can pack my bags and leave the Ellington ranch without looking back.

"Congratulations," the principal says.

Three steps later, a photographer takes my picture,

and I'm ushered back to my seat, where I wait for the rest of the alphabet to be called to the stage.

> Indie: Stop playing with my emotions. I know you're not here.

Milo sends me a picture of *me*. Me sitting in my chair, sending him that message while the row behind me stands to line up at the stage. It's impossible to breathe while I scan the crowd in the direction from which the picture was taken. And then ... I see him.

"You're here," I mouth, wiping a runaway tear from my cheek.

Milo winks and puckers those lips to blow me a kiss.

I don't know how he's here, but it doesn't matter. The most important person in my life just witnessed the most important day of my life thus far.

After a final word and a flurry of hats dancing in the air before tumbling to the ground around us, we march out of the auditorium to the band playing "Pomp and Circumstance."

I shoulder my way through the tangled mess of hugs and congratulatory high fives to the rear exit. Grandma and Faye are meeting me by the front of the school, but I need to find Milo first.

"Hey, smarty pants, where you going?"

I stop. Grin. And close my eyes for a few seconds to compose myself before I start bawling. Then I turn toward him.

Shit.

My strategy doesn't work. The tears are uncontainable.

"How are you here?"

He shrugs. "Strategic planning—oof." He chuckles with a grunt when I throw myself into his arms, hugging him as tightly as I can.

"I love you. I love you. God ... I love you so much."

Love ... it's every possible emotion stuffed into the heart—stretching, wriggling, bubbling until you reach that thin line separating euphoria and complete despair.

I feel both in equal parts. This kind of love can't exist without the promise of pain.

Milo buries his face into my hair next to my ear and whispers, "My. Whole. World."

His whispered words excavate a deep hole in my chest ... maybe my soul. I've never been anyone's whole world. Ruthie loved me dearly, and I always felt it, but she also loved Fletcher beyond words.

My mouth finds his, and I kiss him with everything I have inside me. I don't care who sees us. I don't care what questions I'll have from friends or overly curious parents.

Milo doesn't pull back one single inch. His tongue slides against mine, and he hums with me. His fingers comb through my hair. Eventually, they land on my lower back.

Pressing my hands to his cheeks, I lean back to look at him. "Tell me. How did you manage this?"

He lifts his shirt partway up his torso.

"What happened?" I grimace at the bandaged area just below his ribs.

"Officially, I had a run-in with the barbed wire fence this morning after a bull got loose. Unofficially, I took a knife to myself so that I needed stitches, which meant I wouldn't make it to the law school graduation in time because the drive was too long."

My fingertips trace the bandage. "Jesus, Milo ..." My stomach twists. "You hurt yourself just to be here for me?"

"It's just a few stitches."

My gaze lifts to his, and a new round of tears fill my eyes.

He knows it's not "just a few stitches." That's why he averts his gaze for a moment. Is he ashamed? Or is he just as desperate as I am?

"It's no big deal, Indie girl." He looks at me again before kissing my forehead while letting his shirt fall back in place. "Just another scar. I have a million of them."

Again, I hug him, emotion too thick in my throat to speak. When I do find words, I make them as light as possible. "I can't believe he didn't copter you to the graduation."

"His helicopter is down for the next week."

I can't stop grinning. "Listen, I have to go see Faye and Grandma Hill. Wait for me?"

"I only have a couple of hours, and then I have to get back before Fletcher returns home and finds out I'm not there resting my injury."

"I'm going home too, but I don't want to return just yet. We need to celebrate." I turn and take a few steps.

"Yes, we should celebrate one of us graduating high school."

My head whips backward. "Why didn't you graduate?"

Milo shakes his head, slipping his hands into his front pockets. "Life."

I shrug. "I wasn't talking about that anyway. I meant we need to celebrate you being here, not me graduating." I blow him a kiss and navigate the lumpy grass toward the front of the school.

"Indiana ..." Faye opens her arms, and I run into them. "Congratulations, darlin'."

"Thank you." I release her and hug Grandma Hill. She's getting older with pointy bones like an over-sharpened pencil that I don't want to break. And she always smells like apricots. I don't know why. She just always has.

"Ruthie's watching you, honey. And I know she's so proud," Grandma says.

I nod, fighting the tears. "I know," I whisper.

"I have video of the whole thing if Fletcher wants it," Faye says.

With a tight grin, I give her a look. She knows what I'm thinking.

"He's never recovered from losing her. He'd be a different father to you if she were still alive. Grief has slowly killed him." Faye makes excuses for him. She does it because she loved Ruthie, and it's hard to imagine someone so wonderful could ever be with someone so awful.

"Can we take you to lunch?" Grandma asks.

"Um ... actually, I have plans with a ... friend."

"That's fine, darlin'." Faye reaches forward and squeezes my hand. "You're young. Enjoy this time of your life."

"That's the plan."

For a few more weeks, I'm going to enjoy my life. Then I'm going to hate life with a passion.

After Faye and Grandma Hill hug me, I slip off my heels and run back to Milo. As I approach, his grin grows into something so big I can feel it before I reach him.

"Let's go." I fly into his arms, and he catches me without falling to the ground when I wrap my legs around his waist.

When he flinches, I cringe. "Sorry." My gaze slides to his cut.

He shakes his head like it's no big deal. It's a huge deal.

"Where are we going?"

I kiss his cheek next to his ear and whisper, "Anywhere. Just drive."

~

MILO DRIVES.

I open the window and let the warm wind scatter my hair and my imagination in every direction. In a different life, Milo would marry me. Or not. Does marriage matter? If he's marrying Jolene, I don't think there's an ounce of sanctity left in exchanging vows.

Milo doesn't have to marry me. His love is enough. I'd rather be his Indie girl than an appointed wife.

"Where are we?" I ask when he pulls onto a long gravel road with nothing but acres of pasture on every side.

Milo rolls down his window and types a code for the

black iron gates to open. "It's Fletcher's newest purchase. Over five hundred thousand acres of—"

"No." I shake my head.

Milo squints. "What's wrong?"

"Nothing to do with Fletcher. Take me some place he doesn't own. Take me somewhere he's never been."

After a few seconds, Milo's face relaxes into a soft smile. "I can do that."

I lean my head back and close my eyes. "Thank you."

Thirty minutes later, we pull into the drive-thru of a chicken joint.

I laugh. "What are we doing?"

"This is Fletcher's biggest competitor. I thought we'd give them our business."

Nodding, I bite my lower lip. Who cares that I don't like chicken unless they're laying eggs for me to eat.

We order someone else's chicken, fries, and shakes before driving to a park filled with kids playing soccer and dogs chasing Frisbees. It's nothing spectacular, yet incredibly special. I feel normal here.

Just two people in love, eating greasy food in the front seat of a pickup truck while hiding in the shade of Spanish moss-draped Cyprus trees.

"Did you play soccer?" I ask.

He shakes his head.

"Did you own a dog?"

Again, he shakes his head.

"Are you ever going to tell me about your childhood?"

He takes a bite of his chicken sandwich and gazes at the kids playing while he chews his bite. "I hope not."

"Why do you always say that?"

"If the day comes that I'm sharing something that awful with you, it means I'm in a worse place than I was when my world imploded. As long as I can keep looking forward, it means I'm still alive."

I pause a fry at my mouth and tap it to my lips a few times. Milo twists his neck, shifting his gaze to me.

"When did you know Fletcher bought me?"

"Don't look back, Indie. Didn't you hear me? It's a slow death. Look forward. Chase something better. Don't ever fucking look back."

"If I don't know where I've been, how will I know where I'm going?"

He removes his hat and tosses it onto the dash before running a hand through his hair. "You'll know where you are when you get there not because you know where you've been. You'll know it because it's where you're supposed to be. It will be a feeling of belonging that can't be explained. It's just a feeling you'll know. And all you have to do is keep following that feeling, and you'll be fine."

"How do you know?" I ask. "Have you felt it?"

Milo nods. "I feel it right now." He smiles, but it quickly fades. "Sometimes, happiness is fleeting. But I can now say that when I die, I'll have known that feeling. I'll remember how it felt to be *home,* if only for a few breaths. I'll remember it forever; I'll remember *you* forever."

I can't toss my food into the bag and the bag into the back seat fast enough before crawling over the console and wedging myself between the steering wheel and Milo, careful not to bump his stitches.

He holds out his hands, one with a greasy paper bag and the other with the last few bites of his sandwich. I rip them from his grip and toss them in the back seat with mine.

He stiffens, and I know he's protecting his wound.

Pulling up his shirt, I brush my fingers over the bandage. "If this is love ..." I can't even finish. Why does our love have to be forbidden? Why does it have to involve cutting flesh and lying to everyone?

"I'm fine."

I glance at him. Pressing my hands to his cheeks, I kiss him. It takes him a second to relax his arms and wrap them around me.

"Drive," I murmur against his mouth. "Drive us so far away from here no one will ever find us. Be with me, Milo." I kiss his jaw to his ear. "We don't have to be fleeting. We can be forever. Get lost with me." I sit up straight, returning my hands to his scruffy face. "I don't need much. We can live out of a car for all I care. We'll be broke and happier than we ever imagined. We'll make love every day."

Only now do I realize I'm crying happy, *hopeful* tears. "We'll never fight. And when we save up enough money, we'll buy one of those panini makers and burn the hell out of our grilled cheese sandwiches."

He gives me a sad smile while wiping my cheeks, and if I didn't know him better, I'd say he's fighting back the tears. Not my Milo. He's never cried. I'm sure of it.

I grin big enough for the both of us, but it doesn't keep his from vanishing. A sadness corkscrews into my chest, slowly mangling every bit of hope I've brought to life over the past thirty seconds. Like Fletcher rapes the earth and steals its precious oil, Milo's destroying my innocence and the dreams it's held since the day I knew I loved him.

His knuckles feather along my cheek, pulling me into him. I close my eyes.

"Life isn't fair, Indie girl. But as long as you're alive, it's really fucking beautiful. As long as you're alive, there's a reason to open my eyes, stand up, and breathe in and out."

"You don't owe him anything," I whisper. "He's an awful ... awful man."

Swallowing hard, Milo tips his head into a slow nod. "He's awful. And I owe him everything even if you don't understand." He curls my hair behind my ear and smiles. "Had I not met Fletcher, I wouldn't have met you."

"No." I rest my hand on his, keeping it pressed to my cheek. "Don't say that. I don't want to believe that everything happens for a reason."

With a chuckle, Milo bends forward and kisses my neck. "Cause and effect. Everything does happen for a reason, but not in the cosmic or biblical way you're suggesting. I'm a bigger believer in happenstance. You are the best happenstance."

My fingers comb through his thick hair while he deposits a hot trail of kisses down my neck to my shoulder.

"Can I go to my favorite place?" he whispers.

I grin, closing my eyes. "What took you so long to ask?"

Milo chuckles. "Just trying to be a gentleman." His hands grip my ass, pulling me closer.

We drive just outside of town and find a less-traveled road. Milo digs a horse blanket out of the back seat and spreads it in the bed of his truck. Then he gets lost inside of me. And I focus on this and only this.

The way we fit perfectly together.

His hands molded to my curves.

Our mouths fused into a long kiss filled with soft moans.

Then he pulls back just enough to look into my eyes.

Lips parted.

Sweat beading along his brow.

My eyes fight to stay open when I reach the top and tumble down the other side into that pool of euphoria. Milo quickens his pace and arches his back, letting an explicative fall from his lips attached to my name when he releases inside me.

And I think ... what if I stopped taking my pill? What if I got pregnant with his baby? What would Fletcher do?

Milo collapses onto me, his labored breath a whisper at my ear.

I know what would happen. Milo would still marry Jolene. And I'd be shipped off to abort the baby or worse ... Fletcher would sell the child to some bastard much like himself. Deep in Texas, where a handful of white men own everything and everyone, freedom doesn't exist. I have to wonder if my dreams are nothing more than an illusion. As long as Fletcher owns Milo, he will also own a part of me.

20

JUST STAY DRUNK

MILO

As a pre-fuck-you ... I mean ... *pre-wedding gift*, Fletcher asks Pauline and Jolene to stay at the main house so I can be "in on all final wedding details." Total bullshit. There's no way every detail hasn't already been planned down to the times and locations where I'll be allowed to take a piss on the special day.

Indie.

He wants help keeping an eye on Indie and me. We've been allowed to see each other at breakfast and dinner. That's it. Jolene drags Indie's ass around like a designer purse dangling from her arm. And Fletcher works me to the bone from sunrise to dinnertime and for another two hours after dinner—just long enough for Indie to be locked in her ivory tower for the night.

I've stopped taking her calls again. It's torturous to hear her voice, and we're days from the wedding ... I can't handle it.

Indie: Just use the middle finger emoji if you're not going to take my call.

Milo: There's a middle finger emoji? And all this time I thought the blowing a heart kiss emoji was a kiss my ass emoji. Well I'll be damned.

Indie: Haha. I'm not falling for your humor or any more of your charm. I need to hear your voice.

Milo: Fletcher cut my tongue out.

Indie: It's not funny. He probably would do that, especially if he knew where your tongue has been. (She ends with a pussy cat and tongue emoji.)

I grin, and my dick stirs a bit in my jeans while I make a late-night sandwich, black as sin, of course.

Indie: Where are you honeymooning?

Milo: We're not talking about this

Indie: It's okay. I'm drunk.

Milo: ???

Indie: Whiskey. That expensive shit you and the devil drink. I stole the new bottle before Micah refilled that glass thingy

Milo: Decanter

Indie: Whatever

> Milo: Are you still going to Canada this summer?

> Indie: Where are you living?

> Milo: I hear Canada is beautiful in the summer

> Indie: Don't be a dick. Just answer me

I sigh, taking my burnt grilled cheese to the sofa. Indie's hell-bent on making herself miserable with the finer details.

> Milo: We're living in the main house for a while.

> Indie: Sounds cozy. You can sleep in my room.

I chuckle. Why? I don't know. This fucking hurts. I'll be sleeping in a bed with Jolene, probably less than twenty feet from Indie's bedroom. She needs to get out of that house, out of this state. Far ... far away from the Ellingtons.

> Milo: That's a nice offer. Thanks.

Three dots appear, but no message.
Then nothing.
Again, three dots.
Then nothing.

> Milo: Stop drinking. Go to sleep, Indie girl.

Nothing.

Has she passed out? Is she asleep? Mad? Is she okay?

> Milo: You still there?

Now, I'm going crazy. I pace the room a few times, tossing the rest of my sandwich in the sink. Before I lose what's left of my mind, I call her.

It only rings once before she answers. "Breaking your own stupid rules and calling me?"

"Jesus ... what are you doing?"

"Waiting for you to call me. The wait is over, and I couldn't be happier. Is it really so torturous to hear my voice?"

"Yes."

"Aw, that's sweet. Listen, Jolene dragged me to buy lingerie today. She's wearing all white under her wedding dress. Please tell me you're not having sex with her like ... ever." Indie hiccups. "Oops ... excuse me." She giggles.

Maybe the whiskey is a blessing—anything to keep her laughing in the face of the upcoming event.

"Stop drinking. Go to sleep. Okay?"

"Is that a yes or no? Are you going to have sex with her on your wedding night? I need to plan accordingly. If you're having sex with Jolene, then I'm having sex with my wedding date. So ... it's up to you."

"Indie, it's not a game."

"It's the *worst* game, Milo. And you're the biggest pawn!"

I pull the phone away from my ear while her words slay me. It's her tone more than the actual words. An unfamiliar tone. It's poison or the jagged edge of a knife.

Not drunk words.

Not pleading words.

Not hurt words.

Indie's livid ... at me.

"I'll be too drunk to have sex ... ever again." I want to mean it. Comfortably inebriated seems like my best chance at a happy marriage with Jolene.

"Good boy. Listen ... don't get sloshed and impotent on your wedding day until you fuck me. It's all I want for my birthday this year, Christmas ... and all future gift-giving holidays."

I laugh. "For me to *fuck* you?"

"Technically, it's to fuck Jolene's husband before she does on the day she becomes his wife. Can you imagine? There isn't anything more humiliating than that. It's like eating someone's whole birthday cake while the candles are still lit."

This is a new side to Indie. I've always thought she was like Ruthie, the gentle yet strong type. Clearly, I never want to cross her.

"Indiana ... I think you should be sick on that day. You should do whatever it takes not to be at the wedding."

"Wow. You don't want me there?"

"No. I don't."

She doesn't respond. I won't take it back. It's the truth. I don't want Indie watching me marry Jolene.

"That's rude."

"Indie ..."

Another long pause fills the space between us.

"I know," she whispers. "I don't want to be there either."

21

'TIL DEATH

INDIE

The Wedding

I WANT to crawl out the window and run to the barn, but I don't.

I want to make myself vomit and bow out of my personal attendant duties, but I don't.

The list of things I want is forever long, but I know I'll cave to the pressure and conform. I'll put on the ugly dress and curl my hair.

I'll smile on cue and wait on Jolene, fulfilling her every request.

Staring at my phone, I contemplate sending Milo a message. But what would I say? This is happening.

Do I make him feel any worse than he already feels?

"Rise and shine, Indiana. Today's the day." Pauline's cheery voice drifts down the hallway, eating at my skin like acid.

I toss my phone aside. If Milo thought there was anything left to say, he'd call or text me.

It's been almost a month since graduation, almost a month since we've had sex. Almost a month since we've been alone. It feels like a lifetime.

"There you are." Pauline makes me jump when I open the door to my bathroom, one towel around my head, the other around my naked body.

"Chop. Chop. We have hair and makeup in thirty minutes. Don't keep the bride waiting."

"I can do my hair and makeup." I tighten the towel around my body.

"Afraid not. We have a stylist who will decide what's best for you today."

As long as I live here, I will never make my own decisions. This is it. This is the very last day Pauline and Fletcher will dictate over me. I'm doing this for Milo. His trip to Hell should be as smooth as possible.

"Give me five minutes to get dressed." I practice my best smile. I might as well use them up; it's unlikely I'll smile again after today.

"Perfect. Breakfast will be served in the limo on the way."

"Perfect."

Pauline narrows her eyes. "What's up with you today?"

"What do you mean?"

"You're ... cheery."

"There's a wedding today. It's a joyous occasion. Why wouldn't I be cheery?"

Studying me for a few more seconds, she nods. "Five minutes."

On the way to the stylist, I gaze out the limo window and wonder where I'll be in a year. Five years. Ten years.

Will my heart have mended? I can't imagine ever loving someone the way I love Milo, but maybe there's someone who can make me smile again. Maybe Milo will grow to love Jolene if they have a family together. And one day we can see each other, and things won't hurt so much.

Maybe.

"Indie, I think you'd look cute with bangs," Jolene says while a short black-haired lady curls Jolene's long brown hair.

"Respectfully, I disagree." I smile while caped in black, and my stylist combs my damp hair.

"What do you think?" Jolene asks my stylist.

"You have the face for bangs." The stylist shrugs.

Jolene has the face for punching, but I'm not going to plant my fist into her nose. Well ... hopefully not.

"I don't need a haircut. Just style it."

"What do you think of a tight bun with bangs?" Jolene eyes my stylist like I'm not here.

"It would be quite sophisticated."

"Then let's do that," Jolene replies, directing her attention to her phone.

"I don't want—"

"Who's the bride?" Pauline's whiplike tone silences everyone.

The bridesmaids scowl at me like I'm some inconsiderate bitch for not wanting my fucking hair cut.

I hate her.

Milo will never love her, no matter how many children they make together. He will love his children, and he might respect her in front of them, but he will never love her.

I shift my attention to the stylist's reflection in the mirror while the whole room waits for my response.

I can't remember the last time I pulled my hair back in a ponytail. And I don't ever remember having bangs. I like my long hair. I liked the way Ruthie used to brush it.

Don't ever cut your beautiful hair, Indiana. It's angelic.

When Ruthie died, I think all of her dreams for me died too.

"It's your call," the stylist says.

"Whatever the bride wants," I murmur, closing my eyes and letting the hum of dryers lull me into an alternate universe where Jolene doesn't exist.

I don't look at my reflection, not even when it's done. And I don't complain when they pluck the fuck out of my eyebrows only to fill them in with a pencil.

Not a word when they cake on foundation and powder.

Fake eyelashes.

Thick lipstick.

And then it happens ... on the way out of the salon, I catch a glimpse of myself. And I don't recognize the reflection. I look old. And ugly. Not myself at all. Jolene doesn't look this way, and neither do the bridesmaids. They look young. I'm the only one with my hair up. I'm the only one with bangs. I'm the only one with green eye shadow. Their makeup is far more natural looking.

"Coming, Indie?" Jolene says when everyone else is out the door.

Dragging my gaze away from the mirror, I tip my chin up. "Yes."

"Green is your color. What do they say? Green with envy?" She winks before letting the door close in my face.

This is a game. A game of revenge. She doesn't need my help today for anything but getting back at me for ... Milo? Something else? I don't even know.

Over the next few hours, I fetch coffee, champagne, and a vaping stick for one of the bridesmaids, and I wipe Jolene's ass when she takes a nervous, runny shit. Her fake nails are too long to do it herself.

"Are you going to ask Milo to wipe your ass on your honeymoon?" I wrinkle my nose and retch while flicking the toilet paper in the toilet.

She stands, waiting for me to pull up her satin under-wear. "I'll have different nails for the honeymoon. Uh ... wash your hands before you touch my underwear."

Drawing in a long, slow breath, I stand straight and plaster on the smile. "Of course. Your squirts were pretty nasty. You'd hate to smell like shit when you walk down the aisle," I mumble on my way to the sink.

"What did you just say to me?"

"Nothing." I keep my head down while scrubbing my hands.

She waddles toward me.

I turn and pull up her underwear.

"I know you have a crush on my husband. It's a little pathetic that you can't find someone your age."

"He's not your husband."

"He will be in less than an hour." She stares at her reflection in the mirror and dabs her glossy lips together. "So feel free to fantasize about *my* husband, but keep your distance. You make him look bad." Her gaze slides a fraction to me.

Don't say it. Don't do it. Take the high road ...

Sometimes you have to be eighteen and reckless.

"I've fucked your *husband* ... more than once. I know what he feels like inside me. And he knows what I taste like. And you can't wish that away, no matter how much of a total entitled princess bitch you try to be today. So remember ... I had him first. And since we'll be one big family ... don't fucking turn your back or blink because there will never come a day that his dick doesn't get hard when I walk into a room." I bare my teeth and tap on one of them. "And uh ... you have lipstick on your teeth. You're welcome."

Jolene doesn't blink. I'm not sure she's breathing. Not even the artificial color in her cheeks can hide the blood draining from her face. In the next breath, I exit the lounge.

"Oh, there you are. Is Jolene in there?" her maid of honor asks.

I smile. "She is, but I'd give her a bit. She has a bad case of wedding jitters in the form of lethal diarrhea."

Her nose wrinkles. "Oh. Okay."

Brushing past her, I grin, and this time it's genuine. I found my voice with Jolene for the first time. Was it bad timing? Maybe. But it won't change anything, and I know it. This wedding is a merger, not a love story. She will still marry him. He will be in her bed tonight and every night. I may never eat a burnt grilled cheese with him again. We may never race in the pond, ride Ranger at sunset, or pick figs together.

She's pissed off, but for the wrong reasons. But one day, she'll really see Milo and love him because it's impossible not to love Milo Odell. When that day comes, she will think of me and live the rest of her life never knowing if he loves her back—always wondering if he loves me more. And that will plague her for eternity.

"There you are." Pauline rushes to Jolene while the rest of the women do last-minute primping. "Are you okay?"

Jolene is a statue. An impeccable actress. She'll make a fantastic, cut-throat attorney. "Let's do this." She slides her gaze to me. "I'm done with you, Indiana. You can leave now. I'll take it from here. I'll take *everything* from here."

Handing her the bouquet, I look her up and down just to fuck with her one last time before she marries my Milo. "Break a leg." I wink the same way she winked at me.

That's for the dress.

The green makeup.

The ass-wiping.

The bangs.

Every degrading comment.

Every condescending look.

Every reminder that I'm not real family.

And Milo. That's for taking the only thing in life that matters to me.

Literally ... break a fucking leg, bitch.

I turn the corner toward the grand sanctuary constructed with two-story arched ceilings and entire walls of stained glass. "Oof! Shit ... shoot." I cover my mouth, eyes wide at Milo.

He fixes his white tie, wearing the hell out of that black, three-piece suit. I don't see my Milo. No jeans. No chaps. No hat. And he smells like weird cologne instead of leather, coffee, and cinnamon. A slow smile works its way up his face.

"Sorry. I ... uh ... should've watched where I was going."

He doesn't say a damn word. He just ... smiles at me with a mischievous twinkle in his eye. Maybe he's high. If I were him, I'd have to be high to marry Jolene, to promise to love, honor, and cherish her.

I open my mouth to say more stupid words, but Fletcher, Ty, and two guys I've never seen before walk up behind him.

One of the unfamiliar guys rests his hand on Milo's shoulder. "It's time, man."

Milo ignores him for several more seconds while taking his sweet time to inspect me. My gaudy green dress, old lady shoes, clownish makeup, and ... my bangs. It's not until he really zeros in on my hair that his smile falters.

I pull back my shoulders and smile. "Jolene wanted me to have bangs for your wedding."

Milo's brow tightens a fraction, and I know he has

something to say, but it's too late. We have an audience, and he has to get to the front of the sanctuary before his bride makes her grand entrance.

I stare at his mouth. The next person to kiss his lips will be Jolene. And it breaks. My. Fucking. Heart.

"There you are." Judah, my pre-law date, saunters toward me. "I was going to go ahead and be seated, but since you're here, we can be seated together."

"Let's go, son," Fletcher says to Milo.

Milo gives Judah an unreadable look before returning his attention to me. No smile. No life. The mischievous sparkle in his eyes has been extinguished. Fletcher, Ty, and the two other men lead the way, and Milo follows, his hand lightly brushing mine.

That tiny brush of his flesh against mine sends an unbearable pain straight to my heart, and I gasp a silent, shaky breath.

Judah holds out his arm to me. "You okay?"

Swallowing, I nod and take his arm.

"Love your hair. It makes you look older," he says while we wait to be ushered to our seats.

Older.

I don't want to look older. I want to look like Milo's Indie girl.

We're seated in the second row. Minutes later, Pauline is seated in front of us. And all too soon ... Milo and his groomsmen enter through a door close to the altar. They stand with their backs to the guests while the bridesmaids make their way down the aisle.

Then the guests stand, and a string quartet plays the processional. Fletcher walks Jolene down the aisle. He kisses her cheek over her veiled face and hands her off to Milo, who turns to see her for the first time today.

He smiles. It's a pained smile, which should comfort me, but it doesn't. Milo's happiness is my happiness. His misery is my misery. Does he feel the same? Can he feel my heart coming apart one chamber at a time? Does he find it as hard to breathe as I do?

We're seated, and I don't feel anything. I don't hear anything. Everything's numb. I imagine it's what death feels like when there's not enough life left inside to *feel* anymore.

The minister speaks.

Someone sings.

Candles are lit.

Another song.

A prayer.

Vows.

Exchanging rings.

"You may kiss your bride."

I bow my head. I can't watch it.

Not when they kiss. Not when the string quartet plays the recessional, and they walk down the aisle as man and wife.

"Here," Judah whispers.

I glance at his hand nudging mine. He's holding a tissue. My gaze lifts to his.

He nods toward me. "Thought you'd want to wipe your tears before your makeup gets smeared."

My fingers touch my wet cheek. Swallowing the lump in my throat, I say, "Thank you."

Everyone waits outside the church with baskets of

rose petals for the newlyweds to emerge. Butterflies await in cages to be released. And an old white Rolls-Royce convertible in mint condition awaits the mister and misses. Nobody has beckoned me to do personal attendant duties, so I embrace my demotion to an ordinary wedding guest. Maybe this means I can leave early.

The crowd erupts into cheers, and as much as I don't want to look up, I do it on instinct. Jolene and Milo descend the stairs in a flurry of rose petals and butterflies.

She's a beautiful bride, almost ethereal in all white, and he's the most handsome groom anyone could imagine.

And I'm the million-dollar orphan.

I turn. "I ... I" My head shakes. "I can't. I have t-to ... go." Every heart has a limit, and he is mine.

"Where are you going?" Judah asks. "Are you okay?"

Okay? I will never be okay.

Pushing and shoving, I worm my way through the crowd. I can't breathe. I just ... can't ... breathe.

"Where are you going, darlin'." Fletcher's hand grabs my arm, and he squeezes until it hurts.

"Please just let me go."

He pulls me to stand beside him, right next to the Rolls-Royce. Front and center to watch Jolene and Milo climb into the back.

After Jolene and her long train are tucked into the far seat, Milo starts to step in after her, glancing up at the last second and locking gazes with me.

If I blink, my world will fall apart into big fat tears at his feet.

You have me.

For how long?

For as long as you need.

Forever?

Today is the end of forever.

Milo breaks first, dropping his gaze before climbing the rest of the way into the back of the car.

"Where's your date, Indiana?"

I jerk my arm out of Fletcher's grip and turn toward him. "I fucking *hate* you." My chin tips up.

His jaw clenches. On any other day, his hand would meet my face. But not today, not in front of friends and family. I want to say a million other things to him, but those four words work for now.

Before he can make a threat or utter one word, I retrace my steps back to Judah while the Rolls-Royce pulls away from the curb.

"Take me home," I say to Judah.

"Wait. What about the reception?"

"I'm not going to the reception." I head toward the parking lot, having no clue where he parked since I rode to the church in the limo.

"Indiana, shouldn't we go for a little—"

"Take me home," I erupt, an explosion of emotion, and instantly cover my mouth with a cupped hand while the tears burst from my eyes. I'm no longer numb.

I feel everything.

And it's too much.

"Indie ..." Judah says softly when I turn toward him.

"T-take me h-home ... p-please."

He hugs me. "Okay," he whispers. "I'll take you home."

22

PENANCE

MILO

YEARS AGO, I learned to shut off my emotions, put on a brave face, and do what needs to be done. I've been stripped of such luxuries as free speech and free will in exchange for someone else's version of freedom.

I've done some awful things. I've hurt many people. I've killed people.

Now, I'm doing my time; it's just not in a prison cell.

There's a reception with no Indie.

A night in the presidential suite of Dallas's fanciest hotel.

And now, we have two days at the house before we leave for our honeymoon in Switzerland.

Two days in the same house as Indie.

"I won't make you carry me over the threshold until we come home from our honeymoon." Jolene shoots me a grin before opening the door to Fletcher's house.

I carry our bags inside while she calls for Pauline.

"Mr. and Mrs. Odell, welcome home," Micah says before we make it to the stairs.

"Where is everyone?" Jolene asks.

Micah shoots his gaze to me and then back to Jolene. "Sorry, I assumed you knew, but I'm sure they didn't want to disturb you."

"Know what?" she asks.

"Indiana is in the hospital."

My chest nearly folds in on itself, crushing everything inside me. "What happened?"

"I'm not sure. I haven't been given an update. When Mr. Ellington and your mom arrived home after the wedding reception, they found Indiana in her room, unresponsive. I called for an ambulance right away. That's all I know."

"What ..." I clear my throat, but it's fucking hard to speak when I can't catch my breath. "What do you mean unresponsive? Was she ..." Again, I have to clear my throat. "Breathing?"

Micah shakes his head. "Sorry. I really don't know."

"Well..." I run a hand through my hair "...we need to get to the hospital."

"Milo, we just got here." Jolene frowns. "Let's not panic until I talk with Mom."

Is she serious?

We don't know if Indie is dead or alive, and she wants us not to fucking panic? "Jolene—"

She pulls her phone from her handbag. "I'll call her now."

I fight to keep my shit together, but I can't help but pace in a circle while she's on the phone.

"Hey, Mom. We just got home. Micah said Indie's in the hospital. What's going on?" Jolene nods and rolls her eyes. "Figures. Okay, then we'll just see you when you get here. Bye." She drops her phone back into her bag. "That girl is messed-up."

"Jesus, Jolene, what happened?" My clipped tone earns me another scowl from her.

"She had too much to drink. She'll be fine. They'll be on their way home soon."

"Can I get you something to eat?" Micah asks.

"We're good. We had a fantastic brunch delivered to our suite this morning." Jolene stares at her phone screen, texting someone. "Milo, dear, would you take our bags to my bedroom?" She glances up at me and smiles. "*Our* bedroom."

I nod without making eye contact. If I look at her, she'll see it on my face, every ounce of concern for Indie. Before I make it to *our* bedroom, I stop at the door to Indie's room, letting the bags drop from my hands and taking cautious steps toward the empty whiskey bottles on the floor. The broken mirror and Fletcher's shattered decanter next to it. And vomit on the bed.

This fucking hurts.

Fletcher took away my ability to protect her. And look what happened.

"Sorry, I'm late. I'll get this cleaned up right away. I went home for the weekend with my family." Linda, the housekeeper, shuffles into the bedroom with a bucket of cleaning supplies and a big trash bag. "I do hope Miss Indiana is okay."

She dons her gloves and bends down to pick up the largest piece of the decanter.

"Don't," I murmur.

She glances back at me.

"Sorry, did you say something?"

"Just ... leave everything. I'll clean it up."

Her eyes narrow. "Mr. Odell. It's fine. I'm here now. Your lovely bride is downstairs. You should be with her. Congratulations on your wedding."

I can barely speak. "Leave. Leave everything."

She slowly sets the decanter piece next to the trash bag and just as slowly exits the bedroom, closing the door behind her.

It takes me several minutes of nothing more than surveying the room over and over again, trying to imagine what happened before I pick up the glass and other empty bottles, before I clean up the vomit and I strip the sheets from her bed.

"What the hell are you doing?" Jolene opens the bedroom door just as I tie the trash bag and deposit the dirty bedding next to it.

"Cleaning things up before they get home," I say in a monotone voice.

"Linda's here. That's her job." Jolene crosses her arms.

Eyeing her, I nod. "I'll put our bags in the bedroom." I brush past her, and she grabs my wrist, fingernails digging into it.

"This ends now. Do you understand me? Whatever sick relationship you had with her ... it ends now."

I glance back at her. "Sick relationship?"

Pulling in a long breath, her expression hardens. "I know you were grooming her."

"Grooming?"

"Befriending her. Gaining her trust so you could manipulate her into doing ... inappropriate things."

What. The. Fuck?

"She told me, Milo. On our *wedding day*. Why do you think she wasn't at the reception last night? Why do you think she tried to drink herself to death? She told me everything. And I assured her she would never have to be alone with you again. And Fletcher doesn't know. He would end you, Milo, and you know it. So here's how this will go ... when she gets here, you leave. Go to the barn, stay in our bedroom, and do whatever you have to do to stay out of her sight. We'll get you help; no one else has to know."

My gaze slides to her grip on my wrist, and I jerk my arm out of her grasp, grab the bags, and carry them to the other bedroom.

23

FREE

INDIE

"WERE YOU TRYING TO HARM YOURSELF?" the psychiatrist asks.

I stare at her. "No."

"Have you had thoughts about harming yourself before?"

"Before?" I narrow my eyes.

"Before last night."

"You're implying I was trying to hurt myself last night when I *just* told you I wasn't."

"Tell me about yesterday and the events that led you to turn to alcohol."

"For someone with what I assume is a degree that took many years to acquire, you are a terrible listener and incredibly shortsighted. Are we done here?" I slide off the edge of the hospital bed and shove my feet into the sneakers that aren't mine but seem to be here for me.

They're brand new. Fletcher must have sent someone to get them for me.

"Indiana, I recommend you see me once a week. We can meet at my office from now on."

"See you for what?" I crane my neck, looking for Fletcher, Pauline, or better yet, Faye or Grandma Hill.

"The depression will hit again, Indiana. And your outcome might not be so lucky. I should admit you, but I know your family, and I'm comfortable discharging you into their care with the condition that you come to see me every week."

When I don't see anyone I know, I return to the gray-haired woman sitting in the chair with her legs crossed and a notepad on her lap. "It was a wedding. I celebrated by drinking too much. Today, I have a killer headache and feel like shit, which is the definition of a hangover. Did I drink too much?" I shrug. "Probably. Doesn't mean I was trying to end my life. It just means I lost track of how much I'd had to drink. Lesson learned. No need to follow up."

"But you weren't at the wedding reception. You were by yourself at home. Excessively drinking alone. And you're eighteen. I'm also going to recommend you attend AA meetings."

"Super. Maybe Fletcher can attend them with me. He drinks himself into a stupor most nights. He drinks until he has no control over backhanding me for asking simple questions."

She frowns.

"Sorry. Does knowing that make you uncomfortable? You know … since you're a 'family friend.' Or does

Fletcher pay you to harass me and ignore his years of indiscretions?"

The good doctor continues to study me, tongue idle, hands fiddling with the pen and pad of paper.

I laugh. "It sucks, doesn't it? Being owned by such a rich man. You can't be yourself. You can't make your own decisions. Like right now, you're conflicted. On the one hand, you know you should report what I've told you. I'm eighteen, but was he abusing me before I turned eighteen? Can you safely recommend releasing me into his care? Could you lose your license if anything happened to me, and you knew the risk? We know the answer is no because that would require a board to hear your case and decide to revoke your license, but Fletcher would pay off the board before he'd lose one of his pawns."

"Are you ready to go home?"

I turn toward the devil himself.

"Where's Faye or Grandma Hill?"

He nods toward the psychiatrist, and she leaves the room.

Wow. Should one man hold so much power?

Will this be Milo someday after Pauline and Fletcher die?

"Let's go." He turns his cold shoulder and expects me to follow.

I do, this time. But when I get home, I'm leaving and never coming back.

When we reach his truck, Pauline eyes me from the front seat. It's pretty Cruella de Vil of her. "Are you going to live?" she asks when I climb in the back.

"Sadly for you, yes."

"Indiana, that's not fair. No one in the family has ever wished anything bad upon you. But your timing yesterday wasn't the best. I'm glad you chose to act out at home alone instead of at Jolene's wedding, but still ... it's not what we wanted to come home to last night."

Fletcher pulls onto the main road, and I stare out the window, trying to keep from laughing. It's not funny. It's sad. She's happy I chose to drink, pass out, and get alcohol poisoning alone. I could have died alone. No wonder Jolene is such a piece of work.

When we pull into the driveway, Pauline twists her head to glance back at me. "I'll have Micah bring you something to eat in your room."

"I'm not hungry."

"You need to eat and continue to hydrate, so he'll bring you something, and I'll check on you later."

"I can eat in the kitchen."

"I think it's best if you stay in your room. Jolene and Milo are having a small gathering to open their wedding gifts tonight."

"And this is all happening in the kitchen?"

"Indiana ..." Fletcher glances at me in the rearview mirror. "Go inside. Go to your room. I don't want to hear another word out of you today."

I climb out of the truck and make my way to the front door, ripping off the taped gauze from my arm where they placed my IV. Opening the front door, I'm met with a moment of déjà vu, only this time I'm at the door and Milo's standing at the top of the stairs.

He doesn't hesitate before descending them.

"Oh, Indiana, you're home." Jolene appears just

behind him. "We were just heading out to—" Her words die harder than shooting a horse between the eyes.

Milo hugs me.

I don't move. I'm not sure this is happening. It might be a dream.

"Indie ..." he whispers.

"Indiana, you need to rest. Go," Fletcher says behind me as he and Pauline walk in to see what's happening.

I'd go to my room, but Milo's holding me too tightly. I couldn't break free if I wanted to. And I don't want to.

A thick silence settles in the foyer. Our onlookers are at a loss for words.

In Milo's time, not anyone else's, he releases me. Concern lines his face, but he remains quiet.

Jolene steps between us. "So glad you're okay, Indie." She hugs me, but it's not the same. "I certainly hope you get the help you need."

I push away from her. "For what?"

Jolene eyes Pauline and Fletcher before returning her attention to me. "Indie, you tried to take your own life. You need help."

"I had too much to drink. I didn't—"

"Too much to drink involves a little vomiting and a headache. You had alcohol poisoning. You tried to drink yourself to death," Jolene frowns; it's condescending.

I look past her to Milo, but I can't read his expression. Does he think I tried to kill myself? Is that why he hugged me the way he did despite our audience?

"Let's go, Milo." Jolene sidesteps me and takes his hand, pulling him toward the doorway.

"Everyone will be here in two hours; don't be late,

you two," Pauline says with a much cheerier tone than she uses with me.

"We won't. We just need a little alone time. We'll be in the barn."

I head toward the stairs. I'm done listening to Jolene. She doesn't want alone time with Milo; she wants revenge. And I did this. Maybe she never had any intention of having sex with him, but after the things I said to her yesterday, I'm sure she will do whatever it takes to claim what she thinks is hers.

MICAH BRINGS ME FOOD. I don't eat it. And nobody checks on me.

Hours later, I hear laughter from the main level, so I sneak down the stairs and listen.

"It's perfect," Jolene gushes. "Not that I plan on cooking. We'll hire that out, but it's a lovely Dutch oven."

"Maybe Milo knows how to cook," someone else says. I don't recognize the voice.

"I've never asked. Do you cook, Milo?" Jolene asks.

She doesn't know if her husband can cook. She knows *nothing* about him.

"Depends what you call cooking," he says, and it draws a round of laughter.

I can't see his face, but he doesn't sound miserable or excited. Milo is adaptable. He's a survivor.

Leaning against the railing, I sit sideways and pull my knees to my chest, listening to people I don't know and people I wish I'd never met. Milo doesn't say much ... until now.

"I'm going to grab a water from the kitchen. Can I get anyone else anything?" he asks.

"Milo, honey ... we have people to do that," Jolene says.

"I need to stretch my legs."

"I'll take more champagne," Pauline says. "Thanks, Milo."

Down the wide hallway, Milo crosses from the living room toward the kitchen. At the last second, his head turns in my direction.

My heart wakes up, beating harder, as it always does when he looks at me.

Milo glances over his shoulder toward the roomful of guests and then back to me. He jerks his head once before continuing to the kitchen.

I tiptoe toward the back entrance to the kitchen, a small hallway with a half bath on one side and Ruthie's sewing room on the opposite side. Milo converses with some of the staff. Then ... he turns the corner, and it's just us.

My out-of-control heart makes it hard to hear past its thundering beat. Milo eyes the bathroom; then his gaze slides to the sewing room. Again he jerks his head. I step inside, and he follows me, quietly closing the door behind us.

"What the fuck, Indie ..." he whispers while his eyes redden and his fingers dive into my hair, holding me captive. "What did you do? You don't get to leave this fucking world while I'm still in it. Do you understand?"

Tears burn my eyes. "I-I didn't. I was just so angry and hurt and …" I try to shake my head despite his hold on me. "I didn't try to kill myself."

Milo swallows hard, slowly shaking his head. He doesn't believe me.

"It was…" I fight to get the words past the lump in my throat "…too much. The dress. The makeup. She had them cut m-my hair." I swallow my tears. "And you said 'I-I d-do.'" I sniffle while my lower lip quivers. "And you k-kissed her. And it was too much."

"No, Indie girl …" His thumb brushes along my bottom lip. "It's not too much. You are the strongest person I know. The brightest person." He smiles. "The *best* person. We find a way."

"A way to what?"

His posture slumps. "I don't know yet, just … a way."

I'm not strong. He's the strong one. I don't know how to hold on to hope when everything feels impossible.

"I can't stay."

His brows slide together. "I know." He kisses me.

My fingers curl into fists, clenching his shirt. I don't ever want to let go.

"I have…" he pulls away, breathless "…to get back."

I rub my lips together, staring at his while nodding. Then I crash my mouth to his again. My hands tug at his belt. It's so quick, I don't even try to think, and neither does Milo while his hands shove my sweatpants and underwear past my butt. His foot lifts to the crotch and rips them down my legs. I step out of them while releasing him from his briefs.

It's too quick.

I can't think.

I can't speak.

I can only feel.

And what I feel is *need* as strong as the demand for my next breath. Milo lifts me, pressing my back to the wall next to the sewing table. My legs encircle his waist, and he drives into me.

The world has fucked us over and over. It's time to fuck the world and everyone who won't let us be together.

I tug his hair while one of his hands skates up my shirt. He rocks into me over and over. It's not enough. Not close enough. Not fast enough. Not deep enough. This moment will never be long enough. The need eats me alive. I want him ... all of him. Always.

"I love you," I whisper in his ear after I orgasm.

Milo pistons into me several more times, and I know it's the last time we will be together like this. The unfairness of life has never felt as unbearable as it does now.

I love him.

He loves me.

Why isn't that enough?

"Fuuuck ... I love ... you ... Indie girl." He lifts his head and stares at me while our hot breaths mingle.

He doesn't move.

I didn't have sex with Jolene's husband. I had sex with *my* Milo. There will never be a day that it's wrong for him to be inside me. He's mine as much as that beating organ behind my chest is mine ... an integral part of who I am. The reason I'm alive.

"Milo?" Jolene calls.

"He might have gone upstairs, ma'am," one of the catering crew says.

Silently, Milo eases me to my feet. It's an instant, excruciatingly painful loss. He pulls up his jeans while I step back into my sweatpants.

Milo reaches for the waist of my pants and pulls them the rest of the way up my legs, taking his time to tie the drawstring. Even now, when we are out of time, he steals extra seconds to dress me. Care for me. Love me.

There is no pretending that everything is okay or ever will be okay. I don't even try to keep the tears from running down my face. I don't try to steady my hands while they rest on his forearms. The most I can do is bite my lips together to silence the sobs.

This is a death. My heart feels just as devastated and lost as it did the day Ruthie died. I love Milo with my *whole* heart. What's its purpose if he's not with me? When all it wants to do is love him?

After he runs his hands through his hair, he frames my face again and ducks his head, lips at my ear. "Be free. I know this hurts, baby. It hurts *so* much. Be everything you were meant to be." His lips drag along my cheek to my mouth.

He blots my tears, and my hands rest over his while I shake and choke on a sob before whispering, "Yours. I'm meant to b-be y-yours."

Milo's face scrunches, jaw clenched, and he nods several times. With one last kiss, he turns and cracks open the door. When it's clear, he steps out and shuts it.

PART TWO

24

THE SPERM DONOR

Four years later ...

MILO

THE LAST TIME I saw Indiana Ellington was in Ruthie's sewing room. I told Jolene I was using the restroom. Then, one of the servers said they saw me come out of the sewing room, and a few minutes later, they saw Indie leave the same room.

Jolene had a breakdown as soon as the guests left, believable only to Fletcher and Pauline, the only two people who mattered. Fletcher had Ty take me to the back of the barn. One day, he was standing at the altar with me as a witness to my marriage; the next day, he held a gun to my head all the way to the barn and pistol-whipped me until I passed out. When I awoke, my hands were tied behind my back, and Fletcher kicked the living shit out of me with his steel-toed boots. I coughed up blood for the first half of my honeymoon, and Jolene shook her head, silently scolding.

Indie?

No one's seen or heard from her since the server snitched on us.

She hasn't touched her bank account, and her phone was left on her bed next to a note that read: *Nobody owns me.* And she signed it, *Million Dollar Indigo.*

That day, I felt like Archer, taking it all, bearing the most significant burden, and choosing someone else's life over my own. Three months later, my brother died by lethal injection. Fletcher forced me to go with him to watch.

"You fucking own your fate, your place in life, and bear witness to the sacrifices made so that you could live." He put Archer right up there with Jesus.

That day hardened me in ways I never imagined possible.

"Two more weeks. Are you ready?" Jolene asks when I walk into the bedroom a little after nine at night.

She eyes my holstered gun and frowns. "I don't want that in the house."

"Then you don't want me in the house because it goes where I go."

"Maybe if you didn't make so many enemies, you wouldn't have to look over your shoulder all the time."

I shake my head and grunt while making my way to the bathroom.

"Fletcher doesn't carry a gun," she chirps.

"You're correct." I unbutton my shirt. "The three-hundred-pound man always at his side is the one packing." I roll my eyes. Some days I can't deal with her. *Most* days.

"Did you hear me say two more weeks? You're going to be a dad."

"Sperm donor," I mumble to myself. "I'm a sperm donor."

Barely two minutes into my steam-filled shower, Jolene steps into my space, wearing a grin. "I won my case today. A forty-two-million-dollar payout. I think that calls for a celebration."

"Not tonight." I squirt shampoo into my hair, massaging my aching head with crimped fingers that ache just as much. If I ignore her ... will she disappear?

"You need a trim, baby." She presses her front to my backside and slides her hand through the back of my hair. That same hand glides along my shoulder to my abdomen and down to my dick.

I grab her wrist, drawing in a deep breath to control the repulsion I feel when she touches me. If I'm not highly intoxicated, I can't stomach it. Right now, I'm sober. "Not. Tonight."

She rips her arm away from me with a huff and stomps out of the shower. "I hope you're a better father than a husband because you're an asshole husband."

After a long shower, I drag my tired ass to bed.

Jolene is perched at the foot, wrapped in a black satin robe, hair pulled into a bun. The room reeks of her godawful perfume. "If you're fucking someone on the side, it ends now. We will be a family when we bring our child into this house. You will step up and be a real husband and father. Do you understand me?"

"Sure." I collapse into the bed and shut off my light.

Even in the dimly lit room, I sense her glowering at me. "If I were pregnant, would you treat me better?"

"Sure."

"Nice, Milo. Do you not have anything else to say other than *sure*?"

Praying for an easy way out of this conversation, I throw an arm over my head. "What are you looking for? Praise for hiring the surrogate? Excitement over a child who doesn't feel real to me yet? I jacked off to a five-minute porn video. Someone took the cup of donated sperm. And a woman I've met once is carrying a baby that's genetically half mine. Sorry if I'm not appropriately excited. This child feels like the next expected step in our business arrangement."

"This baby is part of you and part of me. We can't undo what's been done. Don't you want what's best for him?"

I sigh. God, I'm so exhausted. "What's best for him? Are you going to quit your job, stay home, and raise him? Playdates? PTO? Trips to the zoo? Are you going to sew Halloween costumes?"

"Jesus Christ, could you be more misogynistic? Why do *I* have to stay home? If you're such a family man, why don't you quit your job and go to playdates, trips to the zoo, and join the PTO?"

"Done. I'll tell Fletcher tomorrow. If he asks questions, I'll refer him to you. And you can explain that I'm doing what's best for our son without being a misogynist."

"Stop being so ridiculous. We have a full-time nanny. Neither one of us has to quit our job."

"So we have a full-time nanny. A house the size of a hotel. And more money than God. You're worried about what exactly?"

She stands, cinching the sash to her robe. "I need to know you're going to love him."

"Define love, and I'll let you know if I'm going to love him."

She stops at the door to the bedroom and turns around.

I lift onto my elbows. "When you think of love, what comes to mind?"

Jolene shrugs. "My mom loves me."

"How do you know?"

With a huff, she frowns. "She's my mom. That's how I know."

"And you argue cases with that logic?"

"Fine, Milo. How do you know if someone loves you? And it can't be that person saying it because people lie."

Really? She's telling *me* this?

"A look. A touch. Sometimes it's just a feeling."

"Should I feel this from you? Because I don't. It's been four years, and I don't feel your love. We made a baby, and I don't feel your love."

"I donated sperm, and you donated an egg. Saying we *made* a baby feels like a stretch."

"Many women use surrogates or adopt. It doesn't make them any less of a mother."

I chuckle. "Women who can't carry a baby. You have no clue if you can carry a child."

"Sorry. Did you want to make love to me and create a baby the old-fashioned way? Looking deep into my eyes and thinking just how much you cherish me? It would be a nice change to you fucking me from behind like an animal."

I recline to my back and stare at the ceiling. "Sorry, did we fall in love when I wasn't looking?"

Jolene deflates with a long sigh. "She's gone, Milo. I am your life now. Our child will be your life."

"It's a business arrangement."

"A child is not a business arrangement," she snaps.

"Tell that to the nanny you hired."

"Jesus ... you are a bitter man. If she were here, she'd no longer want you."

I clench my jaw, biting back all I want to say ... words I've wanted to say since the day Fletcher kicked the shit out of me for loving the wrong Ellington.

"Milo ..." Her voice softens. "I'm the only family you have. But in two weeks, you're going to have a son. You can hate Fletcher and Pauline. You can hate me. But you can't hate him. He's an innocent life. I know you're better than this."

Click.

The door shuts behind her.

25

IT'S BEEN AWHILE

H*E CRIES ALL THE TIME.*

Probably because he heard his name: Benjamin Iverson Ellington-Odell.

I had to fight to have it be Ellington-Odell instead of Odell-Ellington. Iverson is Jolene's birth surname, Greg's last name, but Pauline wanted her to be an Ellington. I suggested we name him Archer, but Jolene refused to name our son after a man who died by lethal injection. Benjamin is Fletcher and Pauline's dad's name.

Ben has my blue eyes, and I think it irks Jolene, or maybe she's pissy because she hears him crying. Leah, the live-in nanny, doesn't have the magic touch at two in the morning. Jolene added a sound machine to our bedroom and threatened to ask the contractor to add insulation to soundproof it. Instead, she's sleeping on the other side of the house, closer to Fletcher's bedroom.

I don't mind his cries. He has good lungs. He'll be a strong man one day.

"Sorry, Mr. Odell," Leah whispers while dancing

around the nursery with him a little before four in the morning. "I've never dealt with one this colicky."

I don't know why she's whispering; he sure isn't.

"Let me."

She squints. "Uh ... let you what?"

"Take him." I reach for him.

"You're going to ... walk with him?"

"Yes." I take him from her arms and press him to my bare chest.

Leah yawns.

"Close the door on your way out," I say.

"You ... uh ... want me to go to bed?"

Sitting in the rocking chair by the window, I kiss his tiny head. "Yep."

"Are you sure?"

"Leah ..."

"I'm going. I'm going. Wake me if you need anything. I mean anything."

"Go."

I feel her gaze on me for several seconds before she shuts the door.

Benjamin stops crying when I rock him while rubbing his back. He smells like baby lotion. It might be the best smell in the world. Or it might be that I smell manure all day. When I close my eyes, I imagine Benjamin is ours—mine and Indie's. She's been up all night rocking and nursing him, and I decide to give her a break. She's in our bed because we sleep in the same room, in the same bed, and even though parenthood is exhausting, we still make love every day. We can't keep our hands off each other.

And every day, I stop by home around noon to check in on them. Benjamin's in his carrier next to Indie. She's in the garden, wearing a short floral dress and cowboy boots, a dirt smudge on her face. Long hair waving in the breeze. When she sees me, she grins, and I feel it in my bones.

It's the best fucking life.

Only ... it's not real.

I crack open my eyes when the sun rises and slowly stand, laying Benjamin in his crib.

"What are you doing in here?"

Benjamin jumps and lets out a shrill cry.

I turn toward Jolene in her workout attire, covered in sweat. She's had a full eight hours of sleep, a morning workout, and she's sipping a green juice.

Typical mom life. *Pfft* ...

"Good job, Jolene. Better wake Leah. I have to go to work."

"That's my question. Why is Leah not with him?" She follows me to the bedroom, totally ignoring our crying baby.

"I gave her a break."

"We pay her to be with him twenty-four hours a day if necessary. She's *very* well paid. She doesn't need you giving her a break. She naps when he naps."

Before she can follow me into the bedroom, I turn at the threshold. Opening my mouth to say something like, *"You're a unique piece of work."* I, instead, hold my tongue and close my mouth just as quickly. I'm too tired of exchanging barbs. She's not worth my time. If the day comes that she shows a glimpse of humanity, I'll reciprocate and make time for her in some capacity. This is all a big "if."

After throwing on clothes and brushing my teeth, I pass Fletcher in the kitchen while grabbing the coffee Micah has waiting for me. "I'm on my way to the bank to sign the papers," I say to Fletcher.

"Good. Then you need to visit Annie."

I freeze, slowly turning back toward him while his words punch the air from my chest.

He doesn't look up from his mug of coffee. "She's not doing well. It's an infection. She's been transferred to the hospital." His emotionless gaze meets mine. "I think it's time, Milo."

Swallowing hard behind gritted teeth, I head to my truck.

"She's at Southwestern, Milo."

AFTER THE BANK, I sit in the hospital parking lot for a coward's hour. It's reminiscent of visiting Archer. Only this time Indie won't be calling me to check in. She won't make me smile. Her voice won't settle into my chest like a shield from the bad things in life.

It's just me and my past. It's just me and ... my future.

Annie is the reason I work for Fletcher.

Annie is the reason I let Indie go.

Annie is the reason I'm married to Jolene.

Annie is the reason I have a son.

Everything about my life feels like it begins and ends with Annie.

Climbing out of my truck, I shove my phone into my pocket; heavy, numb feet carry my weary body toward the entrance. The smiley lady at the information desk sends me to the ICU.

"But only family is allowed," she says as I head toward the elevators.

"I'm family," I murmur.

It's been eighteen years since I've seen my twin sister. When I step into her room, it takes a minute to let reality come to life in a very tangible way. She's hooked to so many lines and tubes. And she looks nothing like the girl I remember. The giggly blonde with bouncing curls is a ghost at best.

Annie's hair is short and matted. Pale, lifeless skin. Wrinkled and dry.

I feather my fingers over her hand. It's cold. The machine keeping track of her pulse and heart rate says she's alive. I'm not so sure I believe it.

"Hey, Annie. It's Milo. I ... I wanted to see you before now, but I couldn't. I'm sorry. Sorry for everything. I don't know if you can hear me, but if you can, please know that I'll never stop doing whatever it takes to give you the care you need. The care you deserve." I laugh a little to keep from falling to my fucking knees and bawling. "You should outlive both of us. Archer already left us, and I'm a moving target most days, so ..." I blow out a long breath. "You stand a chance of surviving everyone else if you fight this nasty bug."

Her eyes crawl open, and I suck in a slow breath. They're my eyes. They're the eyes of the giggly girl with bouncing curls. I see her. She's still in there.

Her fingers twitch before her hand lifts toward mine. I squeeze it while simultaneously wringing tears from my stinging eyes. I stifle a sob and chuckle again. "Oh god ... there you are, beautiful Annie." My other hand wipes my face. "Hey ... do you hear me?"

She has a tube up her nose, but she gives me a slight nod and parts her cracked lips. Nothing comes out.

There's so much I don't know about her. I know she has brain damage. I know she's blind in one eye. I know she can't walk unassisted. And I know it's my fault.

"Don't try to talk. We'll talk later." I sniffle again, wiping my nose with my sleeve. "I'm just ... so happy to see you."

Something resembling a smile touches her lips. And I wonder what she remembers from the past. If she knows who I am. Does she know her doctors don't think she'll leave here alive?

"They're fixing you. Then I want you to see my son." I grin. "Can you believe I have a son? I uh ... didn't exactly get him the way I ever imagined I'd have a child, but he's mine. He has our eyes. And he's strong, just like you. So yeah, you need to fight this. Okay?" I bring up a picture of Ben on my phone and show it to Annie.

She looks at it and then at me. I think she can see it with her good eye.

Everything inside my chest falls to pieces. I don't want to completely lose my shit in front of her, but god ... it's hard.

For the next hour, I sit beside her bed, holding her hand, and I reminisce about our childhood, the happy times. There were a few. I'm not ready to talk about the day our lives took a plot twist into a horror story. We'll discuss that when she gets better.

As her eyes drift shut, I squeeze her hand. "I'm gonna let you sleep, but I'll be back tomorrow and the next day and every day until you're better. Okay?"

Annie opens her eyes, and they blink heavily.

I kiss her hand and then head toward the door.

"M-Mi-lo."

I turn. Wiping my eyes as fast as possible but fuck if I can keep up with the tears. She said my name. My fucking name.

"L-lov-love y-you."

My face scrunches. I can barely speak. "Love you too ... so much."

I leave my contact information with the nurse, so I get the updates before Fletcher. If she lives, I can't be apart from her again. I've done the work. Put in my time. Fletcher owes me this.

The elevator dings, the door slides open, and a running bouquet heads in my direction. "Hold the elevator, please." It's a strained, high-pitched voice, a little out of breath. The running bouquet rushes past me and straight into the elevator while I try to hold open the doors. The bouquet turns, and familiar eyes peek out from the stems of tall flowers just as the doors shut. "Milo—"

And as quickly as she ran into the elevator, she disappears.

My finger pounds the button repeatedly, but it's too late. The elevator stops on the second floor, third floor, fourth floor ...

"Fuck," I whisper, smacking my hand against the doors.

Pacing the lobby, I gaze at the elevator every time it chimes.

Not her.

Not her again.

Again ... not her.

Maybe I dreamed it. After all, I didn't sleep well last night or any night since we've had Benjamin. I'm three months sleep-deprived.

Ding.

The doors open again, and she steps out, eyes scanning the lobby. She nervously bites her thumbnail for a few seconds before her gaze locks with mine.

I don't move, and neither does she. I'm scared out of my fucking mind to so much as blink.

"How do you know if someone loves you?"

"A look. A touch. Sometimes it's just a feeling."

Then it happens, and I can't stop it. I grin.

It's by far the biggest grin since Benjamin's eyes met mine for the first time.

Her bangs are long again. All of her hair is longer. She flips it behind her shoulders and makes her way to me. She's beautiful.

As I take a step toward her, she stops, head shaking over and over while her hand cups her mouth and tears fill her eyes.

"Indie ..." I take another step, but she retreats a step and holds up her finger, signaling that she needs a minute.

There's nothing I want more than to open my arms

and let her walk into them like she's done so many times before. But a lot has happened in four years.

Wiping her eyes, she draws in a shaky breath and releases it while finding a smile for me. "It's really you," she whispers.

Fuck. This hurts.

Indie shoves her hands into the back pockets of her jeans, taking yet another step backward.

It hits me hard. I feel every day and hour of the four years we've been apart. Our divergent lives.

I'm married to another woman.

I have a child.

I have no idea where she's been for four years or what she's been doing. She could be married with a child of her own.

Yet ... everything inside of me comes to life like *nothing* has changed. I love her as much as I did the last time we were together.

More.

I love her more.

I return an easy nod. "It's really me. What are you ... where have you ... I ..." My head shakes. "God, I'm fumbling my words. It's been an exhausting day. I'm bone-tired ... every day. Now I'm just ... shit. Tell me to shut up."

Her gaze crawls along my body from my hat to the toes of my boots, like she's unsure if I'm real. A somber, heartbreaking expression accompanies it. She clears her throat and finds another sad smile. "I would never. Keep talking. I think I caught something about you being tired. I think that was the gist of it. Right?"

I roll my eyes at myself, mirroring her by sliding my hands into my front pockets, so I don't grab ahold of her. God, I want to touch her more than anything. "Yeah. That's the gist of it. So ... you're in Dallas? I never dreamed you'd be uh ... so close."

She shrugs. "It's hard to get very far without much money."

I nod several times. She left everything behind, including the money in her bank account.

"I had five hundred dollars cash. I couldn't waste it on a plane ticket. So I grabbed an Uber to Dallas."

I can't fucking believe it. All this time, she's been *this* close.

"It's been four years. Surely you've made enough money doing something to buy a plane ticket."

Again, her gaze slides down my body and back to my face. She can't hide the shock on her face. I don't know what she sees on my face, but it's pain and regret.

"True." She clears her throat. "But I met someone. So I stayed here."

Three words my heart wasn't ready to hear. I'm not stupid. Of course, she met someone. Indie's a beautiful, kind woman.

"That's good. You look good. You must be doing ..."

She chuckles. "Good? Yeah. I'm good. How about you?"

Me? Oh, I'm a blubbering idiot because I'm as much in love with this girl as I was the day she left with nothing more than a note in her wake.

"I'm surviving."

Her smile fades a little. "I suppose surviving with the Ellingtons is as good as it gets."

"Says Indiana *Ellington.*"

She shakes her head. "Indiana Hill. I legally changed my name. Grandma Hill and Faye love it."

"You see them?"

"Of course. They're my family."

This angers me, but I don't let Indie see it. Fletcher said he's always in touch with them, always looking for Indie. I think I've always known it was a lie, but I couldn't deal with the truth: He could find her, he just didn't want to find her; he wanted to keep her away from me.

"Are you visiting someone?" I ask.

"No. Well, sort of. I work at a flower shop." She lifts her arm, looking at her watch. "In fact, I have two more deliveries. I need to keep going."

"Yeah, of course."

There's an awkward pause in our conversation. We look at each other, smile, then look away.

"Well, uh ..." She forces her gaze to mine again.

I slide my hands out of my pockets. "Can I give you a hug?"

"Oh," she laughs. "Probably not a good idea."

My hands go right back into my pockets. "You're seeing someone, that's right. I don't wanna—"

"No. I mean ..." She closes her eyes and shakes her head. "I don't think it's a good idea because ..." Her nose wrinkles, and she bites her lip. "We're not that good at *just* hugging."

I blink a few times. Is she really saying what I think she's saying? I don't blush easily, but Indie's managed to bring heat to my face. I wet my lips and glance over her shoulder, scrounging every last bit of confidence I can find. "I get it." I shrug. "You don't trust yourself. I mean, it's been four years, but I'm pretty unforgettable."

"Pretty full of yourself is what you are, Milo Odell."

I smirk, and it feels good even if she can still see me blushing like a pathetic teenager witnessing a pair of titties for the first time.

"But really..." again she looks at her watch "...I have to go."

"You should give me your number or something."

Her eyes narrow. "Did you get a divorce?"

"No."

"Did your wife die?"

"No."

She bites her lips together and stares at her feet for a second before pivoting and waltzing toward the door. "It was truly nice seeing you, Milo."

That's it? She appears out of nowhere after four years, and I don't get a hug. An invite for coffee? Or her phone number?

COWBOY CONFIDENCE

INDIE

"CAN YOU MAKE ONE MORE DELIVERY?" Lincoln asks as soon as I push through the shop's front door.

I hear him—sort of.

I saw MILO!

And I tried to play it cool.

My heart nearly crashed and died ... bleeding at his feet.

I didn't think I had a zero chance of running into him. However, with a population of over one-point-three million, and my working in a floral shop and delivering to private homes and hospitals, the chances felt close to zero.

He was nervous. And he blushed. I have never seen Milo Odell blush. He fumbled words and couldn't stop grinning. It didn't feel like four years; it felt like four seconds.

Same Milo, just ... more.

Bulkier muscles.

Thicker beard, but still well-kept.

Sexy jeans.

Same hat.

And that smile.

It was all too much.

"Can I hug you?"

Gah! I couldn't hug him.

I've never been able to hug Milo Odell and willingly let him go. And today would not have been the exception.

"Hello? Earth to Indie?"

I glance up at Lincoln, my elbows on the counter and my face cradled in my hands. "Huh?"

He laughs. "I asked if you could make one more delivery?"

"Sure."

"What are you thinking about?"

I shake my head and stand straight. "Nothing. I just saw an old friend at the hospital."

He lifts an eyebrow, removing the thorns from the roses. "Should I be jealous?"

"No. Why would you ask that?"

"Because of that look on your face."

"What look?" I check the delivery on the counter for a card.

"It's the look you have after sex."

"What?" It's my turn to blush.

"Listen, I know what we have is casual, but I'm not seeing anyone else, so if you—"

"I'm not seeing anyone else. And I didn't have sex with my friend at the hospital. That's just weird. And the answer to your question is no, you shouldn't be jealous."

"You sure?"

I lift onto my toes and kiss his soft cheek, inhaling his rose scent. "Positive."

Lie. Lies. Liar.

"Can I see you tonight?"

Lincoln's jealous whether he should be or not, and he has a primal male urge to claim me. I don't blame him, but I can't be with him tonight after seeing Milo Odell. I need a minute to gather my thoughts about our encounter. Sort through these complicated feelings.

"Sorry. Girls' night."

"Since when?" He frowns.

"Since I invited my girlfriends out for drinks." I grin and head toward the door with the final delivery for the day. "See you in the morning."

"I'm available tonight ... even if it's late."

Yep. He needs to mark his territory.

"Okay. But really ... I'll see you in the morning."

IT HASN'T BEEN EASY, but I've found a life.

A job.

Friends.

And friends with benefits.

I've found intimacy, and I even allowed myself to enjoy it.

So why am I so miserable? It's been three weeks. I should have hugged him, I think. Or at least given him my phone number so he could call me and ... what? Tell me about his marriage?

Seeing Milo didn't set my heart back four years. It didn't rip open every scar. But it tore a few small holes, leaving me bleeding again. I'm not sure I can walk away from him with my heart completely unscathed.

"Bailey's not coming in today, so I have to set up for the wedding," Lincoln grumbles about his sister, scuffing his feet along the floor and sipping his coffee.

"Good morning to you too." I arrange the last bouquet for the outdoor stand.

He gives me a half grin. "Sorry. I hate weddings. That's all." He stares through the glass doors of the refrigerator. "Wow. The bride's bouquet looks ..."

I smile. "Like a work of art? I completed it at six this morning."

"I was going to say it looks like I might keep you around after all." He turns and cozies up behind me, arms around my waist, face in my neck. "Now, if I could just convince you to stay over at my place. It's been forever."

I giggle and squirm; his unshaven face tickles my neck. "It hasn't been forever."

"Nearly a month."

I roll my eyes. "Three weeks. And I see you're keeping count. Should I be worried that you don't know what *casual* means?"

He sips his coffee and raises an eyebrow. "No. I think it's you who's keeping count. You might be a little *too* casual."

With a shrug, I redirect my gaze to the last bouquet. "I track my period. That's all."

"And are you having your period?"

With a laugh, I carry the bouquet outside and place it in the last slot on the display. "You never ask a woman about her period."

"Fine. Then I'll ask you to help me load the van and give me a quickie before I have to leave and you have to flip the open sign."

"Can't ..." I open the fridge door to help load the wedding flowers. "I'm on my period."

"You're so sadistic," he grumbles while I giggle.

Lincoln spends the morning setting up for the wedding across town, and I watch the shop, take last-minute orders, and call in Russ, Lincoln's retired dad, to make today's deliveries.

"It's just three today. They're all in the box on the counter. Thanks, Russ," I say when the door chimes.

Russ doesn't respond.

I pull off my gloves and turn toward the front of the store. "You're not Russ."

Milo removes his hat and grins. "Not to my knowledge. I'm just a guy who's visited every floral shop in Dallas over the past three weeks." He glances around and back out the front door. "You're not exactly in the safest part of town."

My heart's doing that happy dance that makes it hard to speak, that makes me sound breathless. "Cheap rent," I manage to say without a full-on dog pant.

He sets one of the bouquets from the sidewalk display on the counter.

"You've been searching all of Dallas for this particular bouquet?" I wrap it in paper for him.

His gaze slides to mine while he digs money from his pocket, and a tiny grin plays on his lips. "So it would seem."

"Your wife will love this. It's filled with fragrant hyacinth and ranunculus."

Milo tosses a hundred-dollar bill onto the counter. I open the register to get his change.

"Keep it," he says.

I set his change next to the bouquet. "You don't tip a florist unless we deliver, and you feel generous."

He frowns at the money for a few seconds before folding it and shoving it back into his pocket. "It's for my sister, not my wife."

My giddy heart slows to a dull, pulsing thud in my chest. "Sister?"

"She's in the hospital. That's why I was there when we ran into each other."

"Sister?" I'm not sure how many times I have to say the word before it makes sense. Maybe never. "I didn't ... know ... I mean, why didn't you ever mention your sister?"

He lifts a shoulder, eyes narrowed a fraction while he stares at the wrapped flowers on the counter. "I couldn't."

"Why not?"

Milo's lips twist. "It's complicated."

I start to speak but clamp my mouth shut. I want to say, "What's not complicated?" But I refrain from going there. Milo has never shared his life with me, and the more I think about it, the angrier I get at my stupid heart for always having such a visceral reaction to his nearness.

"Well, I hope she likes the flowers." I can't keep all the bitterness out of my voice, but I do my best. It's not the least bit soothing, but I still chant in my head: *Not my circus, not my monkeys.*

I escaped the fucked-up world of the Ellingtons. Even if Milo Odell still carries around a big chunk of my heart in his pocket, I can't go back. Not physically. Not emotionally.

Maybe he has ten siblings, four wives, six kids, and a pet crocodile. It's none of my business anymore.

He picks up the bouquet and brings it to his nose before pulling a ranunculus. "Can we get a cup of coffee or something?"

"I'm the only one here. No coffee breaks for me."

Twisting his body, he inspects the front door. "Sign says you close at four. How about a cup of decaf at five?"

"I eat dinner at five."

"Then have dinner with me." He leans forward, slipping the flower behind my ear.

I stiffen, suffocated by his nearness. And leather ...

He grins before slipping his hat back onto his head.

God ... he's only gotten sexier.

"It's just dinner."

"What if I have a boyfriend?"

"What if I have a wife?"

Our gazes lock, a silent standoff. I can't imagine the day when I can share space with Milo and not feel like he has more power over me than any other human.

More than Ruthie.

More than Fletcher.

More than Pauline or Jolene.

Power isn't taken; it's given. It's too intangible to steal.

When Ruthie died, it was Milo's hand that took mine. It was he who fed me. It was his arms that held me, that made me feel safe. He didn't carry me. He watched me stumble my way into womanhood. He didn't give me strength; he showed me strength. When I gave him my trust, I gave him power over me.

As we stand here, I ask myself, *do you trust him?* And if the answer's still yes, then Milo Odell still has tremendous power over me.

He's baited me with a piece of his past—a sister. I should say no. I *need* to say no. I absolutely should not say yes to dinner with Milo Odell.

With a quick nod toward the window that causes him to glance over his shoulder, I say, "Right there. They have the best tacos in Dallas. I'll be there at five. I won't wait to order, and I'm leaving when I'm done eating."

Milo faces me again, a slow grin blooming along his face while he tips his hat to me. "Five o'clock."

Where is the word-fumbling man I encountered at the hospital three weeks ago? Nowhere to be found. This guy struts out of the shop, confidence rolling off him in crashing waves with not so much as a glance back at me.

This isn't good.

27

TACOS IN SILENCE

MILO

I CHECK my watch while Fletcher yammers on about someone stealing a horse. One fucking horse. Not even a good horse.

"Someone's going to pay for coming onto my property, breaking down my fence, and stealing my fucking horse. No excuses. No second chances. Just put a bullet in their head. Do you hear me?"

It's four fifteen. Traffic's gonna be a bitch.

"Milo?"

"Yeah?" I jerk my attention back to him.

"Is there someplace more important that you need to be? You keep checking your watch instead of answering me. Did you hear me? Shoot to kill. Understood?"

It's fucked-up that the man who saved me from doing time for murder has spent so much time training me to kill people.

"Shoot to kill." I nod, stand, and make my way out of his office.

"Oh, Milo?"

"Yeah?" I turn.

"I'm glad Annie's doing well. She's a fighter."

I nod slowly. I don't trust him.

"I had her transferred to a safe place where well-qualified people will continue to care for her."

"A safe place? Where?"

He laughs, and I'm reminded that he's more monster than man. "You don't get the keys to the castle just yet."

"I want to see her."

"You did."

"I saw her in the fucking hospital a handful of times." My voice escalates while I make two hard fists at my sides.

"You're welcome." He smirks.

"I've done everything you've asked," I say between clenched teeth.

"Good." He shifts his attention to his phone while he leans back in his leather chair. "Keep doing it, and Annie will be fine. You'll be fine. Everyone will be fine because of you, Milo. You're a goddamn hero."

It takes everything I have, every last shred of self-control to keep from planting the muzzle of my gun between his eyes. When I close the door to my truck, I blow out a long breath and glance at my watch. I'm going to be late.

On my way to the taco joint, Jolene calls me. It's tempting to ignore her call. But now that we have a child together, I have to take all calls. I can ignore her, but I can't ignore Benjamin.

"Yeah?"

"Milo, where are you? I just saw you pull out of the driveway. Leah is sick, and I have court tomorrow."

"I'll be home by tomorrow."

"Don't be this way. I have so many files to go through tonight."

"He'll sleep."

"But if he wakes up—"

"Then soothe him back to sleep."

"Dammit, Milo. When will you be home?"

"I have a meeting."

"Where?"

I roll my eyes while barreling down the road toward Dallas.

"Turn around and come get Benjamin. You can take him with you."

"No. My meeting is not in the best part of town. The last thing I need is a baby with me. Call your mom or have Fletcher watch him. I'll be there when I get there."

"Milo—"

I end the call. If she has so much work, then she'd better get to working instead of wasting time whining to me.

Twenty minutes late, I park in front of the taco joint. The lights are off at the floral shop, and I have no idea what car Indie drives. My patience is gone. If she's not here, I'm going to lose it. I *need* her to be here, especially after Fletcher has taken my sister again.

"Hi. Did you have a to-go order, or will you be dining in?"

I barely hear the man behind the counter. Indie snags my attention, and she doesn't know I'm here. With a book in her hand, one knee is drawn toward her chest. She scrapes her teeth along her bottom lip, enthralled in the book before her instead of finishing her half-eaten plate of tacos.

"Sir?"

I shake my head slowly without taking my eyes off Indie. "I'm meeting someone ..." I trail off while making my way to the back of the restaurant.

Burnt fajita veggies and the aroma of seared meat fill the air, along with the sizzle of hot plates being served around me.

Indie glances up at me as I approach and presses her lips together, but it doesn't completely hide her smile. "You're late."

"Not really. I've been watching you, getting up the nerve to invite myself to eat at your table."

She giggles, marking her place in the book and setting it aside. I've spent more time with Indie than I have with Annie. I know her better. She's the only person on this earth who makes me feel at home. She's the only person who erases a lousy day with nothing more than a smile.

"Well, I'm about done, but you're welcome to sit with me for a few minutes."

I pull out a chair, resisting the urge to lean forward and brush my lips along her cheek. Resisting the urge to draw a long breath at her neck just to see if she still smells like lavender.

"Can I get you something to drink?" the waiter asks.

"I'll have what she's having."

"Her drink or her meal? She's just drinking water."

I don't look at him. I can't. Indie demands my attention with her tiny grin while she brings said water to her red lips.

"All of it. The water she's drinking, the food she's eating, the air she's breathing. Just ... everything."

He chuckles. "Sounds good. I'll be back with everything in a bit."

"The air I breathe?" She sets her water glass on the table.

I lift a shoulder. "It's been one of those days. I'll take whatever I can get."

"You must have a shitty job."

"The worst." I take her glass and gulp down most of the water, dumping a few pieces of ice into my mouth.

Indie raises a brow at me. "Help yourself."

"Oh ..." I smirk while chewing the ice. "I plan to."

She shakes her head, again biting back her grin. "Oh boy ... you're a little extra today, aren't you?"

"Extra what?"

"Just ... extra."

My eyes narrow. "I think you stole my line. Are you quoting me?"

"Milo, Milo, Milo ..."

"Say it again, but deeper, breathier."

"Stop," she snorts, covering her mouth.

"Sorry, I'll behave. Let's see ... how did you end up working as a florist? I mean ... it's very Ruthie of you. But no college, Smarty Pants?"

She runs her fingernail along a crease in the table. "College is expensive. I'm no longer rich. I'm—"

"Free," I remind her.

Indie lifts her gaze. "Yeah," she whispers. "I don't know. I had no clue what I wanted to study. So why go? And when I left everything behind, I realized my dreams and life were mine again. I didn't have to rush anything. I didn't have to live up to anyone else's expectations. So here I am. I'm fantastically poor, yet content with my lower income status."

I nod slowly. "But are you happy?"

A sadness ghosts along her face. "I mean ... I'm good. Are you happy?"

"I'm fucking miserable." I chuckle. "My norm, I guess."

"Did you build a new house? That was the plan, right?"

I don't want to talk about my life, but it's an unavoidable subject. "It's in the process of being built. Things keep getting delayed. Plans keep changing. The cost keeps increasing." I roll my eyes.

"I bet it's going to be larger than life. Larger than Fletcher's house."

I shrug. "It's a house—a place to eat. Piss. Shower. Sleep. It's overkill for my needs. In case you forgot ... I lived in a barn."

A smile fights to bend her lips, but I can see it warring with an underlying sadness.

"Still have Ranger?"

"Of course."

"Does ..." She shakes her head. "Never mind."

"Yeah."

Indie eyes me.

I grin. "You were gonna ask if he misses you. The answer is yes."

There it is, that soft radiance that is my Indie girl. The shy blush. Eyes averting. Lips rubbing together.

"Well," she glances out the window, trying to be coy with me. "How could he not?"

"I know how he feels."

When Indie looks at me again, emotion builds in her eyes. She clears her throat. "I don't really care, but I don't want to be rude, so I'll ask ... how's Jolene?"

I want to tell her everything. And I want it to be okay. Why does sharing everything with her put lives at risk? It's so fucking unfair. It makes me feel weak, like every ounce of strength I have is just an illusion that Fletcher allows.

"She kicks ass in the courtroom. And ..." I can't say it. I want to share the only good thing in my life that's not Indie. But I can't. It feels too cruel. And I know this because I would feel ripped apart if she told me she had a child with another man.

"And? Is that it?"

The waiter brings my tacos and water. When he leaves us alone again, I remove my utensils from the napkin. "That's it."

"She's good at her job. Fair enough. I didn't want to ask about her anyway."

"Me neither." I bite into my taco and chew it for a few seconds.

Indie watches me. Indie has watched me for as long as I care to remember.

Rope.

Herd.

Brand.

Build.

Repair.

Ride.

Play in the mud.

Sweat in the sun.

Swim across the pond.

Everything is better with her eyes on me.

"I suppose I should be polite and ask about your uh ... personal life. Tell me about your boyfriend."

Her eyes narrow like she's thinking too hard. "It's less complicated than your life. His name is Lincoln. His family owns the flower shop. They're great people."

"Sounds serious."

Indie laughs. "Does it? I don't know about that. I'd use other words to describe it."

"Such as?"

"Easy. Casual."

"I see." I wipe my lips, concealing my grin. "That's good to know."

"It is? Why? Because you're gauging how hard the line is that you want to cross?"

I cough with my fist to my mouth while shaking my head. "N-no." I cough some more. "I just think you deserve something easy in your life. Lord knows it was never easy with Fletcher."

"Oh." Her nose wrinkles. "Well, now I'm a little

embarrassed about throwing that terrible assumption out there."

"Not terrible."

Indie folds her hands on the table. "I'm sorry about your brother."

I nod, but I don't look at her.

"I ... I was there," she whispers.

I squint at her.

"Not..." she focuses on her book, tapping the top with her fingernail "...inside the prison. I parked outside. Then I saw you exit with Fletcher, so I left."

"Why ..." I shake my head. "Why were you there?"

Indie's gaze finds mine. "I thought maybe you would need someone's arms." With a sad smile, she shrugs. "I thought maybe you would need mine."

I did.

I fucking needed her that night.

She chuckles. "But I know you're strong. And while I drove home that night, I thought of how stupid it was for me to think you needed me when you never really told me about your past. And I was reminded that I had never been those arms for you. So why ... why did I make such a stupid assumption that you would suddenly be comforted by me?"

"Indiana ..."

"Don't." She shakes her head. "It's been years. I'm not trying to make you feel bad. I just wanted you to know that I was thinking of you that night." The delicate hint of a smile rests on her lips. Then she clears her throat. "You have a sister."

I take a few seconds to let my mind shift from the fact

that she was waiting for me after Archer died to her knowing I have a sister. I can't protect her *and* share everything. It makes me look like an asshole, an uncaring asshole incapable of reciprocating the same kind of love.

"Yeah, listen ..." I blow out a long breath. "Fletcher can never know I told you about her."

"Well, you didn't tell me about her. I know nothing about her. Like I know nothing about your brother. Like I know very little about you."

Nice right hook. I deserve it.

"And I don't see Fletcher. How would he know when he doesn't know where I'm at?"

"Indie." I toss my napkin onto my plate. "Fletcher doesn't know your whereabouts because he doesn't need to. If ... *when* the day comes that he wants to see you or talk to you, he will find you. And I'm just saying you can never breathe a word about my sister."

"Why?"

I pinch the bridge of my nose. "It's best if you don't know. The less you have to lie about, the better."

Her gaze drops to her half-eaten plate of food as her mouth falls into a frown. "What are you doing here? You told me to leave and never come back. Your life hasn't changed. Fletcher still pulls the strings. Jolene is still your wife. So please ... tell me why you're here with me?"

My boot slides next to her white sneaker, and she glances up at me. "I needed to catch my breath," I murmur.

After several long blinks, she moves her other foot next to mine, trapping my boot in the middle. "Have you caught it?"

I frown while slowly shaking my head.

Indie grabs her book and opens it. "They close at ten."

For the next hour, Indie reads her book, occasionally glancing in my direction when she turns a page. And I ... well, I watch her ... and I breathe.

Laying cash on the table for her dinner and mine, I push back in my chair. If Benjamin's having a rough evening, I fear Jolene will let him scream in his crib while she holes up on the other side of the house with earplugs in her ears. And Fletcher will no doubt be drunk and passed out.

Indie looks up. "Home?"

I nod.

She closes her book and stands, sliding her cross-body bag over her shoulder and her book into the bag. "Thanks for dinner. I could have paid for mine."

"You're welcome. Do you need anything? Money? Transportation? Stamps?" I follow her outside.

"No." She laughs. "I have a scooter. And I can't believe you remember the stamps."

"A scooter?"

Indie nods. "Yes. An electric scooter. I had a car, but the payment was too much. So I rented scooters for a while, but since then, I've saved up and bought my own."

She saved for a scooter.

I moved from a barn apartment to a ten thousand square foot home, and Indie moved from a Texas mansion to saving for an electric scooter.

"Well, I guess this is it." Her hands slip into her front pockets. "It was nice catching up." She rocks back and forth on her heels, the wind catching her long hair. So beautiful.

"Remember our last time together?"

Heat turns her cheeks extra pink, and she stares at her feet. "How could I forget?"

I shrug. "Time steals many things. Memories are vulnerable. Emotions fade. Every moment feels irreplaceably important. Until the next. In four years, you've had a lot of *next* moments."

Indie looks up at me. "Like a video game with the top scores? Over time, someone else takes the top spot?"

"Yeah."

"Mmm ... I see." She turns and looks both ways before crossing the street to the scooter chained to the light post by the flower shop.

"Ranger would feel betrayed," I call when she frees her scooter.

Erupting into a fit of laughter, she takes off on her scooter. "Night, Milo."

"Night, Indie girl," I say to myself, mesmerized by her figure fading into the distance.

28

LET HIM DIE

"I'VE GOTTEN NOTHING DONE. Thanks for that." Jolene passes a fussy Benjamin to me the second I remove my boots and hat. "I'll tell my client she has you to thank when we lose this case tomorrow." Her feet pound toward the other wing of the house.

"Why didn't you call your mom?"

"My mom had book club tonight, Milo."

"And her book club was more important than helping her only daughter?"

She pivots, arms crossed. "*We* are his parents. We shouldn't have to ask family to help us out all the time."

All the time? I can't remember the last time Pauline watched Benjamin. "Whatever, Jolene. I'll take the blame." I kiss Benjamin's head, and he immediately calms down.

When I glance at her, Jolene gives me a frown. "How do you do that?"

"Do what?"

"Get him to stop crying so quickly?"

"You don't wanna know. Just go do your work."

She takes several steps toward me. "What's that supposed to mean? Why wouldn't I want to know?"

"Because you'll be offended." I head toward the kitchen to grab a glass of water. My little guy will heat me up rather quickly, nestled on my chest.

Jolene's bare feet slap the floor behind me. I feel her inches away like a dog nipping at my ankles. "You've never spared my feelings before."

Oh, Sweetheart ... you have no idea.

I drink the whole glass of water and calmly set it on the counter. "This."

"This what?" She blows at the hair falling into her face.

"This. You're losing your mind. I can physically feel your anger from five feet away. He can feel your frustration, anger, and impatience; it makes him uneasy. When he's uneasy, he cries. But I remain calm even if something is messing with my head. Like now, your willingness to have this conversation with me when you're supposedly going to lose your case tomorrow *because of me* makes me want to ram my head into the wall." I smile, showing my teeth. "But I let that shit stay in my head. From the neck down, I stay calm."

Jolene rolls her eyes and huffs before pounding her feet away from me again. "It's because you have no stress in your life. You ride a stupid horse all day and drive around in your truck. You have no clue what it's like to have a real job."

Again, I kiss Benjamin's head. "Mommy's an entitled bitch. Sorry, buddy. We don't get to choose our parents," I say in a soft, cooing tone.

He pulls in a breath and releases it in a shaky exhale.

"Yeah, my thoughts too. This is why daddy needs Indie in his life. She's a gentle soul. You'd like her." I carry him into the family room. "You'd crush her heart, but you'd like her. And eventually, I think she'd like you. You're irresistible." I ease into the corner of the sofa and prop up my feet. "I think you get that from me, but don't tell your scary mommy."

~

SEVERAL SOMEWHAT HARD SLAPS TO my cheek bring me out of my sleep. My hand bats the pesky slapper away while I peel open my eyes. "What the fuck, Jolene," I whisper, jackknifing to sitting.

She's in a black skirt suit with high, pointy heels. "What are you doing?" she whisper-yells while her finger jabs past me.

I glance back at Benjamin sleeping. "What?"

"Why is he in here?"

"Because he sleeps soundly next to me. Who knew? All this time, Leah's been pacing the house with him half the night. Problem solved."

"Problem *not* solved. You cannot start this. He needs to be in his crib."

I swing my legs off the side of the bed. "That's rich coming from the person who has never gotten up with him in the middle of the night and sleeps in the room farthest from his," I say through a series of partially stifled yawns.

"Put him back in his crib *now*. Leah will be here any minute."

I stare at her for a few seconds. I didn't think it was possible for her to get worse than she was when I married her. The fact that I've put my dick into her a handful of times (drunk and desperate times) over the past four years is cringeworthy.

I salute her. "Yes, ma'am."

This seems to anger her more, but she leaves my room in a hissy fit because she needs to get to work. Thank god.

After Leah arrives, I get chores done around here and mount my horse to check on the new calves. When I return to the house an hour later, flashing lights come into view. I speed up, fly off Ranger while one of the ranch hands takes him, and run into the house just as the paramedics wheel Fletcher out on a gurney.

"What happened?"

He's barely conscious, brace around his neck, and the medics don't acknowledge me. They're in too much of a hurry to get him to the ambulance.

"Micah, what happened?"

Micah shakes his head, watching the medics. "He got sick after breakfast. He thought it was something I made him. But then he complained about the lights being too bright and affecting his vision. The next thing I knew, he tumbled down the stairs."

"I'm following the ambulance. Have you called Pauline?"

"Not yet. I've been with him waiting for the ambulance."

I jog to my truck. "Call Pauline!"

Morning traffic poses a big challenge for the ambulance. They should have life-flighted him. Hell, they should have taken his copter. When I park and make it to the ER, I'm told to wait for news from the doctor.

I text Jolene instead of calling her, knowing she won't pick up her phone if she's in court, but she might glance at a message, or her assistant might see it.

It takes hours for an update.

When the doctor finally emerges, Pauline jumps out of her chair. "Oh my god, how is he? What's taking so long?"

"He's in surgery," the doctor says.

"Why?" Pauline rests her hand on her throat.

"He had an aneurysm rupture."

"Oh my god. Is he going to be okay?"

"We'll know more when he comes out of surgery. The bigger issue is his spine. It fractured from his fall. But I'll let you know as soon as I know anything new."

I back away ... feeling conflicted, like a terrible person. Fletcher was Archer's best friend. He helped keep me out of prison, and he ensured Annie got the best care money could buy. But all of it has come with a considerable price. And as long as Fletcher's alive, my life will not be mine. Not completely.

A dark voice speaks a truth I will never share—*I don't want Fletcher to come out of this surgery alive.*

"Jolene should be here soon. She couldn't leave in the middle of court." Pauline hugs me like I need to be consoled, and she's willing to take on the job until "my wife" gets to the hospital.

If she only knew ...

29

WHO'S YOUR DADDY

INDIE

IT'S BEEN two weeks since I had dinner with Milo. It didn't feel like closure. I don't know if closure with Milo Odell is possible in this lifetime. He still carries so much baggage.

Baggage he's not willing to share with me.

Maybe I should be grateful. I'm in a better place, physically and mentally.

"These Dahlias are stunning," a customer says of the arrangement on the counter that's a special order.

"They are." I smile.

"Is Lincoln in today?" she asks.

"He should be within the hour. Can I help you with anything?"

Before she can answer, the door chimes. I glance around the bouquet, and Milo's gaze locks with mine.

"I'm supposed to talk to him about my wedding in the spring."

"Oh ... uh ..." I force my attention back to the customer. "Did you make an appointment to talk with him?"

"Well, no. He said just to stop by anytime."

I choose a friendly smile instead of rolling my eyes at what I'm sure was Lincoln's casual reply to the woman. His mom would scold him for not insisting the lady make a proper appointment.

"I'll call him, but I'm not sure he can get here any earlier. Or I can have him call you to schedule an appointment?"

"What if I grab a cup of coffee and come back in an hour?"

"Yeah. Sure. That works too." I watch Milo browse around the shop, stealing a glance here and there in my direction.

"Okay. Well, I'll be back."

"Sounds good."

Milo makes his way to the counter.

"Hi." I do my very best to rein in my grin.

"Hey. How are you?"

"What's wrong?" I ask.

"Why do you think something's wrong?"

"Because I can read you."

He hesitates for a second before relinquishing a single nod. "It's Fletcher."

"What about him?" I cross my arms. I don't want to hear anything about him.

"He had an aneurysm rupture and a subsequent stroke."

"Is he dead?"

Milo flinches. I'm not sure if it's because Fletcher is, in fact, dead or if it's my emotionless question.

"He's in a wheelchair. And rehab. He fell down the stairs as a result of the aneurysm. He's paralyzed from the waist down."

Ruthie would be in a panic. But I'm not. I don't feel anything right now. It's just a regular old Tuesday.

"It happened two weeks ago. The day after we had dinner. I didn't have your number, or I would have called you. And I grappled with the decision to say anything at all since I highly doubted you would—"

"Give a shit?"

Milo frowns.

"I don't. And if that makes me an awful person, so be it. He's not my father. He's not family. He's been dead to me for years. Him dying won't affect my life. So as you can imagine, his incapacitated state doesn't interest me."

Milo rubs his lips together and returns a half dozen quick nods.

I sigh. "Listen, I appreciate you thinking about me, but don't. I'm not an Ellington. I've never been one. Beyond Ruthie dying, I don't care about that family. They are not, nor have they ever really been, my family. So ..."

Using his middle two fingers, he massages small circles on his forehead. "What if ..."

"What if what?"

He drops his hand. "I have all these things. Secrets. And keeping them is so exhausting, but necessary for now. And I thought I'd know if or when the day ever came that I no longer had to keep them. I thought it would be clear, but it's not. Not anymore."

"What are you talking about?"

Milo stares at me with a pained expression.

"What do you want to tell me?"

He gazes at the ceiling for a moment. "Everything." When he looks at me again, I know he will not tell me everything.

"One. Tell me one thing. Trust me with one. Thing."

His brow wrinkles, and his mouth opens. "Fletch—"

"Hey, sexy ... thanks for ... oh ... oops." Lincoln cringes when he sees Milo. "Sorry, I didn't know you were with a customer." He rests his hands on my shoulders and kisses the back of my head. "I'll be unloading in the back. Let me know when you're done here."

Milo eyes Lincoln a little too intently.

"Okay," I manage to whisper. "Sorry." I wrinkle my nose. "What were you going to say?"

Milo shakes his head. "It doesn't matter. I just came to let you know about Fletcher. I'll let you get back to work. And your boyfriend."

"What were you going to tell me?"

He steps backward. "Nothing. It's not important."

"I don't believe you."

"Well, you should. I'll maybe see you around." He turns toward the door, and I rush around the corner and chase him.

While he climbs into the driver's seat, I open the passenger door and hop inside the truck.

Milo doesn't look at me. After he fastens his seat belt,

he rests his hands on his legs and stares out the windshield.

"Is it you, Milo? Are you sad about Fletcher? Am I your safe place?"

He shakes his head.

"Did you really think I'd want to know that he had an aneurysm?"

Another headshake.

"Then why?"

"He's your father."

I laugh. "He's not my father. He's the man who purchased me. He's the man who loved Ruthie. He's the monster she left behind. But he's not my father."

"Indie, he's your father."

"Jesus, Milo ... stop saying that. I thought you understood. You were the one who told me to get as far away from him as possible. What has he said to you? Why are you on his side? I thought you were on my side."

"I *am* on your side." He looks at me for the first time since we got in the truck. "You are his biological daughter, who he didn't want because of Ruthie. And when Ruthie couldn't have kids, he paid your biological mother a million dollars to give you up and walk away forever."

Some things in life don't register—floating pieces to a puzzle that don't seem to fit but you've been told they will work. Milo's words don't fit. They're floating in the air, forcing me to acknowledge them. But they don't fit.

I shake my head. "That doesn't ... no. Just ... no. Who told you that?"

Milo frowns, stealing his gaze from mine. "Your mom," he whispers.

"My ..." Something catches my voice. It might be my heart figuring out what it's feeling. Shock? Anger? Betrayal? I think it's feeling all three and a storm of other emotions. "Ruthie?"

Milo pinches the bridge of his nose and slowly shakes his head.

"My biological mom?"

He nods, blowing out a long breath before his regret-filled eyes find mine again. "Several years after you moved in with Fletcher and Ruthie, your mom showed up. Fletcher had me remove her from the premises before Ruthie or you saw her. I wasn't even sixteen yet, but I had a gun. So I did what I was told to do. I didn't even know who she was until she started yelling all this stuff about him. She called him a bastard for knocking her up and then stealing her baby. She wanted you back. She wanted to know if his wife knew he got her pregnant."

I fumble for the door handle, ramming my shoulder against the window. When the door opens, I stumble onto the sidewalk.

"Indie?"

"You knew," I say, just above a whisper. Everything spins while I try to find my breath.

"Indie, wait."

I sway a bit, dragging my feet back toward the store. "You knew."

"I wanted to tell you."

"But you didn't." I whip around, eyes filling with tears.

"I couldn't."

"I disagree. You are not mute. And even if you were,

you could write it down or text me. Or sign it and at least give me a chance to figure it out."

"There's so much I've wanted to tell you, but I can't. Not while Fletcher is alive."

My fingers brush away tears as soon as they fall down my cheeks. "If you trusted me, you could tell me anything. I've trusted you. I've told you everything. I've given you my heart, my body, my everything. And you've given me nothing because you don't trust me. I've given you all..." I shove his chest "...the..." I shove him again "...fucking..." another shove "...power."

"I trust you. I just don't trust Fletcher. I don't trust him not to drag information out of you. And I wouldn't even blame you. He's the goddamn devil. He has a way of bringing out the worst in people while keeping absolute control over them. He's done it with you. He's done it with me. He can't take something from you if you don't have it to give. So while he's taking breaths on this earth, I refuse to give him one more inch of my life."

I sniffle, tipping up my chin. "So why tell me this now?"

He shrugs. "I want to know when he dies that you've made an informed decision about your last words to him, your last minutes with him. I know you think I'm late telling you, but I'm not *too* late. So now you know. And maybe it changes nothing, or maybe you want to have words with him, ask him questions, or maybe you want to spit on his face or burn his house to the ground with him in it. But I want you to know that you've lost your father when he dies. Whether that's a good or bad thing in your life is not for me to decide. It's simply a fact."

325

Squinting against the sun, I gaze over his shoulder for several seconds. "I walked away from the man I love. And I never looked back. If the man I hate dies tonight, I won't shed a tear. Father. Warden. Monster. Doesn't matter. He's nothing to me. And that's by choice." Turning, I return to the store, wiping my face to gain as much composure as possible before seeing Lincoln. He knows so little about my past. Does not sharing the awful parts with him mean I'm no different from Milo?

I don't know anymore.

30

CAUGHT

MILO

"How is she?" Fletcher asks, staring out his bedroom window from his wheelchair.

I haven't made it past the threshold—he senses everything, even since his health crisis.

"We didn't say more than two words this morning, and I just got home. I haven't seen her yet."

"Not Jolene," he says. "Indiana."

I take a few steps into his bedroom, using the extra seconds to measure my words and tone.

"I'm trustworthy enough to marry your niece, to run everything in your absence, but I'm not trustworthy enough to venture into town without someone following me?"

Fletcher rolls his wheelchair around to face me. "*Are you trustworthy?*"

"Are you asking me this because I stopped by a floral

shop or because you've taken my sister away from me for a second time?"

He twists the end of his mustache. "Milo, will I live to see a day that you aren't pissed off at the world and everyone in it even though you are the only one in your family who is alive *and* fully functional?"

I'd prefer he not live to see his bedtime tonight, so this is a tricky question for me to answer, even if it's rhetorical.

"Have you been in touch with Indiana for the past four years?" He lights a cigar and puffs it.

Why can't he just die?

"Is that a real question or a test?"

"Maybe it's both. Are you going to answer the question and pass the test?"

I shake my head. "No. I only recently ran into her."

"And are you fucking her again?"

"And by her, you mean your daughter? Your biological daughter. The one who is blood to you? The woman I didn't marry in a brilliant partnership to ensure your family's legacy lives on in prosperity?"

"I don't care for your tone, Milo. It's funny. Since my incident, I find my humor and patience aren't what they used to be. I think it has to do with being confined to a goddamn wheelchair instead of on my horse or driving my truck. It might have something to do with needing assistance to get dressed, bathe, and take a shit. So I'm only going to ask you this one more time ... did you fuck my daughter?"

"Not recently."

His lips bend into the hint of a smile. "Why do you hate me so much?"

I shrug. "I could ask you the same thing."

"Is that so? You think I hate you? I'm hurt, Milo. You're getting the keys to the empire when I die. Why do I sense that you're hoping that day comes sooner versus later?"

"When you die, I get my sister back. Is that not reason enough?"

He barks a laugh. "Milo ... Milo ... Milo ... Did you not take a good look at her when I granted you a visit? She's not in great shape, despite the exorbitant amount of money I've donated to the cause over the years. Private care. Therapists. Chefs. Afternoons in the sunlight. If she doesn't leave this life first, she'll leave it when I leave it. I've made sure of it. Then you'll know."

My fingers curl into fists. "Know what?" I grit my teeth.

"How it feels to have everything money can buy ... yet nothing at all. Cancer took Ruthie. And you took my best friend with your recklessness. And that put me in a predicament. Seek revenge or honor Archer's request to take care of you and Annie." He chuckles. "I figured out how to do both."

I *hate* him more than it should be possible to hate another human.

"What's my play? There's always a play. Something you want from me as an exchange."

"An exchange for what?" Fletcher asks.

Gritting my teeth harder, I swallow. "Annie."

"No game. No play. No exchange. I want you to experience what Archer experienced. Helplessness. Doom. Maybe even some regret." His lips twist. "Maybe not regret. I honestly don't think Archer regretted anything. Admittedly, he was a better man than both of us combined. You need to practice some gratitude. One day, it will just be you. The rest of your family will be gone, and you'll have no choice but to cling to your new family. Jolene and Benjamin and the future children you'll have together."

"You're a fucking bastard."

Again, he chuckles while nodding and puffing his cigar. "I won't argue with you on that. It's what your wife and son will say about you someday. Misery has nothing to do but rot. You will rot into something unrecognizable, and you'll see me when you look in the mirror."

"I will never be you."

Fletcher holds his tongue; a practiced defense he's perfected. He turns his chair back to the window.

31

HOMECOMING

INDIE

"Who's Fletcher?" Lincoln asks, an unexpected punch to my gut the second I make it in the door.

He's finishing an enormous arrangement.

I give him a nervous smile and nod toward the flowers. "Who died? That's quite the arrangement. I didn't see a wedding on the schedule. And it's a Wednesday."

"They're for you." He bites the inside of his cheek for a second before offering me a tight smile and wide, expectant eyes.

"What do you mean they're for me?" I laugh it off and deposit my purse on the counter.

"They're from a Fletcher."

Bile crawls up my throat. I slowly reach for the card printout that Lincoln hasn't placed in the holder.

My Darling Indiana,
I miss you. It's time for a visit.
Fletcher

"Listen, Indie, I know we said we'd keep things casual, but over the past few weeks, you've found any excuse not to hang out with me outside of work. And now this? I'm not mad. I just want to know if you've met someone else? And is it serious?"

Why did Milo tell Fletcher about me? He had no right to do that. What was the point of telling me to get as far away as possible if he was going to help Fletcher find me?

"Are you open?" A young man peeks his head in the door. "The sign's not on, but your posted hours say you should be open."

"Yes. I forgot to flip it on." Lincoln brushes past me to the door.

"Do you have pre-made bouquets? I'm proposing to my girlfriend." The young man beams.

"In the cooler." Lincoln points to the far end of the shop.

"It's your lucky day." I grin. "First customer through the door gets this arrangement." I nod to the flowers from Fletcher.

"Indie." Lincoln frowns.

"Are you serious?" the man says, eyes bulging from his head.

"It's easily a three-hundred-dollar arrangement, and it's yours. Congratulations! I hope she says yes." Snagging my bag from the counter, I retreat to the back room.

"Fuck. Fuck. Fuck you, Fletcher. Fuck you, Milo." I stab my fingers through my hair.

They've left me with no choice. It's time to leave Dallas. Setting my phone on the prep counter, I take a pair of pliers and break it. Then I exit the back of the building to get out of here for good.

"I need you to come with me."

Jaw set, I tighten my grip on my bag.

Ty holds open the door to his truck, windows tinted black like the paint.

My head shakes over and over. "I'm not coming with you. Tell Fletcher to go fuck himself and die."

Ty grimaces. "Sorry, Indie. You're coming with me one way or another. Please just get into the truck on your own."

"No." I bolt to the right. "Stop," I scream when he hooks my waist with his thick arm and covers my mouth with his dirty, calloused hand to force me into his truck.

"Indiana, please don't struggle. I don't want to hurt you or have to restrain—fuck!" He jerks his hand away from my mouth after I bite him.

Whack!

Everything goes black.

"There's my girl. How you doing, darlin'? Ty feels bad it came to that."

Groggy, I peel open my eyes, squinting against the light, wincing from the pounding in my head and the dull ache along my cheek to my ear. He comes into view in pieces.

His jean-clad legs.

The wheelchair.

His hands limp on the arms.

Black button-down.

Gray, unkempt hair along his awful face.

Beady eyes.

And the smell of cigar smoke.

My hand presses gently to my cheek. I'm not restrained. I'm on my old bed.

With a stab of pain to my head, I slowly roll to sitting, legs dangling off the side of the bed.

"Don't worry, darlin', Pauline has arranged for new clothes and anything else you need."

"What..." I clear my scratchy, sore throat "...the fuck am I doing here? You can't just kidnap me, you sick prick."

"It's time for you to be home again. Since you opted out of college or any reputable career, it's best for you to be here with your family. And I have the perfect job for you."

"Fuck—"

"Now, now, darlin' ... you'll need to clean up your language since you'll have an impressionable child in your care."

"What are you talking about?" My fingers rub my temples.

"My grandson. Well," he laughs, "he's not technically my grandson. But since I won't have my own grandchildren, I think of Benjamin as my grandson. He's Pauline's grandson."

His words swirl around in my head, nothing more than mush. Then they take shape. They start to make sense. My heart tries to stop for a second. It's like the whole world stops.

"Jolene won't admit it, but the little guy looks like Milo."

My head and face no longer hurt. The pain in my chest digging down to my fucking soul demands the most attention.

"Their nanny had a family emergency and needs time off. Jolene is beside herself, trying to find a replacement on such short notice. A highly sought-after attorney by day and super mom by night. I honestly don't know how she does it. Anyway ... she and Milo haven't had the time alone they deserve."

Scooting forward, I slide to my feet, taking a second to get my bearings. With heavy steps, I make my way to the window, pressing a hand to warm glass. "She would hate you for this," I murmur.

"Who?"

"Ruthie." I stare at the clouds. "If she sees you now, I promise she wants nothing more than for you to burn in Hell. You are truly deplorable."

"That's enough," he says in a sharp tone.

"It's not." My voice holds no life while my hand slides down the glass. "If you keep me here, I will never stop. You'll have to kill me." I slowly turn. "I'm your *blood*."

Fletcher's jaw clenches, eyes narrowing into tiny slits.

"It's not my fault." I draw in a shaky breath, swallowing back my emotions. "You created me with another woman. That's not my fault. You took me from her, a million-dollar price tag. That's not my fault. Ruthie died. That's not my fault."

I will not cry. I will not cry.

Fletcher doesn't deserve my tears. Not while he's alive. And not when he dies.

"I know why I hate you. You've worked so hard to earn every ounce of it." Again, I clench my teeth to keep it together. "But I don't understand why you hate me."

Fuck.

One tear slips out, and I bat it away.

Fletcher blinks and averts his gaze. I want to believe that he's human, and that something I've said will resonate with him. I fear Ruthie took his soul with her when she died. Now, he's empty.

No soul.

No heart.

No love.

Without another word or even a final acknowledging glance, he turns and wheels himself out of my room.

The first breath of silence hits, and the emotions flow freely.

Milo has a baby with Jolene.

32

I'M SORRY

MILO

"Just in time for dinner," Jolene greets me as soon as I walk into the house.

She's holding Benjamin, and she's smiling. I don't have the energy to ask her why she's suddenly acting so motherly.

"The new nanny moved in today. She hasn't met Benjamin yet, but she will join us for dinner."

"Whatever." I head toward the stairs, stepping around Fletcher's stairlift.

"Where are you going?"

"I'm covered in dirt and manure. Where do you think I'm going?"

"Oh, well ... here she is now," Jolene says.

My gaze lifts to the top of the stairs when I'm halfway up them.

Fuck ...

Indie stares at Jolene—at Benjamin. And it's the most painful thing I've witnessed since Archer died.

I will end Fletcher Ellington if it's the last act I perform before I die. The side of Indie's face is bruised red with darker spots of pooled blood beneath the surface. Someone hit her hard.

That someone's going to eat a bullet from my gun.

"Surprise," Jolene says. "How wonderful is it that Indie's filling in as our nanny until Leah comes back?"

I slowly finish climbing the stairs, stopping one step from the top, putting Indie close to eye level with me. Her dead eyes slide from Jolene and Benjamin to me.

My fingertips lift her hair so I can see the extent of her bruise. "Who did this to you?" I whisper.

"Milo, Indie had an altercation this morning. She works in a bad neighborhood. Thank goodness Ty happened to be there to save her." Jolene's voice shakes a little, as it should. If she thinks I'm going to physically do harm to someone very soon ... she's right.

Indie doesn't move, not even a blink.

"I'm sorry," I whisper.

"Milo, hurry up and shower so we can eat. Indie, come meet Benjamin."

"No one will ever touch—"

"Don't," Indie's low voice cuts through me.

There is nothing discernible between how she looks at me and how she looks at Fletcher. And it guts me.

"You can't tell me the truth. How the fuck are you going to protect me?" she mumbles, shouldering past me to make her way to Jolene.

As Jolene's voice gushes with fake motherly pride to

introduce Benjamin to Indie, I escape to the bathroom. I can't listen to it. And I can't watch it.

I think of Annie. I have to keep thinking about Annie. After my shower, I join everyone for dinner.

"Indie, why don't you take Benjamin to the nursery and get him ready for bed? There should be jammies in one of the closet drawers, and all the diapers are by the changing table," Jolene says like she has a fucking clue where his things are in his room.

"I'll get him ready for bed," I say, reaching to pluck him from his swing in the corner of the dining room.

"Milo, sit down and eat. You don't need to do Indie's job," Fletcher dictates from his wheelchair at the head of the table.

Indie has a full plate of food in front of her. It doesn't look like she's taken a single bite. She pushes back in her chair and ignores me while going to Benjamin.

"One of the partners is married to someone who used to be one of your accountants," Jolene says to Fletcher as I ease into my chair, unable to look away from Indie, lifting a fussy Benjamin onto her shoulder.

I wouldn't say she looks like a natural with him, but she's way better than Jolene, who holds him away from her body as much as possible. It's as if she thinks he will get his baby smell onto her.

This is not how most people live.

Most people marry for love. And children are not insurance policies for family legacies. And families might fight, but most don't go to these extremes to be so flat-out cruel.

I detest every one of them for how they're treating

Indie. It's only a matter of time before I end Fletcher's miserable life. When Annie and Indie are safe, I will take down every single one of these despicable people. If Benjamin never sees his mom again, he'll be better off.

They are the worst stains on humanity. Pieces of shit wrapped in hundred-dollar bills.

"You're quiet, Milo. What's on your mind?" Jolene asks, blotting her lips.

"Ty said one of Rooney's guys took my horse," Fletcher eyes me.

I shove a spoonful of potatoes into my mouth and shrug. "I heard that too."

"I also heard he's still using up oxygen. You getting soft on me?"

Fletcher doesn't make it a habit of talking shop outside of his office. I glance at Jolene and Pauline, but I don't sense any shock from the women's bowed heads. It must be nice to pretend this life is earned and not stolen. Do they pretend the houses, cars, fancy clothes, and diamonds come from good guys working hard on a ranch, doing the right thing?

Pushing back my chair, I toss my napkin onto the table and stand. "I can assure you, I'm not getting soft."

"Where are you going?" Jolene asks.

"I'm going to rock Benjamin to sleep."

She frowns. "Indie needs to learn to do that."

I let the smallest of smiles bend my lips. "Then I'll teach her."

All eyes are on me—and all are filled with distrust.

"I'll be up in a few minutes," Jolene says, giving me a challenging smile.

"Suit yourself."

When I reach the nursery, I wait just around the corner. Benjamin's fussing, but not a full-on cry. He's in his crib, kicking his arms and legs. With her hands resting on the railing, Indie stares at him with an emotionless expression.

"Jolene likes him to self-soothe to sleep," I say.

Indie doesn't move. It's as if I'm not speaking.

"I rock him to sleep." Picking him up, I hug him to my chest and sit in the rocking chair that faces the window. "He didn't ask to be born into such a fucked-up family. The least I can do is try to give him something that might cultivate a little compassion and decency in him."

Indie hasn't moved. She stares down into the crib as if he's still there.

"I wanted to tell you," I whisper, the words almost too heavy in my chest to reach my lips. "I just didn't want to tell you everything at once. It felt like telling you about Fletcher was enough."

Still, not a single glance.

"I'm going to fix this."

A breath of sarcasm pushes through her nose, and she slowly shakes her head. "Fix what?" she mumbles, moving to the opposite side of the nursery, staring at the horse mural on the wall. "My imprisonment? Outing me to Fletcher?"

"I didn't out—"

"Or the baby?" Her head tilts a fraction like she's studying the horse's head. "Are you going to unmake that baby with Jolene? Are you going back in time to tell me about the day my real mother came to get me?

Are you going to rewind every time Fletcher or Ty hit me?"

"Ty will never lay a hand on you again."

"It's okay, Milo. He didn't hurt me nearly as much as you did."

"Indie, you can go to bed now. Milo and I will take it from here tonight and give you a chance to settle in. You'll have him all day tomorrow. Might as well get some rest," Jolene says.

Milo and I?

"I'm going to take a bath, babe. Feel free to join me when you get Benjamin down." Jolene leans down to kiss me.

I turn my head slightly so her lips land on my cheek instead of my mouth.

What does Jolene want me to say that she doesn't already know? I just showered. I don't take baths. And I've never taken a bath with her. Oh, and she's been sleeping on the other side of the house and using a different bathroom. But I want her to get out of here as quickly as possible, so I don't respond.

Not that it matters.

By the time Jolene stands straight and adjusts the belt to her skirt, Indie's gone.

I take my time, holding Benjamin until I can barely keep my own eyes open, then I lay him in the crib and check the monitor before closing his door.

"There you are." Jolene smiles from the bed, rubbing lotion on her legs and wearing a short black nightie. "Want me to massage your shoulders and back?"

I make my way to the bathroom to brush my teeth. "I want you to sleep in your bed, not mine."

"What are you talking about? This is *our* bed."

"Since when? I haven't seen you in this bedroom since Benjamin was born."

"Well, that's about to change. We must do better about being here for each other in every way."

I nearly choke on the toothpaste before spitting it into the sink. Wiping my mouth, I peek around the corner. "If Indie being here makes you so paranoid, why'd you let Fletcher kidnap her?"

"Kidnap?" she scoffs. "That's a strong word. A little exaggerated, don't you think?"

"If it's too strong, tell her she can leave right now." I shrug off my shirt.

Jolene tips up her chin. "She's not my business. Fletcher wants her here. He wants to give her something to do, so she's watching Benjamin until Leah comes back. I'm trying to be agreeable and pleasant, but if you think I want her here, you're mistaken. I hardly think having her here is a good idea after what you did to her before she even graduated high school. But you're a father now. You're married. You're in line to take over this ranch with me someday. I don't think you want to risk everything for *her,* do you?"

I shake my head and grunt a laugh. "You and your fucked-up perception of my relationship with her."

Her arms cross. "It was inappropriate. She wasn't even an adult, Milo."

I sit on the edge of the bed and set the alarm on my phone. "You dunno what you're talking about."

"I do. She told me. On. Our. Wedding. Day. The things she confessed out of sheer spite and hatred made me want to vomit. They made it hard to smile behind my veil. They made it hard to say 'I do.' And maybe she made it all up. Did she? Did she lie about everything? Did you fuck a high schooler? Did you fuck your boss's daughter?"

I shut off the light and lie with my back to her.

"If you so much as look at her too long, I will make both of you pay. But I'll start with her. Keep that in mind, Milo."

"Morning, son," Fletcher's raspy voice grates along my nerves while I ride Ranger toward the rest of the ranchers waiting to redirect the herd to Sunflower Pasture. A special thanks to Ty for wheeling Fletcher's miserable ass onto the porch just in time to greet me.

"Did Indiana take an instant liking to Benjamin?"

I'm going to end his life. When I find Annie, Fletcher will burn in a fiery hell.

"Did you hear me?"

I don't give a single glance in his direction.

"Milo," he says louder.

If he wants to put a bullet in my head, that's his call. I'm so fucking over submitting to him.

The rest of the day, I keep my head down and my body busy with inventory, checking grass, and making sure the herd gets redirected to Sunflower Pasture without too much resistance. Before heading home, I send Jared to town with fresh meat for Fletcher's favorite butcher, who happens to be his pastor. I imagine he'll preside over the funeral after I kill Fletcher.

"Is there an issue I need to know about?" I ask the security guard outside the front door. Fletcher has guards at the entrances to the ranch but never on his front porch.

"I'm watching Miss Ellington," he says.

"Indiana?"

He nods.

"Well, her name is no longer Miss Ellington, and I'm here, so you're dismissed."

"Mr. Ellington is under the weather and decided to turn in early. I've been instructed to stay until your wife returns."

"I'm here. You're dismissed."

"Sorry, Mr. Odell. I've been instructed to leave *only* when your wife gets home."

With gritted teeth, I give him a tight smile, taking a step closer.

When his hand inches toward his holstered gun, I shove the barrel of my pistol into his neck just below his chin like it's taking his pulse. He stiffens. I retrieve his gun.

The grin on my face swells a bit. "The old man barking orders from a wheelchair can't hold his hand steady enough to pull his dick from his trousers. My hand is steady and faster than yours. Go home. I'll return your gun tomorrow. Understood?"

He swallows before relinquishing a slight nod.

Taking two steps back, I holster my gun and shove his gun into the waist of my jeans.

"He's not going to live much longer. When he's gone, guess who will sign your paychecks?"

"You, sir."

I don't blink until he averts his gaze, a silent surrender. Bowing his head, he scuffs his boots along the paved walk. When I hear his truck's engine fading behind me, I bang the dirt off my boots and open the door.

"No, Milo." Jolene *is* here.

Fletcher's guard is clueless.

"You're a mess. And you smell like manure. Why didn't you come in through the mudroom?" Her heels click down the stairs.

"I'm a rancher. What do you expect me to smell like?"

"Go around back." She frowns.

I shake my head. Her demon-eyed gaze follows my hands while I remove the extra gun, my holster, and every scrap of clothing from my body.

"What are you doing?" she hisses.

"I'm gonna shower, Jolene." Snagging only my holster and the extra gun from the floor, I brush past her to the stairs.

"Indiana is up there changing Benjamin's diaper. Stop this ridiculousness." Jolene rarely loses complete control, so the shakiness of her words feels like a reward.

Fuck Fletcher.

Fuck Pauline.

Fuck Jolene.

I'm over it. I'm tired of being a prisoner with a life sentence sold under the guise of freedom.

"Milo ..." She makes a last attempt.

"*Darlin'*, Indiana has seen me naked."

And when I turn the corner, she's right there. Two feet in front of me with Benjamin hugged to her; seeing me naked again.

Passing her, I saunter to my bedroom. Just before turning into it, I glance over my shoulder.

Indie's gaze meets mine. I start to grin at her unapologetic inspection of me, but something in her eyes takes away any joy I feel.

It's lifeless.

The last time I saw such a deep void in her eyes was when I married Jolene.

33

THE MISTRESS

INDIE

"He's amazing, isn't he?" Jolene plucks Benjamin from my arms when I get to the bottom of the stairs. She's said it at least a dozen times since arriving home.

I don't give her a response like I didn't give her one the other twelve times she said it. It's hard to focus on anything but her apparent ineptness when holding a baby. I'm not an expert either, but I'm far from her.

He cries.

She frowns, doing an uneven bounce in her high heels. It's like he doesn't even recognize her as his mother. If her only child can't stand her, that says all that needs to be said.

"You're dismissed." She presses her hand to Benjamin's head while he rears back in a scream. "I'll let you know when I need you again."

I can't turn away from the spectacle. It's a train wreck demanding my attention. Jolene whisks Benjamin toward the kitchen. "Shh ... I'll get you a bottle. Please stop crying."

I haven't looked at Benjamin with any sort of focus. Everything is still too numb.

I change diapers.

Feed him.

Walk him.

Rock him to sleep.

All without looking into his eyes.

It's unbearable to see Milo in him because I'll be forced to see Jolene too. So I've spent the day being very robotic with him. Does that make me a terrible person? Is it his fault? After all, I was the child caught in a mess that wasn't my fault.

She groans from the kitchen. "Why is this bottle leaking?"

When I reach the top of the stairs, I meander past my room to their room. How many mistakes will I make before one of them kills me or I stumble upon happiness with nothing more than dumb luck finally on my side?

Closing the bedroom door, my thumb presses the lock. Light seeps beneath the bathroom door. My feet pad to the light, and I slide open the door, closing it behind me.

From inside the tall glass walls, Milo rinses the suds from his hair and shakes his head, eyes blinking open.

"You made ... a baby with *her*." I've managed a full day, keeping my emotions in check. But I can't do it a second longer.

Milo blinks away the water and frowns. "I donated sperm."

Wiping my eyes, I shake my head.

"A fucking petri dish, Indie. He was made in a petri dish and implanted into another woman."

"Four years, and you've never put your dick inside her?" I try to keep my voice down, but it's hard. I'm livid.

Drawing a long breath, he clenches his jaw and releases the breath through his nose.

I nod slowly, taking a step backward. "That's what I thought."

Milo's finger jabs a button, turning off the water. Keeping his gaze on me, he snags a white towel from a neat stack of them and dries his hair before wrapping it around his waist.

"Don't ever try to find me," I whisper, taking another step backward.

"You can't run. I can't let you do that."

"I will never forgive you for helping him find me. I will never forgive you for hiding the truth from me. And I will never forgive you for sticking your dick inside her." Anger and heartbreak tangle, forming a monstrous lump in my throat while my eyes burn.

"I don't need your forgiveness. I need your cooperation."

"Fuck you." I spit on him.

His eyebrows shoot into tall peaks a second before he tips his chin, watching my saliva slide down his abs. I barely blink before he backs me into the door, a firm grip on my jaw forcing me to look up at him. "I need you to grow the fuck up long enough for me to get my sister back. Hate me all you want. I deserve every ounce of it. But Annie did nothing. So hole up in this goddamn castle of his, keep your head down, and your mouth shut. And when it's over, you can run as hard and as far as you want. You can hate me for a million eternities. But I *need* you to fucking do this for me." His voice breaks on the last few words.

His Adam's apple bobs in a hard swallow.

His breaths quicken.

His gaze drops to my mouth.

In four years, I haven't felt this alive. It doesn't matter that his touch isn't kind, that his words make me bleed.

Loosening his grip on my jaw ever so slightly, his thumb brushes my cheek. I can't move, except my heart ... it throbs, each beat reverberating along my skin, a fire spreading out of control. A harsh breath falls from my mouth as his thumb touches my lower lip.

Milo ducks his head, mouth an inch from mine, breath mingling with mine. His thumb tugs on my lip, brushing along the inside of it. When the tip of my tongue grazes his thumb, his lips part a little wider. I can hear his heartbeat; I think I can feel it.

My hands ball at my side to keep from touching him, but god ... I want to.

Eyes glossed over, each exhale releases a little harsher when his thumb dips farther into my mouth. My lips wrap around it, and his eyes drift shut. The door behind me creaks on its hinges when Milo presses his other hand against it above my head as if he needs it to steady himself.

If his lips touch mine, the last thread will snap. I know it. He knows it.

Memories have never felt as tangible, concrete, and

alive as they do now. I can taste his lips from four years ago. I can feel him between my legs as if he were there now. His tongue laving across my breast, teeth teasing my nipples.

Milo's nose touches mine, inhaling while withdrawing his thumb from my mouth. He's going to kiss me, and I'm going to let him. I'm going to let him do anything he wants to me.

But he doesn't ... he doesn't kiss me. His lips are *right there*.

I lean in, and he pulls away just enough to deny me. The warm tips of his fingers skate down my neck to my shoulder, easing the strap of my sundress to my arm. With one of my bare breasts exposed, Milo rests his forehead on mine, panting like he's ten miles into a marathon.

He doesn't kiss me.

He doesn't touch my breast or rub his thumb along my hard nipple.

He's torturing me as if he's afraid to cross some line that he knows doesn't exist between us. It never has, and it never will.

Do I care if he fucks me right here, with his wife and son within earshot?

No.

A whoosh of air fills my lungs when he drops to his knees, his towel loosening around his waist. It's unexpected, and my heart can't take anymore. If he doesn't touch me ... really touch me ... I will lose my ever-loving mind.

Pressing his forehead against my stomach, he groans

—deep and feral as if it is I who is torturing him. My fingers weave through his thick, wet hair.

Milo's hands slide up my legs beneath my dress. My heart, thrashing around in my chest, feels like it could break the bones surrounding it. He inhales deeply, a trembling breath, while his fingertips barely touch my skin. My palms slap against the door behind me to steady myself. The pain is real. I *need* him.

His patience? Hesitancy? Guilt? I'm not sure what it is, but it's killing me. In this one moment, he's making four years feel like forty years.

Why is he so tortured? What happened to his family? Why does Fletcher have so many strings tied to Milo, each one being manipulated to make him and everyone he cares about suffer?

"Milo?" Jolene pounds on the bedroom door.

I freeze.

Milo doesn't flinch; he simply remains idle, fingers whispering along my skin, shoulders lifting and falling with each breath. What is he thinking?

God ...

What. Is. He. Thinking?

In the next breath, he stands, tightening the towel around his waist—replacing the dress strap onto my shoulder.

My head drops while I step aside to let him slide open the door.

"Milo?" More banging on the door.

He shuts off the bathroom light, leaving me in the dark.

"Yes?" he says, opening the bedroom door.

"Where's Indie?"

"Am I her keeper?"

"Is she in here?"

"Yes. I have her hidden under the bed."

Jolene groans her frustration. "Can you be serious for a second? One of my clients has been arrested. I have to go."

"I need to—"

"Milo, I don't care what you need to do. Take him. Find Indie and tell her to do her job."

Jolene's heels click against the floor, slowly fading.

Drawing in a brave breath, I step out of the bathroom like we didn't just have an incredibly intimate moment. "I'll put him to bed," I murmur.

Milo pats Benjamin's back. "No. He's not your child. I'll do it."

I avert my gaze and nod several times while sidestepping him to get out of the room as quickly as possible.

"That's ..." he sighs. "Indie, I didn't mean it like that. I just ..."

I stop with my back to him, tears fighting to escape.

"I meant he shouldn't be your responsibility."

"Yeah, well, you were right the first time too."

"Indiana ..."

I drudge my way through the emotional baggage chained to my neck and look for any sort of refuge.

34

DON'T LOOK BACK

I STARE at the ground below my window. It's three in the morning. If I fall and break my neck, it will be several hours before anyone finds me. Should be about the right amount of time to die.

My bag goes first, landing with a soft *thud*.

Gripping my ladder of bedsheets, like Ruthie taught me to do if there was a fire, I crawl out the window. Everything tightens, letting me slip a few quick inches as the knots cinch beneath my weight and my breath catches in my throat.

Slowly, I loosen my grip and then tighten it, inching my way to the ground. When my feet feel the earth, a sigh breaks free, and I sling my bag over my shoulders. The entrances to the ranch are heavily guarded, so I have to navigate the pastures and hope I don't get trampled by a spooked horse, angry bull, or mountain lion.

My flashlight illuminates the uncertain path before me. I can't do it. I can't live in this prison.

"Where you going?"

I jump, my hand whipping the flashlight like a saber toward the fence.

Milo's propped against a post, one leg crossed over the other, hands in his pockets.

"W-what are you doing?"

"I finished feeding Benjamin, and I heard something. Never did I expect to see you fleeing out the window at three in the morning. So I'll ask you again, where are you going?"

"Away."

"I didn't tell Fletcher. He had me followed."

"Doesn't matter." I duck to slip between the fence posts.

"I can't let you." He grabs my arms and pulls me toward him.

My feet stumble. "Let go of me." I wriggle.

"Dammit, Indie ... it's been four *miserable* years without you. Every part of my life has been a fucking disaster for as long as I can remember. This is not normal. This life ... it's just ... not even close to normal. Do you know how many days I wonder what I'm even doing? What's the point? Fletcher's gonna let my sister die if I don't find her. And if I put a bullet in his head, I'll walk in my brother's shoes and die strapped to a table with a needle in my arm." He tightens his grip on my arms. "And I'm..." his voice drops to barely a whisper "...I'm okay with that fate if it means you and Annie are free."

His words spin in my head, ricocheting off things that should make sense and crashing into every dream and false perception of reality I've ever had. I don't want Milo to die for me. This is madness.

Nobody escapes Fletcher. Milo's had years to do it, but he didn't. And I'm not going to watch him be some martyr to a sister he never cared to tell me about and me.

"You're hurting me," I whisper, no longer fighting him.

With a sigh, he releases me. "Indie—fuuuck ..." Milo buckles over when I knee him as hard as I can and slide through the fence posts, moving my legs into an all-out sprint. I never imagined the day would come when I'd run from Milo like my life depended on it. Running from the human I love more than any other human.

His boots pound behind me, breaking sticks and rustling brush, sending tears down my face.

Why?

Why didn't he tell me about his sister?

Why don't I know what happened the day his parents died?

How can I trust him if I don't know him?

I stumble, catching myself with my hands, hair clinging to my wet cheeks. Gripping a rock the size of a baseball, I stand and hurl it at Milo. A shot in the dark. "LET ME GO!" My feet dig into the earth again, kicking it up behind me.

Burning lungs.

Fear whipping my heart like a racehorse.

When I realize the only things I hear are my breath and my body's desperate movements, I glance over my shoulder.

Nothing.

Not a sound.

Just a sky full of stars and my heart racing.

Is he hurt? Did something get him?

The rock didn't hit him.

It shouldn't matter. I need to keep running until I'm free. He's baiting me. I continue running and running. My heart constricts, and it has nothing to do with sprinting.

It's Milo.

He's not the only one with strings attached to him. I have them too. They're all anchored to my heart, and the hand that pulls them belongs to Milo Odell. I stop, resting my hands on my knees, gasping for every ounce of oxygen I can steal. Again, I glance behind me.

Nothing.

I'm free. If I can make it past the creek, I'm free.

So why don't I feel free?

I feel lost and alone.

And my heart's disintegrating into a pile of dust in my chest.

Did he give up on me? Or did he let me go?

"Ugh," I groan, stabbing my fingers into my hair and shaking my head. "Keep going, Indie. Keep going." My pep talk falls on deaf ears. Even in a pile of dust, my heart wins. It's stronger than my self-preservation.

My feet retrace their steps, slowly at first, then they pick up speed. Then he comes into view, a sliver of moonlight on his face, arms resting on the fence.

I slow to a stop a good fifteen feet from him.

This is it.

Everything hits me at once.

I'm willingly giving myself up to Fletcher's reign. I'm willingly taking on the role of Benjamin's nanny. I'm willingly suppressing every last ounce of dignity and self-worth to be near Milo.

Not even *with* him, just near him. I don't care where I am on this earth; I need to feel the sun. I need to feel Milo.

More tears fall. My knees buckle, and I drop to the ground, the unforgiving dirt and rocks digging into my knees. My face falls into my hands while the sobs rattle my body. It's as if they're trying to shake sense into me.

I'm not sure my feelings for Milo make sense. They simply were, are, and always will be.

Through my tear-blurred eyes, I first see his boots.

"Indie girl ..."

Indigo.

That only makes me cry harder. Ruthie would die a second death if she could see me, the abuse my heart has weathered at the hands of Fletcher. If I died, would Milo lose his soul and harden into an out-of-control monster feeding his rage with innocent bystanders?

"It s-should have been m-me ... you were m-mine."

He lowers next to me, pulling me into his arms. "It *is* you. I'm gonna end this. I'm gonna end Fletcher and everyone who has laid a hand on you. And then I'm gonna give you the keys to the kingdom. And if you want to burn it down, I'll light the fucking match for you. Okay?"

"Milo, you have to t-tell me about your f-family."

"Indie, nobody wants to know—"

I shove him, backing away and climbing to my feet. "I am not nobody."

"My need to protect you is—"

"Protect me?" I shake my head. "Are you kidding me?" I sniffle and wipe my nose. "I'm here. Armed guards who have been told to keep me here are surrounding this ranch. This..." I point to the bruise on my face from Ty "...is not you protecting me."

Milo winces.

"If I'm going to die in this fucking hellhole, I at least deserve to know why."

He stands, wiping the dirt from his jeans. "You're not going to—"

"YOU DON'T KNOW THAT!" I cover my mouth before I wake anyone up, and a new round of tears fills my eyes. Shaking my head, I whisper, "You don't know that."

Milo's face wrinkles. A breath later, he nods. "You're right. I don't know that. But you won't die while I'm still breathing."

"Tell me."

He shakes his head.

"Milo ..."

He continues to shake his head.

"If you don't, he will. Fletcher will tell me his version of your story. I'm his pawn too, and he's going to use me to destroy you." I wipe my face. "Take away his power."

His gaze settles at his feet, shoulders curled inward. "She'll die," he whispers.

"Your sister?"

He nods.

"Why?"

"Because I'm the keeper of his secrets, and he's the

keeper of mine. Fletcher no longer has anything to lose, but I do. *He* holds the power."

"Take it away."

Milo shakes his head.

"Then I'm going to ask him. I'm going to poke and prod until he can't help but spill everything. I know he's dying to tell me why he hates you yet holds onto you tighter than anyone." I get two steps toward the house.

"I shot her."

Everything stops. *Everything.*

My breath catches while the night air delivers his chilling words.

"My twin. I shot my twin sister."

His words are not only shocking; they're paralyzing.

"I stole my dad's gun. The shot was intended for him. And everything just..." Milo sighs "...happened so quickly. My mom tried to stop me, and the gun went off; a bullet landed in Annie's head. My dad took one look at Annie and charged toward me. Then *boom.* His body fell to the floor, and blood from the hole in the back of his head spilled onto the faded wood floor. Mom screamed, frantically attending to Annie and then to Dad. She ... just ... wouldn't stop screaming. Then *snap!* Another shot, but that one landed right between my mom's eyes."

Milo slowly shakes his head, face blank. "We hadn't seen Archer in weeks. He was busy. Always busy working with Fletcher. I needed him, and he was never around. Then the day I decided to handle things on my own, he just ... appeared."

His gaze lifts to mine, and he blinks slowly. "Archer wiped my dad's gun and put it in his hand. Then he told me to ride my bike to the park, play with as many kids as possible, and not come home until dinnertime. I ... I said no. But he held his gun to my head and told me to go before he put a bullet in my head for being so fucking stupid."

My lips part to speak, but I can only find a shaky breath.

"My parents are dead. Archer is dead. I really, *really* need you to help me save her before he lets her die. I can't ..." His voice cracks, and he swallows hard. "I can't let her die. She's the only one of us who deserves to live."

Biting my quivering lips together, I blot my eyes.

Milo's boots scuff along the dirt, past the fence, toward the house. He stops without turning back to me. "If you decide to stay, I'll leave the back door unlocked. Skip the third and seventh steps; they creak."

His head twists, chin at his shoulder, but his gaze doesn't quite find me. "If you decide to leave, I understand. You're an innocent victim too. And I love you, Indie."

I choke on the emotions, holding them hostage until he reaches the house. Then I lower to the ground, knees to my chest, head bowed. And I cry for Milo Odell and his sister, Annie.

35

THAT'S FOR INDIE

MILO

WHEN TY's wife left him, he moved into my old barn apartment.

"Hey," Ty says, opening the door a little after five thirty in the morning, holding a cup of coffee. No shirt on yet. No holster. No gun. He's much bigger than I am, but timing is on my side.

Thud!

I land my boot in his gut. He buckles over, spilling his coffee. Then I ram my knee into his nose, sending blood splattering everywhere.

Click.

I hold my cocked pistol to his temple while he's on all fours, moaning.

"It's not your fault that Satan pays so well. I get it. You need the money. But you have a daughter. You have no excuse. If you *ever* lay a fucking finger on Indiana again, I will make sure many lifetimes pass before someone finds your remains. Are we clear?"

"You crazy fucker ..." He sits back on his heels, blood pouring from his nose.

I keep my gun pointed at him. "I am. And I'm not afraid of dying for my cause. You need to decide if you're willing to die for *him*. Maybe chat with your daughter about it." I turn and head out the door, stopping just before shutting it. "Now, I'm going to fuck up your truck so you can blame your nose on an unfortunate accident."

Luck tilts in my direction the rest of the day. Jolene doesn't call me, which means Indie stayed. Fletcher's therapy keeps him out of my business. Chatter about Ty hitting two deer, totaling the front end of his truck and breaking his nose when the airbag didn't deploy, circulates in a believable fashion around the ranch. By nine o'clock, I decide to call it a day, shocked that Jolene hasn't blown up my phone, demanding I quit working and relieve her from her "motherly" duties. An hour with Benjamin seems to be her limit.

Something rustles behind the trees as I unbuckle my chaps to toss them in the back of my truck.

Nobody's on the porch. Maybe I'm hearing things.

Nope.

This time, it's a rhythmic creak.

Reaching for my gun, I take slow steps to the side of the house. In the full moonlight, Indie pads her bare feet along the dock just beyond the clearing. Her short sun dress dances in the light evening breeze like her hair flowing over her shoulders. Always angelic.

Holstering my gun, I make my way to the dock.

"You did that to Ty," she says without turning. "You did that for me."

I don't respond.

"Why were you going to kill your dad?"

Sliding the hat from my head, my breath releases in a long exhale. With a tipped chin and heavy heart, I pull the words from the deepest recesses of my mind, stirring disturbing images and awakening the sick feeling in my stomach. "Annie was pregnant..." I swallow hard "...with his baby."

Indie doesn't move. Did she hear me?

"She was twelve." I close my eyes for a few seconds. Going back still hurts.

"Did your mom know?" Indie murmurs.

"No." Dropping my hat, I thread my fingers into my hair while gazing at the star-filled sky. "She was sick. Early dementia or something. Annie tried to tell her once, but she just laughed. Thought it was a joke. Who jokes about that?" I grunt. "That's why Archer shot her too. He said she was going to die anyway. Why suffer anymore."

A good minute or two passes while Indie remains silently idle. Then ... she lifts her dress, shrugging it off to reveal her naked body, every beautiful inch of it. "I love you, Milo."

Splash!

She circles her arms, swimming to the opposite side. I glance over my shoulder at the house. Every window facing the pond. Every shadow. Then I remove my clothes and dive in after her. At first, I don't see her on the opposite shore. Then I catch the faint outline of her head bobbing in the water a good ten feet from the grassy shore.

It's been four. Long. Years.

I swim to her.

"My Milo," she whispers, arms around my neck; my hands guide her legs around my waist while my mouth covers hers. I'd nearly forgotten what it felt like to want a woman so completely.

To feel this level of passion.

To feel so fiercely protective.

I'd forgotten how that thing keeping time in my chest beats differently just from a woman's touch. *This woman.*

I lift our entwined bodies onto the soft grass.

"My Milo ..." she whispers, threading her hands through my hair while I drag the inside of my lips just below her ear to her shoulder.

Her stomach tightens when I splay my hand across it, not touching her breasts or dipping between her legs. She shivers and squirms, hips slightly lifting from the ground to chase my touch.

I grin.

Her fingers tug my hair with a bit of frustration accompanied by a moan when I draw her nipple between my lips.

Tease it with my teeth.

Suck and squeeze it.

When she arches her back, I tug harder.

Again, I grin when her hand covers mine, trying to guide it between her legs. This will happen on my time.

Tracing the outline of her hips, down the outside of

her leg, my fingertips ghost along her inner thigh a few inches lower than where she wants me.

If Fletcher finds out, I won't be alive much longer, so I refuse to rush one damn moment with her.

On the other side of this moment, a realism I don't want to accept awaits my return. My lips ghost along her skin to her other breast. Indie moves her legs the tiniest inch; her silky, warm thigh brushes the head of my erection, and I can't help jerking my hips like she's doing against my touch.

"Oh god ..." Her breaths quicken.

My tongue circles her nipple before sucking it into my mouth again while my fingers continue to tease her inner thighs.

"M-Milo ..." Her pelvis lurches off the ground serval times, breath catching for a second while her head falls back on a long moan.

And I pause, staring at her lips slowly parting while her eyelashes flutter with each heavy blink. With my hand at her thigh, her knees collapse together—a little shaky.

She opens her eyes.

"I love you, Indie girl."

A ghost of sadness glides across her face, erasing a bit of her joy. And I'm unsure if it's fear of what's coming for us or if she feels conflicted about what we're doing.

Keeping her gaze locked on mine, her hand slides between her legs. As much as I want to watch her touch herself, I can't escape the captivity of her gaze. Covered with her arousal, her hand wraps around my cock. I pull a sharp breath through my nose when she strokes me, her thumb brushing over the swollen head.

And still, I can't look away from her.

"My Milo."

I nod, pulling her to straddle me, sliding into her, my hands at her hips, guiding them back and forth. When I die, this will be the last thing I remember—my favorite place in the world.

It's not that I don't love Benjamin. I'm honored to have a part of my family still here when I'm gone. I'm in awe of his innocence and humbled by his trust and dependence on me. Life leaves little room for genuine regret. It's like the times I watched Indie tend to Ruthie's garden. She had to meticulously pull out the weeds without disrupting the seedlings. I can't regret the bad without disrupting the good. Acceptance is the best I can do. I accept the young life I created with Jolene, and I can love him without loving her.

Indie's hair tickles my face when she leans down to kiss me. Everything tightens, a rubber band stretched to its limit. She slows her hips. Leaving me on the edge of losing my fucking mind. I roll us.

Her legs spread wide, knees pulled back as I move faster, letting go of control and releasing again and again. "Fuck, baby ... fuck ..." I pinch my eyes, stilling deep inside her. It feels ... so damn ... good.

Like I'm floating.

Hell, maybe I just died.

Her hips lift and lift and lift ...

I open my eyes and see it in hers. The need. The verge of another orgasm. It makes me chuckle.

"Milo," she breathes my name, which is between a whine and a plea.

I rock my pelvis once.

She winces, hips pumping into mine and searching so hard.

"Please don't stop." Her fingers curl into my flesh.

Again, I rock into her, stopping to let her rub against me. Watching Indie come undone is an indescribable high. It makes me want to spend every second of every day touching her this way.

She sighs and opens her eyes when her body relaxes for the second time. A shy grin steals her lips.

"*My* Indie girl."

Biting her lower lip, she nods. Then her whole body shivers.

"Cold?" I ask.

Another nod.

"Let's swim back and get you warmed up."

When we reach the other side of the pond, I use my shirt as a towel while Indie pulls her dress over her wet naked body. I already want her again. It's not that I think we can make up for four years, but I'd happily try.

"Don't give me that look." She leans to the side, wringing out her hair.

I pull up my zipper and shove my feet into my boots. "What look is that?"

"Well, I haven't seen it in a while, but from what I recall, it's the look you had the day of the butter incident." Her fingers comb through her hair.

"You'll have to be more specific." I button my wet shirt.

"You don't remember the butter incident?"

"No. I remember. I just don't know what look you're talking about that you think I have right now."

She saunters a little closer to me. "The one you had right before your face went between my legs." Biting back her grin, her nose wrinkles.

I chuckle. "Yes, Indie. It's nothing new. When I'm with you, my mind imagines all sorts of things. And I don't doubt that I have a distinct expression for each filthy thought." My knuckles skate along her cheek, and she leans into my touch. Then I cup her breast over her dress and brush my thumb back and forth over her erect nipple. No man has had a bigger death wish than I have right now. Anyone who knew what they were looking for could see us from the back of the house.

Her lips part, tiny breaths matching the rhythm of my thumb. I no longer know what the fuck I'm doing, but I can't stop touching her.

"Milo ..." Our mouths crash together, and her hands cup my neck while her weight shifts to her toes. "Fuck me again," she mumbles over my lips while one of her hands strokes me on the outside of my jeans.

God, I want her again. The need is painful. I could lift her dress, slide down the front of my jeans a couple of inches, and spread her wide for me against one of the dock posts. Or I could drop to my knees and fuck her with my tongue so that I can taste her the rest of the night.

The answer comes in the form of my phone vibrating in my pocket. The third degree awaits me.

"I can't, Indie girl," I say. My brain does a great job of

coming up with the correct answer despite my hands gathering her dress and sliding it up her backside, gripping her bare ass while shoving my thigh between her legs and my tongue down her throat.

Indie turns me into an animal. With her, every instinct I have is to take and take. Finding that dock post, I do just that.

Indie grinds against my leg, mouth attacking mine, while I tug at my belt and fumble my fly. This might be the most desperate I've ever been to get my dick out of my pants.

"MILO?"

Indie stiffens, hands gripping my shirt, breath at my neck. "Who's that?"

I blow out a long sigh that does little to relieve the built-up tension. "Derek. He must be back with the trailer and needs me to move my truck. I have to go."

Indie takes a step back and mirrors my deflation with her controlled exhale. Her dress falls into place. A fucking shame. And I buckle my belt and button my shirt before dropping my hat on my head.

"Don't get caught." My finger traces her jaw.

Indie turns her head and kisses it. "I won't."

"MILO?"

Hugging her shivering body, she gives me a sad smile. "Move your truck and go to bed with your wife."

I shake my head. "Your cousin. I'm not owning a goddamn person in your family." My boots take me in the opposite direction toward Derek. "Except you, Indie. I own every inch of you."

36

IF YOU LET ME GO

INDIE

THE FOLLOWING MORNING, I wake at the crack of dawn and thank all the stars in the Texas sky that Pauline spent most of the previous evening here. Jolene was too busy pretending to be a good mom, or any sort of mom, to notice Milo "working" late or check on my whereabouts. Not that the guards would let me leave. I'm sure they have a photo of me taped to their forearms.

"Oh good, I don't have to drag you out of bed." Jolene dumps her son on me the second I open my bedroom door. Her clicking heels fade toward the stairs while she waddles in her tight skirt, leaving her spicy floral scent lingering with ...

Yuck!

Benjamin's diaper is saturated, as in soaked completely through his jammies. He smells like a urine sponge, seeping through to my clean shirt.

On a deep sigh, I take care of him ... for Milo.

"We need to talk, darlin'." Fletcher eyes me over his coffee mug while I settle Benjamin into his swing next to the dining room table.

Micah smiles at me while placing a plate of food at my spot. "Coffee?"

I shake my head.

"Juice?"

"No. Thank you," I whisper, taking a seat.

"That will be all, Micah," Fletcher says. His dismissal of Micah drops the room's temperature by a good ten degrees.

But I try to act unaffected.

"I thought this would work out," he says, slowly setting his coffee mug on the table. "I thought four years was plenty of time for you to grow up."

I pick up my fork with a shaky hand. When it *tap tap taps* against the plate, I set it back down on the napkin.

"Did you enjoy your swim last night?"

My stomach drops ten stories, and my pulse drives into panic mode. Taking a slow swallow, I force my gaze to his.

His lips twist for a few seconds. "Imagine my disappointment this morning when Sam tells me he saw something a little 'unsettling' last night."

My jaw stiffens, and I think about Milo. Where is he? Has Fletcher said anything to him? Does Jolene know?

"Do you know what happens to women who try to steal married men?"

"He's mine," I whisper.

Fletcher's cracked lips part. It's a rare moment. I don't think he knows how to respond.

Good.

Let him think about it.

Seconds pass, and his shock morphs into something else. Something akin to what I imagine the devil looks like after a bad day. "I think it's time for you to go."

Really?

Before he changes his mind, I scoot back in my chair and find my legs, although shaky like the rest of my body. Still, I'll leave on my knees if I have to; I'll crawl out of this hellhole if that's what it takes.

"Oh no, darlin'." Fletcher cuts into his breakfast steak.

I wish all that red meat would hurry up and stop his heart.

"I fear you misunderstood me. Just because it's time for you to go doesn't mean you're free to leave on your own." He burps.

Everything about him disgusts me. He's ugly through and through.

"It's getting exhausting ... keeping that boy in line. I give, and I give, and I give." He shakes his head. "And what do I get in return? Not a goddamn thing."

"Give him his sister back," I say, barely a whisper.

Brows drawn together, he cocks his head a fraction. "What ... did you just say?"

Inching my head side to side, I take slow steps backward.

"Sister?" His eyes narrow even more into beady little black pinpoints. "Milo doesn't have a sister. His family died. He killed them."

"Archer killed them."

"Archer saved Milo's pathetic little life. He spent years in prison and died so that Milo could live. All ... *all* Milo has to do is show a shred of gratitude. Embrace the life that *I* have given him. Money. Power. A beautiful wife. A child. It's just that fucking easy. Or ... it should be. But for some reason, he's hell-bent on losing *everything* for what? You Indiana? Do you think you're that special? Would you rather see Milo die than not be with him? Are you that desperate? That selfish? Can you not find a man of your own? What's so fucking special about Milo Odell? He's a coward. A murderer. A cheat. A liar. And he'd rather stick his dick in you than save his—" Fletcher's lips press into a hard line.

His sister.

"She's Archer's sister too," I say, feeling the need to be as brave and bold as possible despite being outplayed by the master of games.

"She should have died the day her parents died. Milo shot her in the head. She's physically and mentally impaired. She needs help eating, talking, and shitting. She's blind in one eye. And I've spent more money on her care than the rest of my family combined. Times a hundred."

"So why can't Milo see her?"

"It's called atonement." Control slips quickly while Fletcher's words come out faster, lacking control while his voice escalates. "Milo owes me for taking away my best friend and for everything I've done for his sister. He owes me his life. He shouldn't have shot her if he wanted to see his sister. We all make mistakes, darlin', and we all pay for them."

"Was I a mistake?"

"Half my life has been a mistake," he scoffs. "Don't take it personally."

"Was Ruthie a mistake?"

His expression hardens. She's still his Achilles' heel. "Ty, escort Indie upstairs. Have her pack her things and drive her to her destination."

"What about Benjamin?"

"Don't you worry about him."

Ty, with his taped nose and bruised face, appears from around the corner as I turn around. His hand reaches for my arm, and I turn to the side before he can touch me. His big feet clod up the stairs behind me, and when I reach the top, I turn so we're at eye level.

"He's going to go through you with a fucking bullet to get to him," I say.

Ty's Adam's apple bobs while the overworked muscles in his jaw flex. He doesn't say a word.

He doesn't have to.

It's in his eyes.

He knows I'm not lying. He knows the *he* I'm referring to.

On our way out of the ranch in Ty's truck, I don't see any sign of Milo. Not his truck. Not his horse. He could easily be anywhere. In town. On one of the other ranches. Anywhere.

"What's he have over your head?" I murmur while my gaze strays out my window, hoping for a sign that Milo's okay.

"Nothing," Ty says.

"Bullshit." I shake my head. "People don't work for

Fletcher Ellington because he offers good health insurance and a nice retirement package. He did something for you, something that's given him ownership of your life. Or is it your daughter?"

"You mean Milo's ex-girlfriend?"

I laugh. "Is that the best you've got? Look in the mirror. Who'd Milo beat up for Rae?"

"Watch it. That's my daughter you're talking about."

"You brought her up, not me." I shrug. "Kinda made her sound like one of the many women Milo's fucked in the back of the barn next to his horse. I bet he puts horseshoes on the wall for his conquests instead of notches on his bedpost. I'm sure you're proud of her."

"Fuck you." His knuckles turn white as he tightens his grip on the steering wheel.

"I will," I mumble.

I feel his extended sidelong glance.

"I'll let you fuck me if you let me go."

37

IF YOU HAD TO CHOOSE

MILO

"Where is everyone?" I ask Fletcher just after nine at night.

He stares at his bookshelf, sipping his whiskey.

"Everyone?"

"Benjamin? Jolene? Indie?"

"Pauline took Benjamin ... *away* for a while. Jolene is staying in Dallas. It's closer to her law firm. Just until things get settled."

Settled? I sort through his words. His tone. And the hair on the back of my neck stands erect.

I can't fucking breathe.

It's déjà vu—this calm, calculating side of Fletcher Ellington.

"*Annie is safe. She's being cared for better than before you shot her in the head. She lost the baby. You killed her baby. And maybe that was for the best. But listen, son, I've got you. I'm going to take care of you. There isn't anything*

I wouldn't do for Archer. All you have to do is work hard for me. The harder you work to make me happy, to follow instructions without question, the safer Annie will be. And that's all we want. Right, Milo? We want Annie to be safe and ... alive."

I glance over my shoulder, and Ty's body fills the doorway. The muscles in his face curl into a self-satisfied grin. And for that, I'm going to knock out every tooth in his head with the toe of my boot before I kill him. The man in the wheelchair didn't physically remove Indie from the premises.

"You know, Milo ... *you know* how exhausting it is to break a horse. And sometimes you think they're too stubborn. You think they'd rather die than let you put a saddle on them. But we never give up. Right? You can't give up when you know what's best for them. That's how I feel about you. Jolene's husband. Benjamin's father. I have too much of my goddamn life invested in you to give up now. So here I am, just a guy who wants to retire and leave a legacy for his grandchildren, but you refuse to do your part. Why? Why do you have to make everything so hard?"

He finally turns his wheelchair toward me and sighs, shaking his head. "I'm tired. And I need you to trust me to care for those you cannot care for. You have Benjamin and Jolene. You have all the people who work under you. So many people depend on you. Let me worry about Annie. Let me worry about Indie. You're too invested in how much you've failed them to be able to do right by them now. I've got it. Think of it as 'Jesus taking the wheel'."

Fletcher's patience has been perfected over the years. I know he'll wait for eternity for me to respond. I know he won't let me leave his office until I pledge my loyalty to him in blood. He usually compares himself to God.

Jesus is more fitting. Jesus died.

Fletcher will die. I might even put him on a cross or tie him to a fence post and let the creatures of the night eat the flesh from his bones.

"If you had to choose ... who would it be?" He lights up a cigar and takes a puff. "If I couldn't spare the time and resources for both of them ... hypothetically, or maybe not so hypothetically, who would you choose to live and who would you choose to die?"

"Is it that she died?" I ask. "Ruthie. Is it that she died? Or is it that you cheated on her while the hospice nurse sat next to her bed on one side, Indie curled up next to her on the other?"

"That's it. We're going to the barn," Ty says impatiently, shoving his gun into my back.

Fletcher holds up a hand and gives Ty a slight headshake.

Ty steps back, holstering his gun.

"You don't know what you're talking about," Fletcher says, rolling the cigar between his fingers.

"I know the night before she died, you drank a whole bottle of whiskey, told Ty to get you 'someone,' and when I passed this same office, you were shoving your limp dick in a brunette's mouth while telling her to suck harder. Ruthie died the next morning. You spent the whole day hurling. Everyone thought you were sick from losing

Ruthie. You were just hungover and choking on your guilt."

"I loved her, and don't you ever fucking question that."

"I don't. You didn't have a lot of redeemable qualities, but she saw them. How could you not love someone who saw something good in you when you knew it wasn't much? But she took all the good with her when she died. And I do know how hard it is to break a horse. I also know that when you have one that's so fucking miserable that it can no longer stand on its legs, you have to put it down."

Fletcher eyes his limp legs hanging off the edge of his wheelchair. "Take him to the barn," he says to Ty.

Ranger has seen Ty beat the shit out of me more times than I can count. And I've never fought back. I knew the rules. I knew it would end quickly if I just took it. And for years, I felt deserving of it. My parents were dead. Archer was in prison. And Annie was missing part of her brain and vision in one eye.

Tonight, I can't. Even if I still deserve it, I have to find Indie.

"Annie's gone. You have to be smart enough to know that," Ty says, shoving me to my knees inside the barn, giving Ranger his usual front-row seat.

Sitting back on my heels, I fist my hands on my legs and close my eyes for a few seconds. Annie's not dead. He wouldn't kill her. She's the reason I'm here.

"Sam saw you last night with Indie by the pond. Do your marriage vows mean nothing? I mean, all this for a girl who was willing to spread her legs for me this morning."

What?

Everything turns red. Finding my feet, I slowly turn toward Ty. There it is, that fucking smile again.

He tosses his gun on the ground several feet from Ranger's stall and cocks his arms, hands in fists. "I've been waiting for this."

It's an unspoken agreement on the ranch. When one person tosses their weapons aside, challenging someone to a fight, the other person does the same unless someone's indisputably earned themselves an ass-kicking.

This is the first time that Ty's offered me a fair fight.

"All this for a girl who was willing to spread her legs for me this morning."

"Drop your weapon." Ty nods, taking a step closer to me.

"I told you ..." I say.

Again, Ty nods toward the ground. "Toss your fucking gun aside."

My hand wraps around the gun, slowly pulling it from my holster and holding it at my side. "I told you ... if you ever laid a hand on Indie ..."

Ty eyes my gun, my finger on the trigger. "What makes you think it wasn't consensual?" he asks. Then he dives for his gun.

Bang!

"FUCK!" He trips, hugging his hand to his chest, minus the fingers I just shot off it.

"She wouldn't consent to one fucking finger of yours on her."

"I s-said she was w-willing to—"

Bang!

"Ahh!" He collapses to his side, now with a bullet in his knee. Panting and grimacing, he looks up at me. "You'd b-better plan on killing me..." his face contorts while his good hand covers the hole in his leg "...cuz if not—"

Whack!

My boot lands in his mouth.

He loses consciousness and two teeth while thick pools of crimson ooze down his neck.

Bang!

Right between his eyes.

"It's always been the plan."

Is every person crossing this ranch's gates destined to become an awful human being?

"If you had to choose ... who would it be?"

A man doesn't kill his own daughter. It's what I tell myself, stalking toward the main house. But Fletcher's no longer a man. He's a monster without moral boundaries. And his voracious appetite for revenge can no longer be satisfied with anything less than total domination of everyone around him.

He's not in his office. I follow the cigar smoke to the kitchen, but he's not there. Light seeps beneath his bedroom door as I approach it from the dark hallway. The floor creaks beneath my boots.

"That was quick. Did you make him bleed?" Fletcher asks before I open the door.

When I inch it open, he glances up from his bed, the

back lifted to a forty-five-degree angle. Drink in one hand, TV remote in his other hand.

I see a glimpse of fear in Fletcher Ellington's eyes for the first time.

"Yeah, I made him bleed."

With a shaky hand, Fletcher sets his drink on the nightstand and clears his throat as if it will give him a little composure and confidence.

"Where is she?" I ask, stopping at the foot of his bed.

"Who?" He smiles, but it's feigned confidence at best. "Here we are, once again, facing that all-important question. Who do you save? Your sister? Or your mistress?"

"Both."

Fletcher scoffs. "That's just not possible."

"Why not?"

"Because if I only have one act left on this earth, it's going to be to make you pay. Make you suffer like you've made everyone else suffer."

Jaw filled with tension, I swallow hard. "I was a child. A twelve-year-old child with a sick father who raped my sister, a mother too sick to notice anything outside of her own pain, and a brother too obsessed over making money with his best friend to acknowledge the ugly truth taking place in the house he left, the family he abandoned."

"If you thought you were old enough to take your father's gun, point it at someone, and pull the trigger, then you were old enough to be accountable for the consequences. You could have told the police it was you."

"I didn't shoot them—"

"But you shot Annie!" Fletcher's voice booms,

leaving a slight echo. Blowing a breath out of his nose, he rubs his temples. "You shot Annie. You started it. And you were twelve. You could have taken the blame for shooting all three. Given the nature of your father's relationship with Annie, a jury would have granted you mercy. Instead, you let Archer take the fall, knowing no jury would look at him and show mercy."

"Did you ever ..." I stare at his legs for a moment before meeting his gaze. "Did you ever think maybe Archer felt guilty for not being there to protect Annie? Did you ever think he shot them and faced the consequences because he felt a need to make up for what he didn't see happening? Why do you assume he did it all for me? Maybe he did it for Annie. Maybe he let our mom die without any more suffering. And perhaps he put our dad down like a rabid animal out of control."

In a slow blink, I glance around the room at nothing in particular. "Maybe he felt undeserving of a good life ... or any life at all. I know I felt that way. And I was only twelve. Fucking. Years. Old."

Turning, I slip on my riding gloves and remove the picture of Ruthie from the wall. For a man who hates me so much, he's given me most of his secrets. Six digits later, the safe pops open. I slide the cash aside and take out the gun he gave Ruthie for protection. I don't think she ever touched it. Removing the cartridge of ammunition, I set it on one nightstand before walking to the other side to put the gun on the nightstand closest to Fletcher. Time, I'm buying myself time.

He eyes the gun and then me. I close up the safe and

replace the photo, taking a few seconds to admire Ruthie's kind smile. Her flawless beauty.

Of course, he loved her. Her only imperfection was that she wasn't the mother of his child.

"It's time," I say, pulling my gaze away from the picture. "Put the horse down." I leave the room.

By the time I reach the front door, I hear a pop.

Just one.

I feel it in my chest, a void that will remain that way for the rest of my life. My fingers knot in my hair, clenching it hard while I lower to my hunches. "I'm so s-sorry, Annie ..." I cry.

"When I die, she dies. It's an unstoppable order. It's life insurance. Any way you look at it, Milo, freedom comes with a price."

"If you had to choose ... who would it be?"

I dispose of Ty's body where no one will ever find it. He'll become another missing person. And knowing who he worked for, no one will try to find him. Rae will grieve him, but she'll know ... it was always a risk to protect the devil himself.

And now ... I wait.

38

NOT HIS TEARS

INDIE

"You look like her."

I peel open my eyes, squinting against the sun, while I sit up on the worn leather sofa.

Yesterday, Ty pulled his truck over to the side of the road. My heart sank to the very bottom of my stomach. He was going to take me up on my offer, and I had second —third, all the way to a million—thoughts at that moment. Was I willing to give myself to him like that in the hope of real freedom?

I didn't know. It came out in desperation.

Ty didn't give me a choice in the end. He covered my eyes with a bandanna, tied my wrists, and drove. What felt like hours later, he dumped me off here—a trailer in the middle of nowhere, surrounded by construction and endless miles of trenches and pipelines.

Before I could ask one question, he climbed into his

truck and sped away, leaving a cloud of suffocating dirt and no way for me to leave or contact anyone.

No one came to the trailer last night, so I fell asleep on the sofa.

The blond man with messy hair about the length of Milo's and dirt all over his face opens a can of Red Bull and chugs it down in one shot. No doubt one of Fletcher's men.

"Where am I?"

"Fifty miles west of Waco."

"And you are?"

"Baylor."

"And *who* do I look like?" I run my hands through my hair.

"Our mom." He tosses the can in the tiny sink and wets a towel, rubbing it all over his face, removing a majority of the dirt but leaving a few streaks. With those two words, memories bubble to the surface like they've been suffocated for years. Repressed. Abandoned.

"Baylor, leave your sister alone."

"Baylor, give her half your sandwich."

"Baylor, did you push Indiana?"

"Three kids. Three dads. Same mom." He shrugs before leaning his hip against the counter. "Rosa just graduated from medical school. She has you to thank for that. No debt."

"Indie, Rosa's in charge. Listen to her."

"Indie, Rosa has homework. She can't play now."

Baylor chuckles. "You don't say much."

"Um ..." I slowly shake my head.

"Gotta say, I wasn't expecting this." He pulls an envelope from his pocket. "Twenty grand to let you stay a few days then drive you to the airport and put you on a plane to Switzerland. Are you in trouble or going to some fancy spa in the mountains? I bet you've traveled the world by private jet or a yacht, huh?"

Switzerland? Fletcher's sending me to the place where Milo and Jolene honeymooned. His deplorability has no boundaries.

"Who gave you that?" I find a stronger voice.

"The big guy in the black truck yesterday. Sorry, I had a late shift. You were asleep when I got here. Out hard. And you didn't move when I left at four this morning." He jabs a thumb over his shoulder. "I've gotta get back to work. I just wanted to make sure you were good."

"Um ..." I try to keep my emotions in check. "Can you drive me to Dallas?"

He laughs. "Not today. I took Wednesday off to drive you to the airport."

"Do you have a vehicle I can borrow?"

He shakes his head. "Sorry. Just my truck, and I need it."

"Can you call me a cab or Uber?"

Baylor continues to chuckle. "They don't come out to these parts. Sorry." He opens the door.

"Baylor?"

"Yeah?"

"How is she ... um ... Mom?"

He frowns. "She died ten years ago. Overdosed. The depression won." The door shuts behind him.

On a shaky breath, I quickly wipe my eyes. It's a lot. The past two days have been emotionally more than one person should be asked to endure. My heart can't take anymore.

Grabbing the blanket, I lie back down and close my eyes. I dream of burnt grilled cheese and lazy summer evenings on Ranger with Milo next to me.

I SEE Baylor for less than twenty minutes total over the next two days. He sleeps, welds on the pipeline, and eats on the run. We have a long drive to the airport, and I have so many questions.

"What was she like? I don't feel like I remember much."

"Mom?"

I nod.

Baylor steers his truck with one hand while holding his energy drink in his other hand. Three candy apple air fresheners hang from his rearview mirror. They don't smell like candy or apples. "She worked a lot. When she was in a good mood, she was in the *best* mood. When she was not in a good mood, she didn't get out of bed. And she missed you—her baby. The money didn't matter. Hell, I knew nothing about the money until after she died."

"What?"

He shrugs. "Yup. Apparently, she didn't want to touch it. She felt too guilty. So Rosa and I split it. She went to med school, and I invested my share, so I don't have to live in the middle of nowhere forever."

I don't know how to respond. It's ... tragic.

"What about you? What was it like growing up with a billionaire?"

I stare out the window and grunt. "Overrated."

"After she died, I spent more time with my dad. He's a veterinarian. Rosa's dad owns a restaurant in San Antonio now. Had Mom not died, I wonder how many more of us there would be?" He laughs.

"Because she never settled down with one man?"

"Well, sure. I suppose that too." He shoots me a quick side glance. "She was uh ... an escort. You knew that, right?"

What?

"Our names. You were conceived in a private jet over the state of Indiana. I'm the hometown boy from Waco. She never explained why I was conceived at a university neither she nor my dad attended, and I didn't ask. I was too busy thanking the good Lord that my name isn't Waco." Baylor chuckles. "And Rosa was a New Mexico conception in Santa Rosa. Supposedly it was a scuba diving getaway."

In the next moment, I snort. Then I do it again, doubling over in a fit of laughter—the crazy kind.

"What did I miss?" Baylor asks.

I shake my head, wiping the tears from my eyes while gasping for breath. "Oh ... oh my gosh ..." My stomach hurts from laughing so hard. "I'm ..." More giggles escape. "I'm the million-dollar baby of the devil and his whore."

Baylor clears his throat. "We don't call her that. I mean, she was a pretty good mom."

"Sorry." I wipe my eyes. "I didn't get to see much of

that side of her. Children are supposed to be priceless. I had a price."

"To be fair, I think he held a lot over her head, and the money was just the final nudge to get her to walk away."

Of course, Fletcher held something over her head.

I simmer into sadness, no longer feeling the effects of my temporary nostalgia. And for the rest of the way, I remain silent.

"Will I see you again? Rosa would love to see you too."

I start to open my door when he parks his truck outside my apartment building. And I can't help but wonder if Lincoln's been looking for me. Has he contacted the police?

"I'd like that."

"No phone?" he asks.

I frown. "Not at the moment."

"Well..." he reaches for his glovebox and pulls out a pen, scrawling his number onto a torn-off piece of a fast-food bag and handing it to me "...this is me. Call me when whatever's going on with you gets settled. Okay? And I hope I don't get in trouble with that big guy for not taking you to the airport."

I nod. "Thank you. I'm sure you'll be fine." I give him a second glance before closing the door. There are so many things I want to say and questions to ask, but now, I can only focus on Milo, wondering if I'll ever see him again.

Wondering if he's alive.

～

"Your rent's late," my landlord says, opening her creaking door. Her apartment smells like something's burning.

Grilled cheese.

"I was abducted, but I'm back, and if you let me into my apartment, I'll get you paid."

She rolls her eyes, grabbing a ring of keys. "I'll hand it to you..." she leads the way to the elevator "...you get points for originality. That's the first abduction excuse I've heard in twenty years."

When she glances over her shoulder, I return a tightlipped smile.

Stepping off the elevator on the fourth floor, she rattles her keys, searching for mine. "Texas's wealthiest man died a few days ago. Did you hear about it?"

My gait falters. There are a lot of wealthy people in Texas. Maybe she doesn't know who's the richest. And my name on the lease is Indiana Hill, so she doesn't know who I am ... who I was.

Lorraine opens my door and narrows her eyes at me. "Coming?"

"Who?" I whisper. My body tingles like it's been anesthetized.

"Fletcher Ellington. Blew his brains out. He'd been in a wheelchair after an accident. Maybe he no longer thought life was worth living."

I don't ... I don't understand.

"You okay?"

My body moves in her direction, but I can't feel it.

This is what I imagine it's like to have an out-of-body experience. People talk, but everything echoes. Words mean nothing. Emotions shut off. Your body moves on autopilot.

"You don't look well. Here ... let me help you lie down." She assists me to the sofa, covered in piles of laundry. "Should I call someone?"

He's dead.

"Indiana?" Lorraine puts her face in front of mine. "Do you need me to call someone for you?"

"No," I whisper.

She stands straight. "Have rent to me by tomorrow morning. And whatever you do, don't die in here. Do you have any idea how hard it is to rent out an apartment after it gets out that someone died in it?"

When the door clicks, I fist my hands over my eyes. "No ..." Emotion punches me in the face, and I cry. It kicks me in the gut, and I sob harder. "No!" I'm so fucking angry that I'm having these feelings. I'm mad that these tears won't stop running down my face.

He doesn't get my tears.

"Stop. Stop ... just *stop.*" I shoot to my feet and scrub my face, trying to erase every tear, every last bit of evidence they existed. Clenching my shirt in my tight fists, I rip at it as if I could rip out my heart and stomp all over it for reacting this way to *him.*

Throwing open my kitchen cabinets, I look for any alcohol I can find, settling on a bottle of vodka. Tossing the cap aside, I bring it to my lips.

Then ... I stop.

He would have done this. *He* did do it.

Fletcher tried to drink himself to death after Ruthie died.

Because he supposedly loved her.

Because he couldn't bear a sober day without her.

Because he didn't know how to love anyone else.

It's too easy to imagine his impure spirit watching me, smirking, reminding me that I am his flesh and blood. Like father, like daughter.

Crash!

The bottle of vodka shatters against the wall. I wipe more tears, brushing my arm across my nose to wipe my snot. But I can't stop. My emotional foundation crumbles. And I bleed all the tears and choke on every sob.

His evil spirit can watch me with that self-righteous smile, but he'd better know these tears are not for him. They're *because* of him.

39

SLIGHTED

MILO

"Where's Ty?" Pauline asks while I rock Benjamin and stare out at the trees by the pond. She hasn't said more than a dozen words since returning to the ranch.

I'm okay with her remaining in a state of shock. After his funeral, I will have my judgment day. Jolene should be here soon. She's avoided making the trip home until the last possible minute.

She's avoided *me*.

But today, we say a final good riddance to the fallen master.

"I haven't seen Ty."

"What do you mean you haven't seen him?"

The clouds grow darker. How fitting that it will storm today.

"I mean, I haven't seen him like I don't plan to see a handful of employees who never wanted to be here in the first place."

"Ty was loyal to him. He wouldn't miss his funeral."

"I fear you've mistaken obedience for loyalty."

"Well..." she clears her throat "...when you see him, tell him I'd like to have a word. And later tonight, I will have a word with you as well."

There it is.

I say nothing.

When Benjamin falls asleep, I lay him in his crib, shave my face smooth for the first time in years, and don my whitest shirt, pressed suit, and black silk tie.

We dress our very best to grieve and celebrate. Today is both. A brother and uncle will be mourned. And a new freedom will be celebrated.

"You're not in his will."

Drawing a long breath, I close my eyes for a second before turning toward Jolene.

Her long, brunette hair is pulled into a tight bun.

Her lithe body clad in a fitted black dress. Black gloves. Black heels.

"And in our prenup, you get nothing if you cheat on me."

Adjusting my tie, I don't say a word.

"Was she worth it?" Jolene eyes me with a stern expression and a hatred more intense than anything I've seen from her in our short marriage.

Buttoning my suit jacket, I pull my shoulders back and make my way to the door, to Jolene. I stare down at her until she cowers, averting her gaze. "Yes. She was worth it."

~

FLETCHER'S BUTCHER slash minister presides over his funeral service. His kind words are offered to a filled church. I am one of six pallbearers chosen to carry his casket from the front of the church to the hearse. From the hearse to his final resting place in the Ellington family cemetery next to his beloved Ruthie.

Pauline loses it during the burial service. Jolene passes Benjamin to me so she can console her mourning mother. I don't look at the minister or the casket—my gaze slides along the acres of land surrounding us. And I imagine what my life will be like when it's no longer my responsibility. When I'm no longer a slave to the man in that shiny box.

After the final prayer, family and friends disperse toward their vehicles. No one stays next to Fletcher's grave as he did with Ruthie. I carry Benjamin to the limo and place him in his seat next to Pauline and Jolene.

"I'll walk," I say.

Jolene returns a curt nod before I close the door. When the limo pulls away, I meander to a dead oak tree, facing the hill where Fletcher's casket has been lowered into the ground, where two men are covering it with dirt.

And then I see her.

A bright flowing sundress that sweeps to her knees.

Cowboy boots.

Hair floating on the breeze. A single rose clenched in her fist.

Thunder sounds in the distance while angry clouds converge into thick, dark mountains in the sky. The earthy, musky smell of impending rain permeates the air.

She stands over Ruthie's grave for a few minutes. I

lean against the tree and watch her. Taking a step forward, she lowers, kneeling on Ruthie's grave, and places the rose on her headstone.

Ten minutes pass.

Twenty minutes pass.

Then she slowly stands. Touching her fingers to her lips for a long second, she reaches for the headstone and presses her fingers to it.

Passing Fletcher's grave, she doesn't stop. She doesn't give it the tiniest of glances. It's as if he's not there. It's as if she's not acknowledging he ever existed.

Gaze angled at her feet, Indie makes her way down the hill. Brushing the hair from her face, she glances up. And she stops—eyes on me.

Indie has never looked more beautiful. More free. I should have given it to her years ago.

Her eyes fill with unshed tears, and she smiles. It's blinding.

"Indie girl." I push off the tree when she runs toward me.

"You're alive," she whispers in my ear with her arms around me.

Lifting her from the ground, I bury my face into her neck and breathe. She's lavender and sunshine. She's hope.

Easing her to her feet, I frame her face in my hands. Regret strangles me. I need to know if she's okay. I need to tell her that she's safe. Ty's dead. No other man will ever touch her again. And I'm so fucking sorry for failing her.

"Hey ..." Her brow furrows while her hand presses to my cheek. "What's wrong?"

Slowly, I shake my head, forcing a hard swallow past that lump in my throat. "I'm sorry ... I let him hurt you. But he'll never touch you again."

Indie squints for a second before her head inches side to side. "He didn't hurt me." Her thumb brushes my lips. "He took me to my brother." Her mouth bends into a tiny grin. "I'd blocked out that time in my life. I have a brother and a sister." Indie's smile fades. "Are *you* okay?"

It takes me a few seconds to let the gravity of her words snake around my conscience—a poison to my already questionable soul. I manage a nod.

I lie.

Today I'm supposed to be free.

I'm not.

"Come back to Dallas with me?"

Holding her as tight as possible, I kiss the top of her head. "I have a few things to do. I'll be there tomorrow. Okay?"

"I don't want to leave without you." She pulls back a breath and grips my jacket's lapels.

My knuckles skate along her cheek while I dig deep for a reassuring smile. "It's just one day, baby." I see the concern, the doubt, in her eyes. "I'm yours."

Still, she's conflicted. And I don't know how to ease her mind. It's like she feels everything I'm feeling. Regret is a deep scar that never disappears. And maybe it's not supposed to disappear. Perhaps regret is what keeps us from repeating the past. Regret is the ultimate accountability.

"Milo ..."

I kiss her, closing my eyes to hide the pain that she doesn't need to bear with me. Her fingers find my hair, and she kisses me with a need that envelopes me. It digs its claws into me.

My hands slide to her butt, squeezing and bringing her closer to me. So close, but not close enough.

She buries her face in my neck. "I'm happy he's dead. I hate that kind of happiness."

40

THE UNCOMFORTABLE TRUTH

INDIE

MILO SAID he'd come to Dallas today. It's nearly eleven at night, and he's not here. I don't know his number. I haven't called Milo Odell in over four years and three phones ago.

What if something terrible happened? What if Ty got angry at him? Or Jolene did something terrible? What if he was on his way and got into an accident? How would I know? When would I know?

Over the past ten hours, I've prepared for his arrival —a clean apartment, fresh bedding, and a bouquet from the floral shop. I owed it to Lincoln to let him know I'm alive. He was relieved but angry that I wouldn't give him the details.

The weight of his anger quickly dissipated by the time I got back to my apartment because I knew Milo would be here soon.

I was wrong. No Milo.

Until ... now.

There's a knock at my door, and I sprint to open it, casting all self-control into an ocean of disregard.

It's him!

"I was so worried." I throw my arms around him.

Milo backs me inside, dropping his bag on the floor and kicking the door shut behind us.

"Why do you look so sad?" I press my palm to his face.

He slowly shakes his head, having not said a word yet. His mouth covers mine.

Our clothes are lost.

Our bodies entwine.

Milo takes me again and again, until his eyes finally close, his body relaxes, and he falls asleep with me in his arms. My head on his chest. And all I feel is this deep sadness.

Isn't this it?

Our time?

No more obstacles?

I don't understand.

~

"Morning," Milo says.

Nestled on the sofa with a tall glass of iced tea next to me, I look up from my book. It's almost noon. "Hey. I wondered if you were going to sleep all day."

He stretches and yawns. "You wore me out last night."

I grin. And he does too. It's a friendly grin, but it's not my Milo's. Something's missing.

"I have a Keurig. Make yourself a coffee, and there's cinnamon in my spice rack. I was thinking about lunch. We could go out to lunch."

He starts his coffee. "I was going to eat you for lunch."

My cheeks fill with a good blush. I don't know why. He did plenty of that last night. But in the light of day, in the wake of the past week, everything packs an extra punch.

"I'd like to meet your sister. Have you been to see her since …" I frown. "You know since everything happened? Surely Ty or someone told you where he was keeping her, right?"

Milo slowly twists off the lid of the bottle of cinnamon. "Yeah," he says just above a whisper. "We should go see her."

"Can we talk about Jolene?"

He shakes the cinnamon into his cup of coffee. "It's not a favorite subject of mine, but what do you want to know?" Milo bends down and kisses me before sitting on the sofa, his body angled toward mine.

"Are you getting a divorce?"

He chuckles. "After last night, I hope so. I think we broke a few commandments."

I roll my eyes. "You know what I mean. Have you discussed it with her?"

"Yes. It went something like, she'll take everything, and I'll keep the shirt on my back and maybe my boots.

We'll share custody of Benjamin. She only wants to see me on a need-to basis and never wants to see you again."

I flinch.

Milo shakes his head. "Don't. You're not allowed to be shocked by that."

"I ... I'm not. I just wasn't ... I don't know what I was or wasn't expecting."

"Her husband had sex with you the day after her wedding. And again the day before her uncle died." He eyes me over his coffee mug while taking a sip.

"I love how you're referring to yourself in the third person."

"I'm trying hard to pretend it wasn't me who married her."

I half grin. "I know the feeling."

For a few minutes, we sit in silence. Milo gazes out my apartment window while I pretend to read the words on the pages of my book. But I can't.

"Why do you think he killed himself?"

Milo shrugs, keeping his gaze out the window. "He was disabled and miserable. Lonely. And filled with anger and resentment."

"Who found him?"

"I did."

"I'm sorry you had to see that."

He nods once, gaze a little lost in the distance.

"How did Ty react?"

Tiny lines form along his forehead. "He ... didn't have much to say."

"Did you really think you could take his life?"

Milo turns to me. "Who?"

"Uh ... Fletcher. You said you were going to end his life. I think you said it for me, but do you think you would have been able to do it?"

Milo rubs his eye like there's something in it. "For you, Indie? Yes."

Is there a greater love than a man willing to take a life for you? I can't imagine there is.

I snag his coffee and set it next to my book then straddle his lap and tease the wavy strands of his messy hair. "When did you know you loved me?"

His fingers slide into my belt loops, and he twists his lips.

"Was it one of the summers we spent our free time swimming in the pond and riding horses?"

Milo's nose wrinkles. "What? You were like ... twelve."

"So." I laugh.

"No. When I was twenty, I wasn't having romantic feelings toward a twelve-year-old, despite Jolene accusing me of 'grooming' you."

"She did?"

He nods.

"Bitch."

Milo bobs his head noncommittally, but I know he agrees with me.

"If you say it was when I was eighteen, then I'm calling bullshit." I narrow my eyes.

"The summer before you turned seventeen, I had moments of looking at you in ways that made me uneasy."

I bite my lip to hide my grin.

"When did you look at me differently?" he asks.

"Oh ..." I roll my eyes to the ceiling, lips corkscrewed. "I mean, I fantasized about you from a very early age. And the first time you put me on Ranger with you, I declared you my new obsession. And on my fourteenth birthday, when I saw you screwing some woman in the barn, I ran home and touched myself for the first time."

"Christ." Milo tries to slide me off his lap.

I don't let him. "What?"

"I don't want to get ..." He hesitates.

"Get what? Turned on by my confession?"

"Correct." Again, he tries to slide me off his lap. "Getting a goddamn boner from hearing about you at fourteen touching yourself and thinking about me is wrong, Indie. It's just wrong."

I giggle. "Do you know that, in some countries, girls get married at fourteen?"

"Well, not here."

I tighten my hold around his neck and wiggle my ass on his lap while he groans his conflicted feelings. "The world doesn't care about us. It doesn't wait for us. Why should we care about it? Why should we wait for it? We're not like everyone else."

Milo stops fighting me and relaxes, brushing my hair behind my ear on one side. "Yeah," he whispers.

"Let's go visit your sister."

Again, those lines in his forehead form deep creases. "I need a shower. Come shower with me first."

I grin. "I already showered."

He slides my shirt up my torso. "Not with me."

41

UNEARTHING THE TRUTH

MILO

Some truths can't stay hidden forever. Reality can be an unrelenting bitch that won't be ignored. She wants to be felt and acknowledged.

"What are you doing?" Indie asks when I pull into the parking lot of the cemetery. Her voice is a little uneasy.

It's not a private cemetery like the Ellingtons'. I don't know most of the people buried here. But I know a few.

I kill the engine and inhale as much strength as possible in one breath. "We're visiting Annie."

Indie shakes her head. "I ... I don't understand."

I hop out of my truck and round the front of it, bracing myself for feelings I have yet to fully feel, and I open Indie's door.

She looks at me with red, teary eyes. "How did she die?" she whispers.

I chose you, Indie girl. And I'd do it again.

"A long time ago, her twin brother accidentally shot her in the head. She survived, but it took years off her life. It was ... her time." Everything inside me hurts despite the love and gratitude I have for Indie. She's too good at feeling me. I can't give this burden to her.

"Milo ..." She quickly wipes her eyes.

I take her hand and lead her to a grave I have not seen yet, a grave I can't prove exists. But I knew the rules. And I knew Fletcher. As sure as he took his own life when I left him with the tools to do it, he arranged a long time ago for Annie to leave the world when he did.

He was a horrible man, but he loved my brother too much to be inhumane with Annie. I'm confident she didn't suffer. The suffering was only meant for me.

Indie's grip on my hand tightens when I slow to a stop. That one percent of doubt is put to rest when I see Annie's name etched in granite next to Archer's and our parents'. She's farthest from our dad. I should thank Fletcher for that.

Releasing Indie's hand, I lower in front of the headstone, tracing her name with my finger. "Hey, Annie. I want you to meet Indiana. She's a feisty creature much like you."

Indie sniffles behind me.

"Remember when you used to ask me to lasso the moon for you? Well, now I lasso it for Indie. That should tell you how much she means to me."

Indie rests her hand on my shoulder, giving it a little squeeze.

When I stand, Indie takes my hands and lifts onto her

toes, kissing the corner of my mouth. "Give me a few minutes alone with your family. Okay?"

Well, fuck. I've managed to keep my shit together, but now she's sucker-punching my emotions. I can't say a word or else I'll crack, and it won't be pretty. So I nod and head back to the truck.

An hour. Indie doesn't spend a few minutes with them; she spends an hour with them. Eyes swollen and red, she smiles when she climbs into the truck. It's a beautiful smile. "Okay. We can go."

I watch her fasten her seat belt and retrieve a tissue from her purse. Then I take her home.

"An attorney called me today," Indie says weeks later when I arrive home from my new job.

I found another ranching job for less money. Less corruption. But plenty to do. "Oh?" I hang my hat on the hook she nailed to the wall for me.

The apartment smells like burnt grilled cheese. Indie sets my plate on the table. I think there are figs on it too.

I pull her into my body for a long kiss because ... first things first.

She grins. "Mmm ... I missed you."

"What did the attorney want?" I take a seat at the table.

Sitting across from me, she sips her water. "He said money and property were put into a trust for me. Ruthie left it for me, but I wasn't supposed to get it until Fletcher died. I knew nothing about it. Did you?"

I shake my head, taking a bite of the sandwich. Yep, there are figs on it. I love this woman so hard.

"It's only a hundred acres."

I cough. "Indie, a hundred acres is a nice chunk of land."

She frowns, picking at the crust of her sandwich. "I don't really want to take it. I don't want anything that was his."

I wipe my mouth. "I was his."

"Milo ..."

"It's true. And maybe that land wasn't his. If Ruthie left it to you, it might have been hers."

"How?"

"Her grandparents used to own land. Maybe they left it to her. Did you ask your grandma?"

She twists her lips. "No. Maybe you're right."

My phone vibrates, and I pull it from my pocket.

Rae: If you ever cared about me, you'll tell me if I should continue looking for my father. You'll let me know what Fletcher did with him. You'll give me closure.

"Who's that?"

I shake my head. "Nobody." Sliding the phone into my pocket, I take another bite of the sandwich, but it's hard to chew because I've lost my appetite.

Indie doesn't hide her distrust nor does she question me further. "I'm thinking bees."

"Bees?"

"Ruthie had a few beehives, and Micah helped her

with them. I'd like to have bees. And grow flowers. Fig trees. Maybe I could sell them. Chickens. Goats. What do you think?"

"I think it's a lot of work. I think you'll need to hire help."

She nods. "I think I need a guy who looks sinfully sexy in chaps."

"I don't think chaps are required to make honey, *honey*."

"I'm getting turned on. Why don't you put on chaps ... only chaps, and I'll grab some honey."

I chuckle. "That's a little tempting but also a little weird. If it doesn't go as planned, we won't be able to look each other in the eye anymore. Do we want to risk it?"

Indie's giggles fill the room.

I lean forward. "You have cheese on your face."

She touches her chin while I open the other half of her sandwich and smear the cheese all over it.

"Milo!" She bats at my hand. Then she dives across the table to reciprocate with what cheese is left on the bread.

After she swipes it across my face, I grab her wrist and suck the cheese off her fingers.

Her grin fades into something more serious—the look she gives me when she's turned on.

Our mouths lock together.

The plates get knocked onto the floor, cracking into pieces. I lift her onto the table. Our kiss is hard and deep. Her adept fingers remove my belt and unbutton my pants in record time.

I groan when her hand wraps around me. My hands

snag the hem of her sundress, drawing it up her body and tossing it onto the floor with the broken dishes.

"Yesss ..." She yanks at my hair when my mouth covers her breast.

Her body reclines onto the table, cheese on her face. She's never looked sexier.

I grin, peeling her panties down her legs.

"Don't look so proud of yourself." She bites her lip, resting her heels on the table's edge.

I chuckle, slowly shaking my head. "I'm not proud ... yet." I guide her knees apart. "But I'm getting there."

"Miiilooo ..." Her body arches from the table, and it drives me out of my mind to see her wanting me this much. Am I deserving of Indiana? Probably not. I hope she never figures that out.

"In ... inside me, baby ..." Her fingers tug at my hair.

"Bedroom?" I mumble, dragging my lips up her body while sliding two fingers into her.

She gasps, eyelids heavy, face tense. "Here. N-now."

"Now?" I remove my fingers.

Her eyes peel open, gaze on my cock pressed between her legs. She lifts her hips. "Don't tease me."

I grin.

She scowls.

Then I fill her in one hard thrust.

By the time she announces her orgasm to the neighbors ... the table's halfway across the room, butted up to the sofa. I'm afraid one of the legs has a crack.

"I'm going to shower," I say, sauntering my naked ass toward the bathroom. "Coming?"

"Be there in a sec," she says with a giggle, using a napkin to wipe cheese from her face and breasts.

She doesn't join me in the shower. So after I finish, I wrap a towel around my waist and check on her.

"Rae called," she says in a barely audible voice while sitting cross-legged on the sofa, head tipped to my phone screen. "She told me to tell you to check your messages." Indie looks up at me. "She said she was sorry she missed the funeral—she was too busy looking for her father."

I stare at the phone and then at her.

"Where's her father? He wasn't at the funeral. I haven't seen him since the day he dropped me off at my brother's trailer."

"Indie ..."

"Milo, what happened to Ty?" Her eyebrows squish together. "What did Fletcher do?"

He's my out.

She would never know.

He's the person Rae and Indie suspect. And he's dead. The truth never has to come out.

The truth always comes out.

Pinching the bridge of my nose, I shake my head. "He said ... he said you spread your legs for him." I can't look at her. If she lied to me, if he raped her, I don't know how I'll handle it. I don't want her to see it in my eyes.

"I ... I ... god, Milo ... I was so scared. And I just wanted to get away. I didn't know where he was taking me. So I ..."

My gaze slowly lifts. Where is she going with this?

Tears fill her eyes as she slowly shakes her head. "I

said he could ..." Streams of tears race down her face. "I said I'd have sex with him if he let me go," she whispers.

No. This ... this makes no sense.

Her words come out like a verbal panic attack. "He didn't touch me. Nothing happened. He wouldn't. He was a cruel man who hit me, but he wasn't a complete monster. He took me to my brother's. Why? Why would Fletcher kill him? He ..." She sobs. "He d-didn't d-do anything. It's m-my fault Fletcher k-killed him. And now R-Rae doesn't have h-him."

I ease my phone out of her hand and shut it down. Kneeling on the floor, I brush the hair away from her face and hold it in my hands. And I let her see the emotion in my eyes, the unshed tears I've had for Ty. "Fletcher didn't kill him." My thumbs brush along her cheeks. "I thought he *raped* you. He wanted me to believe that he raped you." I blink, my eyes burning with regret. "Why, baby? Why would you say that to him? I. Thought. He. Raped. You."

Realization ghosts across her face. More tears fill her eyes and her lip quivers. "No, Milo," she whispers. "N-no."

I lay my head in her lap, my arms around her waist, and I let a lifetime of bottled emotion and fear of weakness release from my body.

And it hurts.

It hurts so fucking much.

I cry for my parents. Archer. Annie.

I cry for Ty.

And I cry for the part of Indie that will always feel like she, too, has blood on her hands.

"I'm ... so ... sorry, Indie girl." My body shakes.

So does Indie's. Her fingers comb through my hair over and over. Then she bends forward and rests her head on mine, her lips at my ear. And with two words, I know that this will pass. I know we will survive.

"My Milo."

42

THE ART OF FORGIVENESS

INDIE

"I charge eight hundred an hour. The clock starts now," Jolene says when I walk into her office. She doesn't look up from her computer behind her minimalist glass desk.

Shelves of leather-bound law books.

Framed licenses.

And modern artwork.

No pictures of their family, not even her son.

This office is as sterile and impersonal as Jolene.

I help myself to the chair opposite her. "Why do you hate me?"

Her fingers are still on the keyboard while she lifts her gaze. Long, fake lashes blink several times. "You slept with my husband."

"No." I shake my head a half dozen times. "You've always hated me."

She grips a pen, squeezing it until her knuckles

437

whiten. "What's the deal, Indiana? Did Milo leave you already? Are you lonely? Do you need a friend?"

I wait to respond, letting her live in the echo of her vile words.

She slaps the pen down on the desk and huffs. "I have work to do."

"Did you know I wasn't an impostor? Did you know I was the child Fletcher conceived with an escort in his private jet over the state of *Indiana*?"

Her expression morphs into confusion. Her hand touches her neck, gaze averting to the side. When our eyes meet again, she shakes her head.

"What was my crime? Conception? Birth? Being the innocent four-year-old child sold for a million dollars?"

After a minute or so, Jolene's attention returns to the computer screen, and her fingers resume their furious typing.

"Jolene, I'm sorry for every awful thing I've said to you, thought about you, or done to you." I don't need her to apologize or say another word. She is Benjamin's mother. She will be in his life. He deserves to be surrounded by love. He didn't make the choice to come into this world. He's worthy of a life infinitely more significant than the impersonal conception with which his life began.

When I reach the door, Jolene clears her throat. "She adored you," she whispers.

I slowly turn.

Jolene's eyes gloss over with unshed tears. "Ruthie loved you so much. You were this angelic little fairy in pretty dresses she made for you." Jolene quickly wipes her eyes and gazes out the window. "She laughed with you and ran her fingers lovingly through your long hair. Her eyes were bright and filled with love whenever she looked at or spoke of you.

"And I watched you look at her and Fletcher, you and two parents who were so in love—" Her gaze cuts to mine, and she no longer tries to keep up with the tears. "You were so smart too. Reading all those books, reciting poems, spewing random facts about the plants and bees because you retained everything so easily. And I was the daughter who wasn't quite as smart. Not quite as pretty. My parents never showed each other affection. My mom never looked at me the way Ruthie looked at you."

Slowly, she shakes her head and sniffles. "It's not that anyone compared me to you. My parents knew there was no comparison, so they didn't want to embarrass themselves by trying. But *I* made the comparison—all the time. And the more I compared myself to you, the more I hated you. So imagine how good it felt for me to have something you wanted?"

Jolene laughs, blotting her cheeks and eyes with a tissue. "And it was dumb luck. I didn't ask for the marriage. I thought no one would ever marry me, so why not take the offer presented to me? And when I found out you had feelings for Milo, it felt..." her gaze drops to her desk "...good. For once, I had something you wanted. For once, you didn't have everything."

When she looks at me again, I see a Jolene I have never seen before. She seems a little broken—a little human. "But you really did," she whispers. "You've always had him."

I've told myself many times that there's no way I could ever spare a single tear for Jolene. Here I am, wiping my face. "I forgive you." I open the door.

"I didn't ask for—"

Turning, I rest my chin on my shoulder. "I know. It's not for you. It's for your son."

EPILOGUE

"It's perfect." I stare at the sign.

Annie's Apiary

Milo hooks his hat onto the saddle horn and lifts Benjamin onto his shoulders.

For now, we live in a barn. We have bees and chickens, horses, and a few cows. I've requested an alpaca, but Milo hasn't jumped on board yet. We have acres of flowers and vegetables. Greenhouses. And a pond where we spend hot summer afternoons skinny dipping and making love in the tall grass.

Milo has shared custody of Benjamin. His relationship with Jolene has improved since Pauline started experiencing dementia. She realizes that we're the only family she'll have once her mom is gone. Unless she finds a man brave enough to marry her, but it's not looking promising.

"When will Rosa and Baylor arrive?" Milo asks.

"In about an hour." I open a jar of honey and swipe my finger along the top. "Why?" I smear it on Milo's cheek.

Ben giggles, and Milo narrows his eyes at me.

"We have time for a swim." He turns his head and nibbles Benjamin's leg. "Are you laughing at me?"

Ben giggles more.

"Swimsuits?" I suck the honey from my finger.

Milo grins. "Nah. He's two. I don't think he'll tell anyone."

I laugh. "Until Jolene takes him to a pool, and he thinks suits are optional."

Milo struts toward the pond. "Indie girl, I think we gave up on worrying about things like other people's opinions a long time ago."

I trek through the grass in my boots and sundress, discarding both before I reach the dock.

Milo's grin swells, setting Ben down and removing his clothes.

I pad my naked self to the end of the dock. "Milo, how long can I have you?"

"As long as you need," he says.

"Forever?" I glance at him over my shoulder.

"One day at a time."

"Milo." I narrow my eyes at him.

He shrugs off his shirt and unbuckles his belt, his grin larger than life. "Forever," he mouths.

I dive into the cool water. And I know without question ... this is love.

The End

ALSO BY JEWEL E. ANN

Standalone Novels

Idle Bloom

Undeniably You

Naked Love

Only Trick

Perfectly Adequate

Look The Part

When Life Happened

A Place Without You

Jersey Six

Scarlet Stone

Not What I Expected

For Lucy

What Lovers Do

Before Us

If This Is Love

The Fisherman Series

The Naked Fisherman

The Lost Fisherman

Jack & Jill Series

End of Day

Middle of Knight

Dawn of Forever

One (*standalone*)

Out of Love (*standalone*)

Holding You Series

Holding You

Releasing Me

Transcend Series

Transcend

Epoch

Fortuity (*standalone*)

The Life Series

The Life That Mattered

The Life You Stole

Pieces of a Life

Memories of a Life

ABOUT THE AUTHOR

Jewel is a free-spirited romance junkie with a quirky sense of humor.

With 10 years of flossing lectures under her belt, she took early retirement from her dental hygiene career to stay home with her three awesome boys and manage the family business.

After her best friend of nearly 30 years suggested a few books from the Contemporary Romance genre, Jewel was hooked. Devouring two and three books a week but still craving more, she decided to practice sustainable reading, AKA writing.

When she's not donning her cape and saving the planet one tree at a time, she enjoys yoga with friends, good food with family, rock climbing with her kids, watching How I Met Your Mother reruns, and of course...heart-wrenching, tear-jerking, panty-scorching novels.

www.jeweleann.com

Printed in Great Britain
by Amazon

22464663R00255